# The
# Wagtail
# Murder Club

# The Wagtail Murder Club

## Krista Davis

BERKLEY PRIME CRIME

NEW YORK

BERKLEY PRIME CRIME
Published by Berkley
An imprint of Penguin Random House LLC
penguinrandomhouse.com

Copyright © 2025 by Krista Davis

Library of Congress Cataloging-in-Publication Data

Names: Davis, Krista, author.
Title: The Wagtail murder club / Krista Davis.
Description: New York : Berkley Prime Crime, 2025. | Series:
Paws & claws mysteries
Identifiers: LCCN 2024022395 (print) | LCCN 2024022396 (ebook) |
ISBN 9780593817520 (hardcover) | ISBN 9780593817537 (ebook)
Subjects: LCGFT: Detective and mystery fiction. | Novels.
Classification: LCC PS3604.A9717 W34 2025 (print) |
LCC PS3604.A9717 (ebook) | DDC 813/.6—dc23/eng/20240524
LC record available at https://lccn.loc.gov/2024022395
LC ebook record available at https://lccn.loc.gov/2024022396

Printed in the United States of America
1st Printing

*To my editor, Michelle Vega, with gratitude.*

*We can judge the heart of a man by his treatment to animals.*

—Immanuel Kant, German philosopher

# Cast of Characters

**Holly Miller**
    Trixie—her Jack Russell terrier
    Twinkletoes—her calico cat
**Liesel Miller (Oma)**—Holly's paternal grandmother
    Gingersnap—her golden retriever
**Nell DuPuy Miller Goodwin**—Holly's mother
**Holmes Richardson**—Holly's boyfriend
**Squishy**—black Labrador retriever

SUGAR MAPLE INN EMPLOYEES

**Shelley Dixon**
**Zelda York**
**Mr. Huckle**

THE LAW FIRM

**Ben Hathaway**—Holly's former boyfriend
**Wendell Walters**
    Ella Walters—his wife
**Percy Calhoun**
    Kelly Calhoun—his wife
    Taffy—their dachshund
**Dinah Bonetti**
**Bizzy Bloom**
    Logan Verlice—her son
**Simon LeFavre**

## RESIDENTS OF WAGTAIL

**Sergeant Dave Quinlan aka Officer Dave**
**Cooper Adams**
**Harold and Jean Harvey**
    Jeff Harvey—their son

The
Wagtail
Murder Club

# One

"There is a murderer among us."

My grandmother, whom I called Oma, German for *grandma*, had a great sense of humor. But she wasn't inclined to joke about the macabre. Maybe on Halloween. But it was springtime now. I stared into her blue eyes, hoping to find a twinkle of mischievousness. Her gaze held steady, and no hint of mirth twitched on her face. "I hope you're joking."

"Sadly, I am not."

"Someone was murdered?" While Wagtail had had its unfortunate share of deadly incidents, I was usually the first person to know about them because my Jack Russell terrier, Trixie, and my calico cat, Twinkletoes, had noses for murder. The two of them had an uncanny ability to find murder victims.

I looked down at Trixie, who was doing her best to annoy Oma's golden retriever, Gingersnap. Almost all white,

Trixie had black ears and a large black spot on her rump that went halfway up her tail, which had not been cropped.

Twinkletoes could be a rascal, but her general demeanor was one of feline superiority. The elegant cat sat watching everything slyly through vivid green eyes. Her face and abdomen were mostly longish white fur. Her forehead bore two spots, one chocolate fudge and the other butterscotch, which made her look like she wore sunglasses on the top of her head. She often regarded the world Egyptian style, with her black tail wrapped around her white feet.

"No one has been murdered by this man recently," said Oma. "Not here, anyway. A man called Cooper Adams was convicted of murder. He has just been released from prison and decided to make Wagtail his home. Apparently, he is required to inform the police so we know that this Cooper now lives among us. His name rings a bell for me, but I don't know why."

Part of me wanted to be sympathetic toward Cooper, but a conviction for murder was hard to embrace. "Why? What brought him to Wagtail?"

"I do not know. It is all new to us." A faint smile crossed Oma's lips. "Zelda says the lunar eclipse is a time for new beginnings. Perhaps it is so for this Cooper."

"Maybe it's not as bad as it sounds? Maybe the murder was an accident, not intentional." I sought reasons to convince myself of that. "Maybe it was a stormy night and his car skidded and he hit someone."

"We are having a lunch meeting today where I will learn more."

Oma had brought me on at the inn so she could take it easy and travel, but then she went and got herself elected mayor of Wagtail, which meant she was busier than ever. One of the advantages, of course, was that I heard the town's scuttlebutt.

"Are you still going to Snowball?" she asked.

"I had planned to. Maybe I should stay here today instead."

"Zelda, Mr. Huckle, and Shadow will be here. And I will be a quick walk away. I'm sure everything will be fine."

Probably so. It was simply the shock of the news that caused me to reconsider. There really wasn't any reason to alter my plans or do anything differently, though.

"Be careful, liebchen."

I smiled at her and waved goodbye. Trixie and Twinkletoes followed me to the door. I held up my hand in the "stay" signal. With sad faces, they watched me leave. They would have more fun staying at the inn than shopping for it.

Six hours later, I was on my way home. From my car, I couldn't quite tell what the black thing was near the side of the road. The sun gleamed on it, but tall grasses obscured too much to see it clearly. As I drew closer, it appeared to move or change shape. I was nearly upon it when I realized that it was a black cage. A large black cage with something alive inside it.

Luckily, no cars were behind me. I swerved to the side, gravel crunching under my tires as the car slowed.

When I stepped out and ventured toward it, I paused in terror. Was that a baby bear trapped inside? I glanced around nervously. We were in the mountains of Virginia, well-known for being black bear territory, and where there was a baby, a large, angry, insane mama bear likely lurked nearby.

The black animal in the cage whined and yelped at me. A dog! Definitely a dog! I hurried over to the cage and looked into sad brown eyes. They pierced right through me. Poor baby! What was he doing out here all by himself?

He sat in a wire crate barely large enough for him to turn around in. His food bowl was empty and water, if there had ever been any, was long gone and the bowl lay upside down. A well-worn pink stuffed elephant and several other toys lay around his feet.

His situation was so strange that I wondered if someone could be watching. Was this a ploy to get unsuspecting strangers to stop? To steal a car? To mug them? I gazed around but didn't see anyone. Still, someone could be hidden in the dense trees about twenty feet away.

I hurried back to my car for a leash that I kept there for Trixie. She usually walked off-leash in Wagtail, but on the rare occasions when we left town, I felt it safer to attach a leash to my frisky girl's halter.

I returned to the dog and tried to gauge his temperament. He wagged his tail and licked the finger that I cautiously placed on the wire of the cage. Thanks to a generous donation, my cousin, who owned a rescue transport company called Fly Me Home, had been flying in a lot of dogs and cats who had been cast aside and ignored to the point of starvation, but this guy looked fairly well-fed. Despite his size, I suspected he was still a puppy. He had to be terrified, and who knew what he might have gone through to end up abandoned near the road, confined to a cage. Not all wounds showed.

I knew I didn't have the strength to pick up the cage with the dog in it. I squatted and dared to open the cage door just wide enough to reach one hand inside. He let me pet him and wagged his tail with joy. I reached toward his collar and snapped the leash on it. Moving slowly, I opened the cage door. He bolted out. Wriggling all over, he kissed my face repeatedly, knocking me off my feet.

I couldn't blame him. Poor guy. Who knew how long he'd been cooped up in that cage? Well, I groused silently, someone knew. The someone who had left him there.

When I stood up, he immediately wrapped the leash around my legs in happiness at being released from his awful confinement.

I laughed at him and untangled myself. "What are you doing here?"

He jumped on me with the exuberance of a puppy. Probably a Labrador, I thought, from the shape of his head and a tail that was meant to steer him when swimming. "What's your name, fella?"

He answered by kissing me again.

I didn't see tags on his collar, but I found a piece of paper taped onto it. I unfolded it and discovered a handwritten message.

*My name is Squishy. I am a very good boy. Please take good care of me.*

"Squishy?"

He wagged his tail with joy.

Dragging the cage behind me, I followed along as he proceeded toward my car as if he knew we had to go somewhere else. I stashed the crate in the back and Squishy hopped in to ride shotgun beside me. He was much larger than Trixie, but I managed to attach her seat belt to him. It wasn't perfect, but it was all I had.

I poured some of my bottled water into his bowl and he lapped it up, leading me to believe that he had been out there for a while.

As he drank, it dawned on me that someone had left him very close to the exit for Wagtail Mountain. The town of Wagtail was the premier vacation destination for people who wanted to travel with their pets. Dogs and cats were welcome everywhere in Wagtail. Restaurants had special menus for them. Stores catered to their every need, from collars and leashes to beds and specialized furniture to matching pajamas for people and their furry friends.

I put my car in gear and headed home toward the Sugar Maple Inn.

To protect two- and four-legged residents, cars were left at a parking lot just outside of town. I transferred my purchases to a Sugar Maple Inn golf cart and drove home. Squishy was a good sport and seemed to enjoy the open-air ride.

When we walked into the inn, Trixie, Twinkletoes, and Oma's golden retriever, Gingersnap, rushed us. They greeted me briefly but immediately focused on the newcomer. When I released Squishy from the leash, he romped with Trixie and Gingersnap.

Oma and our desk clerk, Zelda York, bombarded me with questions.

"Who is this dog? Where did he come from?" Oma liked to dress in what she called chic country style, which translated to skirts that fell below the knee, crisp blouses, and matching sweaters. She wore her wavy gray hair cut short and sassy, which suited her face and her personality.

Zelda claimed she could communicate with animals. I couldn't say either way, but she certainly *seemed* to know what they were thinking. She tossed her long blond hair over her shoulder and emerged from behind the registration desk to meet the dog.

"His name is Squishy."

"That is different," said Oma in the German accent she wanted to lose but I found charming. "How do you know this?"

"Squishy," cooed Zelda, scratching the folds of his furry face. "You are adorable! He's very happy to be here."

His tail wagged nonstop. You didn't have to be a dog psychic to know he was happy. Any dog would have been thrilled to be released from that cage.

"It was the strangest thing," I said. "He was in a crate near the Wagtail exit. And this—" I handed Oma the note I had found on him "—was on his collar."

"This was written by someone who cares about him, but it makes no sense," said Oma. "If you love a dog, then you do not leave him in a cage by the side of the road."

"That's right." Zelda nodded. "The person could easily have driven up to Wagtail and brought him to the shelter. Why wouldn't they do that?"

"Maybe they couldn't for some reason?" I threw out the suggestion because it was the only thing I could think of.

"You mean they were in a hurry? Or afraid someone would recognize them?" Zelda suggested.

"Perhaps the person was very young and failed to understand the danger to Squishy. He appears to be an agreeable dog," Oma observed. "No fighting or growling. He is well socialized."

"I bet they come back looking for him," said Zelda. "My heart would be so heavy with grief when I drove away that I couldn't take it."

"Me, either!" I said. "I'll call the shelter—"

Oma stroked Squishy gently and gazed into his melt-your-heart eyes. "Give them a picture and a description. We will keep him here with us and foster him. Yes?"

Zelda grinned and shot me a thumbs-up.

I was all in. The shelter would have had to find a foster home for him anyway. We could save them the trouble.

I pulled out one of the GPS collars we offered guests for their dogs and fastened it to his neck. If he took off, we would be able to locate him.

In the excitement of finding Squishy, I forgot to ask about Cooper Adams, the convicted murderer.

# Two

In the morning, Oma smiled as she watched Squishy, Gingersnap, and Trixie romp in the empty reception lobby. Twinkletoes wasn't so sure about the new dog and watched him from a safe perch on the desk.

Harold Harvey stormed in. A large man, he had no trouble acting as a bouncer for his restaurant and bar, Tequila Mockingbird. As far as I knew, he was generally liked and even respected in Wagtail. Pointing at Oma, he said, "I need to have a word with you. What do you think you're doing allowing a murderer to live in Wagtail?"

I was taken aback by his threatening posture.

"Harold," Oma said softly, "won't you come into the office?"

As Harold trudged after her, I whispered to Zelda, "Call Shadow and get him down here." I didn't really think we needed backup, but Harold was about the maddest I had ever seen anyone.

Although I had not been invited to join them, I followed

him into the office and sat down on a comfy chair. After all, there was safety in numbers. The dogs joined us but quieted down as if they understood there was trouble afoot.

Oma sat behind her desk and intertwined her fingers. "Harold, it's the law. Everyone is very sorry about your son, Jeff. His death was a terrible loss to all of us. I'm certain you must have been in the courtroom when Cooper Adams was tried."

"He should have received the death sentence. It was a miscarriage of justice. At the very least, he should have been incarcerated thirty or forty years. He should have had his opportunities for a good life taken away from him the way he took them from my boy."

"But twelve years is what he received," said Oma. "We cannot change that."

How could Oma keep her calm and speak so rationally?

"He served his sentence. He paid his debt to society," she said.

"The only way that man will ever pay his debt is if he brings Jeff back to life. An eye for an eye, they say." His voice weakened a bit, and he swiped at his eye with the back of his fist.

"He has been released according to the law and has the right to live freely wherever he likes."

"Not in Wagtail, he doesn't." He sounded gruff again and pointed his finger as if he meant to emphasize every word he said. "Mark my words, Liesel, there will be trouble in this town, and Cooper will be at the heart of it. And it will be your fault for allowing him to live here. You're the mayor! You need to run him off. What does he want here anyway?" He rose and planted his palms on Oma's desk, towering over her. "I'm telling you now that there will be blood on your hands if you allow him to live in this town."

"Harold, I cannot change the law." Oma stood, planted her own palms on the desk, and faced him, her head held high. "And *you* will treat him like any other citizen of Wagtail. Because that is his right. If you do not like the law, then I suggest you make efforts to change it."

He shook his finger at her. "I expected more of you. Rest assured that when he murders someone else, I will let everyone know that it's your fault."

He turned and stomped out of the office, past Zelda and Shadow Hobbs, our handyman, who were listening outside. I thought he would have slammed the door if it hadn't been sliding glass.

"Are you okay?" I asked Oma.

"I could use a cup of strong tea." She fell back into her chair. "With cream and sugar."

I hurried to the kitchen and loaded a rolling cart with tea and freshly baked chocolate chip cookies for all four of us. I brought the cart to the office. Oma sipped her tea, and it seemed as if it brought color back into her pale face. *A magic elixir*, I thought.

After two of the cookies, fresh from the oven and with melty chocolate chips, Oma began to speak. "Cooper Adams lived in Wagtail before his incarceration. That explains why he returned here. I do not remember him well, but his name was familiar to me. About twelve years ago, he murdered a young man. Such an awful thing! He threw Jeff Harvey off a cliff. Jeff was the son of Harold and Jean Harvey, who own Tequila Mockingbird."

"Until today I thought they were very nice," I said. "I didn't know they had a son."

"They say Cooper was a model prisoner. Apparently, he is a computer genius. Quite brilliant in his field and highly regarded before the murder. In his spare time he likes to hike in the mountains."

"He came back to the site of the murder? I think I would stay away from the place where I killed someone," I sputtered. "There have to be all kinds of people who will remember him and perhaps be hostile toward him."

"The evening before the murder," said Oma, "he was involved in some kind of altercation with Jeff in a bar here in Wagtail. Apparently, they encountered each other on the mountain later on, got into a fight, and Jeff fell off a ledge to his death."

"I think I remember hearing about that!" Zelda said.

The mere thought of two men fighting on the mountain where we so often hiked and enjoyed nature sent chills down my back. "So what now?"

Oma shook her head. "We treat him like everyone else. He has done his time in prison and is a free citizen who can live wherever he likes."

"But the police will keep an eye on him, won't they?" asked Zelda, wide-eyed.

"They will not be following him or doing anything to make him feel uncomfortable. We should welcome him as we do everyone else."

"Do you have a picture?" she asked. "I don't want to find myself sitting next to him in a bar or something."

"Zelda! We are not putting out his photo. Unless he

shows disturbing signs of aggression, he is welcome in Wagtail."

"Oh!" Zelda held up her forefinger. "I can look him up online. Isn't the Web wonderful? Such a great resource." She grabbed another cookie and hurried off.

Oma gave me a stern look. "Do not let Zelda start something against this Cooper."

I tilted my head at her. "Oh right. Like Zelda is my responsibility? I can't help what she does outside the inn. And it might be good if we knew what Cooper looks like. Just to be on the safe side. He might have a short fuse."

Shadow nodded. "Sounds like a good idea to me. It wouldn't hurt to know."

Oma didn't budge when I brought up Cooper's photo on the computer that was right in front of her.

The image must have been twelve years old. He looked to be in his twenties with dark brown mid-length waves that I associated with surfers. I didn't see any malice in his brown eyes. In fact, they looked warm and kind. He was dressed in a Brooks Brothers–style shirt with the sleeves rolled back.

"He's rather handsome," said Oma.

I nodded. "Of course, he's much older now."

"There are all kinds of people in this world, and we must give him the benefit of the doubt. Help him begin a new life. Ja?"

"Will do," said Shadow. "But y'all see him hanging around here, just call me." Shadow left the office.

I understood Oma's point of view. Cooper had done his time. And for all we knew, maybe he had killed Jeff in

self-defense. But then he probably wouldn't have been incarcerated. Or would he? I sucked in a deep breath. "In
most towns, only the police would have this information. I
feel sort of sorry for him. Wagtail is so small that it won't
be long before everyone knows."

Oma suppressed a smile. "There is much we do not
know about our neighbors. He will be no different."

On that scary thought, I walked away, calling Trixie,
Squishy, and Twinkletoes.


The next week passed in a blur, and I didn't
hear a word about Cooper Adams, so I assumed he was
settling in.

Squishy was, too. He relied on Trixie and Twinkletoes
and simply did what they did. To the delight of our guests,
Squishy often carried his stuffed pink elephant around with
him. The sight of the young black dog with his pink toy
brought smiles to everyone who saw him.

Even though Wagtail focused on dogs and cats, the town
hosted a number of annual events, one of which was the
Spring Has Sprung Moonlight Hike up the mountain.
Wildflowers were in bloom, and this year, the hike happened to be on the night of a total lunar eclipse. Wagtail
expected hundreds of visitors in addition to our usual
guests.

The plan was to hike up the mountain while the moon
still lighted the way. At the top, during the two-hour eclipse,
a lineup of musicians would perform, and snacks and beverages would be sold. The excitement in Wagtail had reached
a pitch as if an alien spacecraft were landing that night.

In addition to that, a company was holding continuing legal education seminars in the convention center, which meant a lot of lawyers were arriving in town for a vacation while they took classes.

The Sugar Maple Inn had been booked solid. Oma was busy making sure the town had adequate police presence and crowd control, which left me to handle the inn.

On the day of the grand event, Zelda and my mom stood at the registration desk checking people in, and I was putting out fires. Fortunately, there hadn't been many.

Shadow carried luggage upstairs and showed guests to their rooms. His sweet floppy-eared bloodhound, Elvis, had retired to the office with Trixie, Twinkletoes, Gingersnap, and Squishy.

Our registration lobby was packed, and I was doing my best to help speed up the check-in process when Mom elbowed me. "Holly," she whispered, "I don't see a reservation for the Ben."

Ben Hathaway had once been my boyfriend. There were a lot of reasons that we weren't together anymore, starting with the fact that he wasn't fond of dogs or cats. Not to mention that he had proposed to me by text! A pity proposal at that. I didn't think I was a prissy person, but I couldn't imagine anything worse. He hadn't even spelled out the words. What would life be like with Ben if he reduced a romantic event to a gibberish text? Admittedly, my life had not been going well at the time. I had lost my job because I'd done the right thing. And there was the undeniable truth that Ben had thought I should give up Trixie and Twinkletoes. As if! Ultimately, Ben went back to Washington, DC, and I made a new home on Wagtail Mountain.

I suspected he was now jealous of my happy life in Wagtail, because he kept returning. Oma wasn't fond of him and called him "the Ben." Unfortunately, that had caught on in my family and among employees of the inn.

Ben appeared to be with a slender man who had a long, thin nose and virtually no lips. His skin was taut against his face, with hollows under his high cheekbones. He reminded me of a lizard. His piercing eyes took in everything.

"Holly!" Ben cried out, waving at me.

What was he doing here? I sighed and made my way around the registration desk. Ben had lugged in a large hardcover suitcase on wheels.

He reached for me, leaning toward me for a hug. Luckily, I managed to turn my head just in time for his kiss to land on my cheek.

# Three

"Hi, Nell!" Ben called out.

Mom had the good sense to stay behind the registration desk. "Hello, Ben."

Ben adjusted his glasses. "This is Wendell Walters, of Calhoun, Bloom, and Walters."

It sounded like a law firm, but it wasn't the name of the one for which Ben worked. I knew we had a group of lawyers checking in for their annual meeting, but I would have known if Ben's name had been among them. "Hi." I stretched out my hand. "Holly Miller."

Wendell's eyebrows raised and he smiled as if he had heard of me. "It's a pleasure to meet you, Holly."

"And this is Nell Goodwin, Holly's mother," said Ben.

Mom nodded at them.

Wendell cocked his head ever so slightly. "Well now, that can't be. You look like sisters."

It was a sappy line. The kind I expected to hear from someone who was trying to get into my mother's good graces. Sadly, though, it wasn't the first time we had heard that. I was born before Mom finished high school, so she had been a very young mother. News of my imminent debut hadn't been received as happily as a first grandchild usually is. But it had all happened a long time ago. My parents married, and when I actually arrived, I'm told, everyone doted on me.

Mom smiled. "You flatter me, kind sir."

Wendell gazed at my mother. "And you are as charming as you are lovely to behold."

Was he hitting on my mom? Ugh.

She didn't show what she was thinking. Probably a trait I should develop.

"I have you in Hike, Mr. Walters. Shadow will take your bags up for you. The inn restaurant is open for breakfast, lunch, and tea. We do not serve an evening meal because there are so many fine restaurants within easy walking distance. A list is on the desk in your room. Enjoy your stay!"

It was a little bit awkward being my mom's boss, but she had such a natural and friendly manner with guests that it really hadn't posed a problem. I figured if she ever did anything terribly wrong, I could go to Oma and let her be the one to talk with Mom. Even though Mom and my dad, Oma's son, had divorced, Oma and Mom got along remarkably well.

Wendell murmured a thank-you and shot Mom a winning smile. "My wife should be arriving later today. Please notify me when she checks in."

Shadow courteously took the handle of Wendell's Gucci trolley-style bag. "Good afternoon, sir. Please follow me."

I had tried not to make assumptions about people based

on their luggage. But after a while, it became second nature, and I couldn't help it. Wendell's luggage told me he had money, a lot of it, and that he wanted everyone to know.

He held his head high, and if you asked me, from the looks of his eyes, I would have said he was a man who didn't miss a thing. Wendell trailed along behind Shadow.

And now I was stuck with Ben. I knew what he expected. He liked to stay in my guest room. But really, couldn't he have told me he was coming? What if I had another guest? "Have you changed law firms? I thought it had a different name."

"Oh. That. There was a big explosion. Remember the guy with the vineyard? He retired, and these days he no longer practices law. Wine is his life now. This is the resulting firm." He leaned toward me. "I'm hoping to make partner. They're having a big meeting here to decide if a Wagtail office would be a good idea." He held up his fingers and crossed them.

For a moment I couldn't catch my breath. Ben? Living in Wagtail? He had long threatened to move here, but this was getting too close to him actually doing it.

He grinned at me. "It's really great to see you, Holly. I've missed you. May I have my key?"

*My key.* He'd said it so easily, as if he thought he had some ownership of the key to my apartment upstairs on the third floor of the inn. I was sorely tempted to tell him that *he* didn't have a key. But I knew everything in Wagtail was booked. He wouldn't find a room until after the eclipse, if then.

"It's in the office. You could have let me know you were coming."

"Why? You're half owner of the inn. And I'm a special friend." Ben followed me into the room where the four dogs and Twinkletoes snoozed. "You got another dog?" he blurted.

"We're fostering him. His name is Squishy."

"Holly, I know you. You're going to keep him. You really don't need all these animals."

Twinkletoes stretched and hissed at him. I was convinced that she knew Ben had tried to talk me into giving her up. The only time she'd been friendly toward him was when he'd rubbed catnip all over his clothes in an attempt to fool someone into thinking cats loved him. You really can't trick a cat or dog in a phony manner like that. They know better.

I fetched the key from a locked cabinet and handed it to Ben. "You're lucky that I don't have a guest. There's not a room in town to be had."

"All because of an eclipse? That's crazy."

"Apparently some people see it as a time for a major life change. Something about moving out of the shadow of something or someone else."

Ben grinned. "Maybe it's good timing for me, then. I might be your neighbor soon."

*Neighbor.* At least he put it that way and didn't think he would be living in my guest room on a permanent basis. "I'm surprised you want to leave DC."

He nodded. "Me, too. But it hasn't been as much fun since you left. Our friends are involved with their own families. You know, having kids, taking them places. Talking endlessly about what school they should attend. Have you been to a birthday party for a one-year-old?" He rolled his eyes. "Everything is about their children now. Nobody is available for brunch or concerts or Frisbee golf anymore. I know I'm more of a city kind of guy, but I like Wagtail. The close-knit community appeals to me more than it did when we were younger. Hey! I might even end up on the town council and work with Oma!"

I choked at the thought and coughed. Oma would hate that. But there wasn't much I could do about it. Ben was free to move wherever he wanted. "That would be—" I sought a nice word "—something!" He turned to leave but looked back at me from the door. "Wendell's wife was in a very bad car accident. She'll be coming straight here from the hospital. She might need a little extra TLC."

"We'll do our best to help her be comfortable."

Ella Walters arrived two hours later. I was glad to have that tiny bit of background information about her because she looked like she'd been through the wringer. Her blond hair tumbled over a neck brace. Her nose and lips were red and swollen. Stitches laced one eyebrow. She walked slowly, carefully, as if she feared she might fall. I wondered if she should have been released from the hospital yet, let alone traveling. Surely she would be more comfortable at home.

A couple arrived just behind her. The woman, who was carrying a long-haired cream dachshund, said, "Ella, is that you?"

Ella turned her entire body toward the other woman as if her neck was stiff and she couldn't turn her head. "Kelly?"

"You poor baby!" Kelly reached out a slender hand. Her fingernails had been perfectly manicured with a light pink polish. She gently touched Ella's arm. "I heard about the accident but had no idea it was this bad."

# Four

"Ella, honey, are you sure you don't want to go home?" Kelly asked.

"No! Wendell expects me to be here. Of course, he might feel differently about that when he sees me." She let out a little half-hearted laugh.

"Percy, maybe I should take her home," said Kelly.

Percy smiled broadly. "I expect they wouldn't have released her from the hospital if she wasn't ready. Maybe it's best for Ella to be here where she can rest and won't have to worry about the house or meals or anything."

"I hadn't thought of it that way. Ella, don't hesitate to call me if you need something. Anything at all. You hear?"

"You're very kind, Kelly. Thank you."

Shadow took Ella's luggage and walked with her at a slow pace.

"Percy and Kelly Calhoun," the man said to Zelda.

"We're glad to have you here, sir."

"Percy, Ella is in no condition to be anywhere but home in bed," said Kelly.

"Honey, I love you for caring, but you can't go judging what a doctor decided. Someone thinks she's ready to get out. She's probably fine, just a little stiff."

Kelly shook her head. "Seriously? That's how she looked to you? Men!"

Percy shot a smile at his wife. "Isn't it lucky you're here to look after her?"

Kelly scowled at her husband. "Well, maybe so if Wendell is too cheap to get her a nurse to help out until she's back to her old self."

Percy's tone was grim when he said, "Kelly, do not start anything." He forced a smile at Zelda. "I hear there's a moonlight walk tonight."

"There is." She gestured outside. "Just join everyone on the plaza in front of the inn at nine thirty p.m. The moon will be full and gorgeous for your hike up the mountain. There will be food and beverages available for sale at the top, and the eclipse should occur from eleven to one."

"Where do we get glasses? Or will they be handing them out?" asked Kelly.

"I'm no expert, but they tell me no special glasses are required for a lunar eclipse. It's only for a solar eclipse that you need to protect your eyes."

"Will I need to wear boots? And can Taffy go with me?"

Percy guffawed. "Any excuse to do some shopping."

"Sneakers will be fine. And Taffy can go anywhere in Wagtail except for the commercial kitchens. You'll find all the restaurants have menus for dogs and cats. You're awfully cute, Taffy!"

Taffy let out a little bark as if she were thanking Zelda.

"Would you like a Sugar Maple Inn GPS collar in case Taffy gets lost while you're visiting? No extra charge."

"Yes, please! She always stays close to me, but I would be devastated if she were lost."

Zelda fastened the collar to Taffy's neck. "There you go! Just remember to turn it in when you depart."

I finally spoke up. "And don't forget the pet parade in front of the inn. It's at five in the afternoon. A lot of the dogs and cats wear costumes. You can see it best from the porch out front. People come from all over Wagtail to watch it."

Kelly gazed at her husband. "Oh, honey, Taffy is going to need a costume."

"Oof. I have a bad feeling my credit card is going to get a workout over the next few days." He grumbled the words with an affectionate grin at his wife.

As they turned to follow Shadow to their room, the sliding doors opened, and more guests arrived. Percy clearly knew them and stopped to say hello.

An attractive woman whom I guessed to be in her fifties greeted Percy and kissed the air over Kelly's shoulder. She wore a loose-fitting travel set that was color coordinated in cream from her long sweater and trousers right down to her shoes. Her hair, cut in a bob, didn't move. A large ring with a golden citrine stone sparkled on her thin finger and a gold brooch was clasped to her sweater. She announced to Zelda, "Bizzy Bloom."

While Bizzy checked in, a younger woman with short orange-red hair in disarray exclaimed loudly, "This is gorgeous! Don't you love all the trees and everything in bloom?" She wore no makeup and had a rounder body type than Bizzy. She wore an eye-catching crescent moon pin of rhinestones or diamonds on her black top. I smiled at the reference to the lunar eclipse.

Percy grinned at her. "I thought you might like Wagtail, Dinah."

A plump man holding a Siamese cat didn't say much. He gazed around while he waited for the others to check in. "It's so quiet," he said. He looked over at me. "Are there really no cars allowed in town?"

"That's right!"

"What about trash pickup and deliveries?"

"All done by golf carts. We've had to modify some vehicles for special purposes, but we don't allow cars anymore."

"I like that." He held out his hand to me. "Simon Le-Favre."

"Welcome to Wagtail, Mr. LeFavre."

At five o'clock, I walked over to the main lobby to check on things. Trixie, Twinkletoes, and Squishy followed me. Everyone had ventured out to the wide front porch to watch the pet parade, leaving Mr. Huckle in the lobby by himself.

Once a butler for a wealthy local family, Mr. Huckle insisted on continuing to wear his traditional waistcoat. I didn't know his exact age, but his face showed the lines of an older man. He had become the darling of our guests. Not only did he give the inn a special upscale touch, but he always found the time to help out guests, no matter the nature of their needs. While Mr. Huckle conducted himself in a most proper way and denied doing anything so vulgar as gossip, he was undeniably nosy and more than willing to share his observations.

He stood at the desk near the entrance. "It's quite the eclectic mix this week. Most of the guests are planning to go to dinner then join the moonlight hike up the mountain."

We stepped outside to watch the parade. I was pleased to see Ella Walters in a rocking chair and smiling despite her injuries. She no longer wore the neck brace. Her husband, Wendell, stood next to her, one hand on her shoulder. Unlike his wife, there was no smile on his face. I wondered what he was thinking about.

To my surprise, Taffy, the Calhouns' dachshund, walked proudly in a yellow-and-black bumblebee costume with gossamer wings on her back. Kelly's husband, Percy, applauded and cheered for Taffy and his wife. He struck me as a good sport.

"Kelly Calhoun didn't waste any time getting a costume for that cute dachshund," I murmured to Mr. Huckle. "She only checked in a couple of hours ago."

Mr. Huckle smiled. "She asked me which store would be most likely to have costumes for dachshunds."

As we spoke, Squishy ambled down the steps to the plaza and joined the line of dogs, cats, and a pig that paraded before us with their people.

"Will you look at that?" Mr. Huckle began to laugh.

He wasn't the only one. Everyone around us was chuckling. I dashed inside for one of the leashes we kept in the coat room for emergencies and hurried back out to the parade. Holding the leash in my hand, I walked along beside Squishy. Not to be outdone, Trixie and Twinkletoes joined us.

When the parade ended, I clipped the leash on Squishy's collar to be sure he wouldn't wander off. Guests gathered around to pet him.

"Squishy will be up for adoption soon if anyone is interested," I said to the people who admired him.

That resulted in more petting and attention for Squishy, who lapped it up.

Mr. Huckle handed out ribbons that said, *Winner! Wagtail Pet Parade*. You have to love an event where everyone is a winner.

Children ran to their parents, excitedly waving their ribbons.

Oma approached me, with Gingersnap walking alongside her. "Holly! I was just going to text you. Are you still planning to walk up the mountain tonight?"

"Yes."

"Very good. I will be with the town council and Mr. Huckle will watch the inn. You will report any problems to me?"

"Oma. You worry too much."

"If only it were so. People will be drinking. But Holmes will be with you. Ja?"

"That's the plan." Holmes Richardson happened to be the first boy I ever kissed. When I was a child, my parents shipped me off to stay with Oma in Wagtail every summer. Holmes and I worked at the inn, along with my cousin, Josh. But there was plenty of time for playing, swimming, and, just for me, teatime with Oma's fine china and delicious pastries. And now that we had grown up and moved to Wagtail, Holmes and I had fallen for each other again.

"Zelda tells me that the Ben is here," said Oma.

I sighed. "Yes, I'm afraid so."

She shook her forefinger at me in warning. "Holmes will only take so much of that. You must be careful."

"Oma! Holmes is the least jealous person in the world. In fact, he *likes* Ben."

"Humph. A flaw in his judgment. Watch out that our Holmes does not become angry with you over the Ben. Is he staying in your apartment again?"

"Oma! Stop it! Holmes knows there is nothing between Ben and me. I'm going inside to grab a bite before the hike."

Oma shook her head. Lowering her voice, she said, "You must be careful." Oma and Gingersnap bustled toward the green, the large park in the center of Wagtail surrounded by stores and restaurants.

I returned to the porch that ran along the front of the main building of the inn, and Wendell approached me.

"Holly, I didn't realize that my wife would still have difficulty walking after her accident. Would it be possible to reserve one of your golf carts for the duration of our stay?"

Squishy pulled on his leash. Instinctively, I reached out to pat him, but found he was actually behind me and had twisted the leash around my legs. "Yes. Of course. If there is anything we can do make her more comfortable, please let us know. We keep a wheelchair just off the registration lobby. If she finds she's too tired to walk, she's more than welcome to use it."

"Thank you. She's trying her best to get around. Ella isn't the type to sit things out. It's quite hard on her to accept that she still needs help. She would love to go to the eclipse tonight, but she may have to pass on it. I don't think she has the strength to hike."

"She's not the only one who can't walk up the mountain. Wagtail taxis will be available to drive people up the back way. She will miss the hike among the wildflowers, but she can join you at the top. All she needs to do is show up on the plaza."

"Wagtail taxis? I thought this was a no-car zone."

"That's just what we call them. They're actually golf carts. You probably took one from the parking area outside of town."

"Yes, I did. Thank you. That will make her very happy."

He returned to Ella and held out his hand to help her out of the rocking chair. Apparently not impressed by his chivalry, she gripped the arms of the rocking chair and stood up on her own. She walked inside with Wendell keeping a close eye on her.

We followed the crowd entering the inn. They clustered in groups, chatting about where to meet for dinner. Ben had joined Wendell, Percy, and his wife.

We turned to the right and trailed behind Ella along the windowed hallway that led to the reservation lobby. She walked by herself, with the benefit of a cane on her right side, and seemed to be doing quite well.

I unlatched Squishy's leash. He really didn't need it inside.

But no sooner had I done so than I recognized my mistake. In his exuberance, he loped forward, heading toward the one guest who wasn't steady on her feet. "Squishy!" I cried out. "No!"

# Five

I ran toward Ella and reached her in time to stabilize her. She looked scared, but for the first time, I realized just how pretty she was. Pretty was actually an understatement. Underneath the bruises and cuts, Ella Walters was stunning. She could have been on magazine covers with her vivid sky-blue eyes and perky nose. "I'm sorry," she said hoarsely. "I'm . . . I'm afraid of big black dogs."

Squishy did not understand that and looked up at her with those adorable brown eyes, expecting to be petted.

"I have to apologize," I said. "I didn't know. He's very sweet. He didn't mean to bowl into you." I latched his leash onto his collar and urged him away from Ella.

"I'll be fine." She watched Squishy and didn't take her eyes off him. "I just would rather not get close."

Not used to being ignored, Trixie sat and swished her tail frantically. She even offered her right paw.

"You're very sweet," said Ella.

"Do you have a dog?" I asked.

"Me? Um, not at the moment."

I'd heard people answer that way before and it usually meant their beloved dog had passed away. "I'm sorry. Maybe you'll get another dog soon."

Ella's husband approached us. His eyes met Ella's. "Looks like a black Labrador I used to have."

"Aren't Labs wonderful?" I said.

He made no effort to pet Trixie or Squishy. He stared at them. "They're highly overrated if you ask me."

One rarely heard that kind of remark in Wagtail. I tried to recover from my surprise quickly and said, "Have a good evening." What a jerk!

With Squishy securely on his leash, I hurried to the registration lobby, pulled the key for one of our golf carts, and stashed it in a drawer with a note appended to it. Reserved for Mr. and Mrs. Wendell Walters. Then I dashed off another note and posted it on the computers so the staff would be informed when assigning golf carts.

We weren't expecting more guests to check in, so I locked the registration lobby doors. Guests could exit but couldn't come back inside that way. A sign directed everyone to the main lobby where they could ring a bell to summon whoever was on duty if they needed something during the evening hours.

Twinkletoes wound around my ankles. It was her way of reminding me that she expected to be served her dinner. I scooped her up into my arms and cuddled her. "Okay. Let's go get your dinner. Fish, I suppose?" She sprang to the desk and leaped to the floor, leading the way back to the main lobby.

"There you are." Ben loped down the grand staircase in

a sport coat and khakis. Relaxed attire, but not completely. "I'd like you to join us at dinner tonight."

I assumed he meant his friends in the law firm. Oma's words about being careful came back to me. I didn't want to look like we were a couple. "Thanks, but Holmes is coming for dinner."

"Oh. In the private kitchen? Wouldn't you rather go out? Oma wouldn't mind. She loves me. You know she would want you to go out. You've been working all day."

He didn't realize that Oma wasn't keen on him? How odd. "Sorry, Ben. I can't do it tonight."

"But I want them to get to know you. You can sell them on Wagtail."

"I would be happy to talk to them about Wagtail, but I can't do it at dinner tonight. Sorry. Enjoy your meal." I walked away.

He caught up to me and hissed, "Holly, it's embarrassing not to have a date."

"Look, Ben. I didn't even know you were coming." I probably would have reserved time for dinner with him had I known he would visit, but that was beside the point. "Maybe I can talk with them about Wagtail tomorrow. Okay?"

I walked away again, but Ben hurried after me and followed me into the private kitchen.

When Oma was raising my father and his sister, she thought they should have a kitchen and family room away from guests. A place for family meals and movie nights in pajamas with the family curled up by the fire. Big enough for homework and school projects and for Oma to cook and bake when she felt so inclined.

My favorite thing about it was the magic refrigerator, so named because it never seemed to run out of food. Extras from the inn kitchen were delivered to local people in need of a helping hand. Even so, wonderful leftovers from the inn's kitchen always filled the magic refrigerator.

Opening it was fun because I never knew what I might find. I pulled out a container marked **Ship Cat's Dream for Twinkletoes**, which turned out to be mostly cod with a few teensy bits of cheese in it. The inn chef knew to add taurine, which is vital for the health of cats. The label on a larger container indicated it was **Turkey Delight for Dogs**. I set them on the countertop and realized that Ben was glaring at me.

"You'd better get going or you'll miss your friends."

The door swung open. "There you are!" Holmes entered with the easy comfort of a person who belonged. "Ben! I didn't know you were in town again. Welcome back." He strode around the counter and planted a kiss on my cheek. "Are you joining us for dinner?"

"He's dining with the hotshots from his law firm," I said. "He's hoping to make partner."

Holmes, who had walked away from a large architectural firm to pursue projects on his own, said, "Wow! Good luck, Ben."

"Thanks. I'll see you at the moonlight hike." Disappointment showed on Ben's face as he left.

"He didn't look very happy about it. Think they'll turn him down?" asked Holmes.

"It's hard to know what's going on there. Apparently, they're meeting here to determine whether to open an office in Wagtail."

Holmes stared at me for a moment, concern etched on

his face. "No kidding," he said softly. He forced a smile. "Wagtail seems to grow more each day. I can hardly keep up." Holmes pulled a spring salad out of the fridge, set it on the table, and returned to search again. "Is Ben staying with *you* again?"

"Yes, but I did not invite him. I didn't even know he was coming. It's as if he thinks my guest room is always available for him. I wish he had found somewhere else to stay." I placed butter on the table for bread and found that the tossed salad only had to be dressed. Black olives, onions, red pepper, bib lettuce, and bits of bacon had been added beforehand.

"How would you feel about Ben living in Wagtail?" Holmes asked.

I shrugged. "Okay, I suppose. He's free to move anywhere he likes."

"I think he's still in love with you." Holmes watched me.

I wrapped my arms around him. "I doubt that's the case." In truth, I wasn't so sure about that. But Ben would be busy with his job, and maybe he would meet someone else. Besides, who was I to tell Ben where to live or work?

Holmes turned me toward him, and we lingered over a kiss. Then he focused his attention on the fridge. "Chicken with pasta, mushrooms, and asparagus?" asked Holmes.

"Sounds good."

"I'll heat it up."

Mr. Huckle pushed the door open. "Sorry! I didn't mean to interrupt."

"Hello, Mr. Huckle," said Holmes. "Won't you join us for dinner?"

"I would be delighted." He fetched dishes and cutlery to

set the table while Holmes watched over the pasta dish and I warmed dinner rolls.

When we sat down to eat, Holmes said, "A guy named Wendell Walters tracked me down this afternoon."

"He's staying here. He's one of the lawyers in Ben's group," I said.

"That's curious. He wants to buy the land that belongs to my parents and me."

"If I am not mistaken, that's a highly coveted piece of real estate," Mr. Huckle observed.

"It is to us." Holmes carved into his chicken breast. "He was . . . How can I say this?"

"Brusque?" asked Mr. Huckle.

"That would be a very polite way of describing his manner. Pushy, rude, and crude are more accurate."

Mr. Huckle nodded. "A man who is used to getting what he wants, I believe."

"What did you say?" I asked.

"I told him it wasn't for sale."

"That's straightforward. Anyone could understand that." I sipped my iced tea.

"Mr. Huckle is right. He's not the kind of man who takes no for an answer. He visited my parents, too. Even went to their house and tried to intimidate them. I'm sorry to hear that he's connected to Ben's firm. He's not someone I would want to deal with. The land isn't for sale, but he left such a sour taste in our mouths that we would never consider selling to him, anyway. Why do people act like that?"

"Did he say he was interested in it for a law office?" asked Mr. Huckle.

Holmes nodded. "But we all know the land is far too

many acres for that. I suspect he has a much bigger project in mind. His interest in it wasn't all that surprising. He's not the first. It was his ugly reaction and harassment of my parents that upset us all. Threatening them with dire consequences if we don't sell to him. I've told them not to open the door to him again. I need to let Wendell know that's not how we conduct business here in Wagtail."

The next couple of hours passed as we ate our dinner and chatted about Squishy's odd circumstances, Ben and his law firm, and Ella Walters's car accident.

"She's quite beautiful," said Mr. Huckle. "I remember when she was a reporter for the newspaper in Snowball."

"I had no idea that she lived here before." I speared a mushroom.

Mr. Huckle squinted. "I don't think she lived in Wagtail or Snowball. A bit farther out, as I recall. On a farm, I believe. I didn't know her personally, but I knew of her."

"Do you remember a young man being murdered about twelve years ago by a fellow named Cooper Adams?" I asked.

Mr. Huckle sighed. "Such a terrible thing. The lives of two young men ruined."

"What happened?" asked Holmes. "I was living in Chicago then. My folks never mentioned it to me that I can remember."

"The two of them had too much to drink and squabbled over a girl. I believe they were both camping on the mountain. They ran into each other a couple of hours later and fisticuffs ensued. Cooper pushed the other man, Jeff, over a cliff and he died."

"Cooper was found guilty of murder and sent to prison,"

I added. "He was recently released and has returned to live in Wagtail."

Mr. Huckle grimaced. "Everyone is talking about it. Some residents are not at all happy that he returned. I remind them that other ex-cons probably live among us and we don't even know."

After we cleaned up the kitchen, Holmes and I left Mr. Huckle to take care of the inn while we joined the crowd on the plaza.

Gingersnap had gone with Oma, but Trixie, Twinkletoes, and Squishy were hiking up the mountain with us. I allowed Trixie to be off-leash, but Squishy wore a harness and leash because I worried that he might wander off. Twinkletoes rode on Holmes's shoulder, her hind legs in a cat backpack. We set off in the bright moonlight with dogs, cats, Ben, and a number of people from his law firm.

We were divided into groups of twenty, each with a leader who pointed out the spring flowers in bloom on the sides of the path where we walked. We drew Logan Verlice as our guide. I knew him as a bartender at Tequila Mockingbird. I was under the impression that he was around thirty and skilled at flirting. It didn't hurt that he was attractive with a well-defined jaw and hair that waved ever so gently in spite of his constant attempts to shove it back off his face.

"Welcome to Wagtail, everyone," he said. "I see a few familiar faces, and one that I'm very happy to see: *my mom*."

Bizzy Bloom blushed and fondly placed an arm around her son. She still wore her cream outfit.

"The vast carpets you see on the sides of the path are white fringed phacelia," said Logan. "The timing for a moonlight hike is perfect because our dogwood trees are in full bloom. That's white mountain laurel and rhododendron gleaming in the moonlight along with wild hydrangea."

"What are these little things?" a woman asked.

"They're clusters of white trilliums. You can see them dotting the woods on both sides."

Most people were quiet, almost reverent, as we hiked. Owls called out warnings as we approached.

Even the dogs and cats seemed inclined to stick to the path. Twinkletoes leaped from Holmes's shoulder to the ground and sniffed the world next to Trixie and Squishy.

At the top of the mountain, a plateau had long ago been carved out for picnics, concerts, and other events. Toilets were discreetly hidden behind a copse of trees. A permanent stage was available for performances and concerts. I recognized some local bands getting ready to play. Assorted vendors selling drinks and food flanked the sides of the stage.

In the daytime, the vista of the mountains and valleys was breathtaking. It was different, but no less impressive, in the moonlight. Small lights twinkled from cabins in the distance.

Holmes threw a blanket over the ground just as Ben steered his law colleagues in our direction. Holmes stiffened at the sight of them.

# Six

Wendell grinned at Holmes. "We meet again. Most fortuitous!"

Ella Walters waved slowly and made her way toward us. When she was seated. I asked her how she felt about letting Squishy loose to play with the other dogs.

"That's fine. When he returns, perhaps you can keep him over on your side of the blankets. I'll be all right if he's under your control."

I released him and to my horror, he went straight to Ella. She stiffened and Wendell shooed him away.

Fortunately, Squishy ran to join in the dog fun.

Twinkletoes snuggled on my lap and purred.

Introductions flew around. I had already met the Walterses, Wendell and Ella, and the Calhouns, Percy and Kelly.

Simon LaFavre seemed a bit older than the others. He wore round gold-framed glasses and breathed heavily after the walk up the mountain. He wiped his brow with a handkerchief and asked Ella if he could share her ride on the way back.

Bizzy Bloom wasn't out of breath at all. She looked as if she had just walked out of a spa. Her makeup and hair were perfect, as were her nails.

"Your son is so handsome!" Kelly gushed.

Bizzy smiled. "If only he would settle down. Get a career with a 401(k) or start a business. Sometimes I think he just needs to meet the right girl." She sighed. "But I can't tell him what to do like I could when he was little."

Dinah Bonetti raised her eyebrows. "He's about my age, isn't he?" She had dressed for our excursion in khaki trousers and layered sweaters. Very practical but without the same attention paid to her attire as Bizzy. She didn't have Bizzy's panache. No polish shone on her short nails, and while her attire was completely appropriate, it was more functional than fashionable. Apparently, Dinah had brought the blankets that they all now shared.

Bizzy appeared to be at a loss for words at the thought of Dinah dating her son.

But Kelly wasn't. "You two would be darling together!"

Percy rolled his eyes. "Please forgive my wife. She thinks she's a matchmaker, always trying to set people up."

Kelly ignored her husband. "Dinah, you're so smart. I can't imagine why you haven't found the right fellow yet."

"Probably because I'm married to my job," she replied. "It's hard to meet men when you work long hours."

The dynamics in their little group fascinated me. I found it remarkable that having just met them, I felt I could already see who liked whom in their group and who didn't!

Dinah proved to be very businesslike. She asked questions about the population of Wagtail and the number of tourists who visited. "Wouldn't Snowball be a more profitable location for an office?"

Holmes nodded. "Probably. There is certainly a larger population. They feature skiing while we're about animals. So there is a seasonal component to consider. Our attraction is valid all year, while their busy season is winter. There are some chain stores and a whole lot more bars, though I think our restaurants beat theirs any day. And while Snowball grabs every major commercial opportunity, in Wagtail we want to preserve our way of life and the quaintness of our town."

Kelly watched her dachshund, Taffy, play with Trixie and Squishy as she chatted with Ella about their antics.

Percy, Kelly's husband, listened intently to Holmes as he spoke.

"Wagtail doesn't have, and doesn't particularly want, all the big-city trappings. We move at a slower pace over here and cherish our small-town ways. If you live here for a while, you get to know most of the residents. There's a steady stream of visitors, and now that we have a big convention center, we can accommodate larger groups. We also have Dogwood Lake, which provides a lot of summertime fun like boating, water-skiing, fishing, and swimming."

"Wagtail sounds like the kind of place I would rather reside," said Dinah. "I've been thinking about getting a couple of dogs, but my schedule in DC is too hectic. It wouldn't be fair to them. Am I correct that they could come to work with me in a Wagtail office?"

"Absolutely," I assured her.

Ben looked worried. It appeared that he had competition

for the position of the attorney who would be residing in Wagtail.

"Count me out," said Bizzy. "It's a beautiful getaway, but I have responsibilities at home. I'm on the library board and the philharmonic and the Women Lawyers Association, not to mention Read with Glee, which provides free books to children up to third grade."

"Well, we all know why you like it here, Ben," said Dinah.

Ben turned red, looked slightly panicked, and glanced at me. "I like the people. DC is great, but the residents of Wagtail are more friendly and involved in the goings-on here. It's not like Washington, where I commute to work and don't recognize a single person on the way."

"Not for me. Though I would love to be closer to my son." Bizzy stretched her legs and rose. "I hope they have something good to drink." She strode away, heading toward Logan.

That appeared to be the signal for their entire gang to get up and check out the various food and drinks available. Even Ella stood with a hand from Percy. She walked away a little more stable than I recalled her being at the inn. Only Ben and Holmes remained.

Holmes leaned toward me. "I'm going to have a word with Wendell."

"Why?" asked Ben.

"I'll fill you in later."

"Hold it!" Ben stretched his hand toward Holmes. "What do you want with Wendell? Don't mess this up for me. You heard Bizzy. That's already one vote against an office in Wagtail."

"It has nothing to do with you. But if I were you, I'd be very wary of Wendell."

"I'm not kidding, Holmes." Ben shouted after him as he walked away.

Twinkletoes stretched and ambled toward the dogs, who romped. She assumed her Egyptian pose and watched them.

And that left me alone with Ben. "Let's go get a drink before they're all gone."

"What does Holmes want with Wendell?" Ben asked as the two of us made our way toward the dim lights of the food concessions.

"Wendell asked Holmes about some property he and his parents own." I hoped my casual tone made it sound unimportant.

Ben grabbed my arm. "But that's fantastic! Why didn't you tell me? It means he's all in for an office here!" Ben yahooed so loud that people turned to look at us.

"Does Wendell have more clout than Bizzy?" I asked.

"Not technically." Ben snorted. "But the reality is that Wendell is very opinionated and quite often gets his way. It's as though he manipulates us."

"It sounds like Dinah might be interested in relocating."

His enthusiasm waned. "I wasn't expecting that. I don't know her all that well. To be honest, I don't think any of us are very close. Maybe Wendell and Percy. I think their wives are friendly. I'm going to look for Holmes and make sure he doesn't mess up this opportunity for me." Ben took off and merged with the crowd.

I watched as Simon browsed the various food booths by himself. He spoke to each vendor, asking questions about their food.

The band that had been playing left the stage and another group began the theme song of *2001: A Space Odyssey*. I looked up and realized that Earth's shadow had already fallen on a good bit of the moon, darkening it.

A hush fell over the crowd. Everyone watched the moon as it became darker and turned red.

Someone touched my arm. It was Zelda, who had come with friends.

"Isn't it fabulous?" she asked. "This is a new beginning. A new start. A time to put old problems behind us and step out of the shadows that others cast upon us. Can you feel it?"

Actually, I couldn't, but I wasn't tuned in to mystical matters like Zelda was. "Are you getting a fresh start?"

"I hope so!"

Twelve dancers twirled across the stage in sparkling outfits.

"You didn't bring Trixie?" Zelda asked.

"Of course I did. She's playing with the other dogs." I looked where the dogs played. The moon felt even darker to me as I gazed around for my little white dog. Panic welled inside me. I couldn't see Twinkletoes or Squishy, either. Though Squishy would be harder to locate in the dark. "Do you see Trixie, Twinkletoes, or Squishy?"

I tried to remain calm, but it wasn't working. I could feel my heart beating in my chest. I ran around to the back side of the stage. Several couples were smooching, but there was no sign of my babies. I returned to the area where dogs raced around and played.

The band switched to fifties dance music and people jumped to their feet to swing dance. They twirled with abandon, many of them singing the lyrics along with the music.

I hoped the dogs weren't underfoot, but I didn't see them.

The music stopped briefly, and while the band prepared for their next tune, I heard Trixie. It had to be her. I knew the sound of that long, melancholy yowl all too well. It meant someone was dead.

# Seven

"Oh no!" Zelda cried. "Is that . . . ?"

I nodded. "I think so."

Zelda's eyes widened. "What do we do now, Holly?"

I pulled out my phone and clicked on the GPS collar app while Trixie continued to howl in the distance. Trixie had the great distinction of having dog collar number one. I pressed on the link. A map popped open, showing me her location. "I'm going to find her. If you see Holmes, let him know."

"I'll come with you. You don't know what you'll find."

"Thanks." I studied the map, trying to get my bearings. "It looks to me like they are northwest of us."

We began to hurry in that direction.

"Holly! Holly!" I turned around and saw Ben running toward us. He panted when he caught up to us. "Come dance with me."

"You hate swing dancing. Besides, we have a problem. We'll catch up with you at the inn."

"What's going on?"

"We think someone has been murdered. Later, Ben."

"What? I'm coming with you."

Great. Just what we needed. I checked the GPS map again. They were in the same location. "Come on, then."

Zelda shook her head. "Ben, you would be so helpless out here alone. You'd better stick close to us."

We began to walk fast in the direction indicated on the map.

"Don't try to ditch me," Ben whined.

"We should put a GPS collar on you!" Zelda retorted.

My bigger concern, aside from the very strong likelihood that someone had been murdered, was that my phone might lose its Internet connection. It was very spotty in Wagtail and worse in the mountains. There was nothing I could do about that, though.

Our path took us through a dense forest of assorted trees. Branches brushed against our faces and grabbed our hair.

Ben moaned and griped about it. "How did the dogs make it through here? Why wouldn't they take a path or something?"

We pointed out how lucky we were that it was spring and the undergrowth was still minimal.

And then my fear became reality. I lost the Internet connection. It wasn't as though I wanted to keep secrets from my friends, but Ben might panic if he knew. Between the tall trees and the darkened moon, the woods only heightened the ominous feeling I had. I switched on my phone's flashlight, which helped a little bit. At least we wouldn't fall over protruding roots.

The soft ground of discarded pine needles turned hard, and my light revealed that we were on stone. I stopped abruptly. The stone only stretched about eight feet before us. There were no more trees in front of us. We had come to a precipice.

"Do you see them? Why have you stopped?" asked Ben.

"We're at a ledge of some sort."

Trixie's howl was much closer now.

"Don't push me," I said. "Stay where you are. I need to look over the edge of this stone."

Ben and Zelda argued between themselves behind me. I tried to put them out of my mind and crawled forward slowly on my hands and knees.

Trixie's yowl sounded as if it came from below. I leaned forward. The drop from the stone looked to be about twenty feet. It was hard to tell in the reddish darkness. I shone my light toward the sides of the rock and spotted an ill-defined trail that skirted around the ledge and led downward. I took a deep breath and called out, "Trixie! Trixie!" I wanted to be sure she was there before I made my way down.

She howled again.

I turned to Ben and Zelda. "Here's what we're going to do. You two stay up here on this rock. I'm going to see how far I can get downhill and whether I can reach Trixie, Twinkletoes, or Squishy."

They agreed. I picked my way to the right side of the ledge and jumped a few feet to the little path.

But then I heard Ben ask, "Is anyone else getting an Internet signal?"

Oh boy. That would be trouble. I shouted, "Ben, don't

go anywhere without Zelda. I don't want to have to get a search party for you."

I hurried down the slope, pushing through old brush and crawling over fallen trees. I hoped no snakes were in my vicinity.

"Trixie!" I called. "Twinkletoes?"

Twinkletoes looked up at me, her mostly white fur dim but visible in the reddish light cast by the moon. "I see them!" It was only Twinkletoes that I saw, but I bet the three of them were together.

I made my way down and glimpsed a very dark movement, like a bear. "Squishy!" He happily romped over, excited to see me. I reached for his neck and stroked him while I snapped the leash onto his harness.

I could see Trixie's white fur, but she wasn't budging, which only confirmed the worst. Gritting my teeth, I moved forward carefully. "Hi, Trixie," I said softly.

She yowled in that pitiful voice again.

Beside her lay a human figure.

# Eight

My light caught the head. The orange-red hair left little doubt in my mind that it was Dinah. She lay on her back, but her head tilted at a troubling angle, making it difficult to see her face from where I stood. I stroked Trixie and told her she was a good girl before I made my way around Dinah. Worried that her neck was broken, I didn't want to touch or move her. I might make things worse.

Once I was on the other side of her, there was no question that it was Dinah Bonetti who stared at me in shock. She wasn't blinking, which led me to think the worst had happened. Even the best rescuer would not be bringing Dinah back to life.

I tried my phone, hoping against hope that I would be able to make a call or text for help. No such luck. I shouted, "Zelda, I found them. Can you walk back far enough to get a signal and call for help? We need the rescue crew!"

"Going right now."

"What should I do?" yelled Ben.

"Go with Zelda."

"Are you sure?"

He wouldn't be of any help here and things would only be worse if Ben got lost. "Go with Zelda!" I called out again.

And then I sat down and petted Trixie, Twinkletoes, and Squishy. He sniffed Dinah and backed away, then sniffed again. To his powerful dog nose, Dinah probably didn't smell right anymore, and it was scaring him.

Feeling guilty that I hadn't checked Dinah for a pulse, I shone my light on her again. She still stared ahead without blinking. That had to be a sign that she was dead. A trickle of blood appeared at the corner of her mouth. Bits of pine clung to her outer sweater. I presumed that indicated she had come through the trees much as we had. Her nails were short and uneven, bitten to the quick. From the stress of her job? Or had she been worried about something else?

Why would she have wandered through the woods? Why hadn't she gotten a drink and a snack and stayed with her group? What could possibly have lured her here, away from everyone?

I angled my phone a bit, wishing I could see better.

I gave up and stared out over the dark vista. At least some stars shone brightly. Would Dinah's death impact the law firm's decision to open an office in Wagtail? Probably.

"Holly! Holly!"

I recognized Holmes's voice. "Down here!" I held up my phone, pointed the light upward, and wiggled it in the hope that he could see it.

"We're on the way," he yelled.

I heaved a sigh of relief. Minutes later, Holmes,

Dr. Engelknecht, and half a dozen people who were part of the Wagtail Rescue Crew descended upon us, along with Zelda and Ben.

Dr. Engelknecht shone a flashlight on Dinah and winced at the arc of her neck. "What happened?"

"I don't know. I assume she took a bad fall from the look of her neck."

He flicked his light on her sweater. "I see. I hear Trixie found her."

"Yes."

Dr. Engelknecht pronounced Dinah dead and took photographs of her, the area around her, and the incline down which she had fallen.

As soon as the crew attached Dinah to a stretcher and began the laborious task of carrying it to the closest trail big enough for a golf cart, Dr. Engelknecht used a can of spray paint to mark the location where Dinah had been found. "We'll be able to see more in daylight," he said to no one in particular.

Ben hadn't said a word.

"Are you okay?" I asked.

"Yes," he murmured. But he didn't say another thing.

"This must be a shock for you," I said, hoping he would feel comfortable enough to express his emotions. After all, Dinah had been a colleague. They might have even been friends outside of work. I didn't know.

Ben stayed mum, which was quite unusual for him.

The moon had begun to shine more brightly again, and I could see a bit better. Maybe not showing emotion made Ben a better lawyer. But given that someone he knew well and worked with had just died a tragic and horrible death, his silence concerned me. I couldn't help wondering if he knew something about Dinah's demise.

We trudged along behind the rescue squad, all of whom panted when they took a break. Twinkletoes and Trixie followed along. Squishy willingly walked beside me on the leash.

Dr. Engelknecht studied his phone. "The Wagtail ambulance is on a walking trail about fifty feet to the south."

One of the rescue crew members nodded. "That ledge is called Drunkard's Folly."

"You know it?" I asked.

He nodded soberly. "It's on maps but off the beaten path."

"Why that name?" asked Ben.

"I can't say for sure, but I've always been told that you'd have to be drunk to go up there. It's not easy to get to."

One of the other members of the crew snorted. "This is where I brought my girlfriends when I was a teenager. It's very private but well-known in Wagtail because a guy named Jeff Harvey died here."

"Jeff Harvey. The one who was murdered?" I asked.

"Yeah. Some guy pushed him."

"Some guy? Do you mean Cooper Adams?" I asked.

"Could have been. I just know about Jeff because he was a friend of my brother's. Nice guy, but he had a trigger temper. Back in the day, he always had the best pot."

When everyone had caught their breath, they continued on their way, cutting back through the trees. We were all relieved when we saw the Wagtail ambulance and a wider path. The ambulance was a retrofitted golf cart set up to transfer people to the parking lot where patients could be transferred to a real ambulance to be transported to the hospital in Snowball.

"Take her to my office," said Dr. Engelknecht. "I'll have a look at her and determine if she needs to go to the medical examiner in Roanoke. I suspect that will be the case." Dr. Engelknecht boarded the makeshift ambulance to ride with Dinah.

It took off just about the time that the eclipse ended. The full moon shone brightly on us as we walked down the path toward the bottom of the mountain and around to the spot where we met up with other eclipse watchers returning to town.

"Someone is going to have to tell the others in the law firm," I said. My eyes met Holmes's.

"No problem," said Ben. "I can take care of that."

I thought it very kind of him. It would be hard to break the news. "I'll go with you," I offered.

At the inn, Holmes squeezed my hand and asked, "Are you all right?"

I nodded.

"It can't have been easy sitting there in the dark with a dead woman."

"I'm okay. I had Trixie, Twinkletoes, and Squishy for company. Thanks for helping, Holmes."

He removed a tiny evergreen twig from my hair and kissed me good night. "I'll walk you home, Zelda."

"Thanks, Holmes!" she said.

Ben and I didn't meet up with the other members of the law firm until we returned to the inn. They had gathered in the lobby.

"Have either of you seen Dinah?" asked Percy. "We lost her back on the mountain."

Bizzy tsked. "I bet she met someone to dance with. She's a big girl. She might not come back to the inn tonight."

Ella backed away from Squishy, which reminded me that she was afraid.

"Ella, why don't you go up to our room?" suggested Wendell. "I can wait for Dinah down here."

"Good night, all." Ella walked away.

"There you are, Ben!" Wendell exclaimed. "We wondered what happened to you." He held a pile of neatly folded blankets. "We took the liberty of bringing Dinah's belongings back."

Kelly nudged her husband. "Now, when Dinah gets here, don't go embarrassing her, Percy. You are not her daddy."

I looked at Ben and back to Kelly again. Had Kelly just intimated a relationship between Dinah and someone? That was news to me. Was Ben going to tell them what happened? Or had Dinah's death hit him more than I realized?

"Maybe you should go into the Dogwood Room and sit down," I said, my hand tight on Squishy's leash.

Ben nodded. "This way."

Percy and Wendell squinted at Ben, clearly not understanding what was happening.

Ben deftly steered them into the Dogwood Room. The rest of us joined them.

Percy's forehead wrinkled. "What's going on?"

Wendell frowned at me as if I had done something awful. He sat down in a large club chair and crossed his legs. The picture of a man comfortable with himself.

Kelly grasped Percy's arm as if she expected bad news.

Bizzy sat primly, her hands gracefully folded in her lap. "I don't understand. Why are we gathered in here? Dinah will come back to the inn when she's ready. We are not her keepers."

Ben blurted, "She's dead. Dinah is dead."

I shot him an I-can't-believe-you-just-did-that look. Really? That was how he thought he should inform them? I gave him a break. I barely knew her at all. Maybe he couldn't say it any other way because he was too broken up about it.

"What?" said Wendell, staring blankly at Ben.

Percy groaned. "That's not funny."

Ben held up his hand as if he meant to signal them to be silent. "I'm afraid it's true. It appears that Dinah wandered off, lost her way, and fell off a cliff."

Kelly blinked at him. "Are you making this up? Is this some sort of gag and Dinah will come leaping in here now?"

With Squishy's leash tied to my waist so he wouldn't frighten Ella, I hurried to the kitchen and loaded a serving cart with liqueur glasses, old-fashioned glasses, scotch, bourbon, and several liqueurs. When I rolled the cart into the Dogwood Room, Bizzy was saying, "This can't be true. I don't believe you."

Simon peered through his glasses at Ben. "Why would anyone make up something so heinous?"

A shiver rolled through me as I watched them. Percy massaged his mouth pensively. Kelly watched her husband. Bizzy appeared to be in shock.

Simon seemed unbelievably indifferent. "What have you got there? Any liqueur? I'm not much for the hard stuff."

"Yes. I thought you might need a drink. Bizzy, can I get you something?"

"Yes, please."

I served each of them while they continued to talk.

Wendell looked from Ben to me. "She fell off a cliff? What cliff? I didn't see any cliffs."

Ben nodded. "I'm afraid so. I don't know why she wandered over there . . ."

Percy stood, jammed his hands into his pockets, and walked to the windows that overlooked Dogwood Lake. At this time of night, I doubted that he could see much. Maybe a few lights on houses or boats.

Kelly watched him with concern. "Where is she?"

"She's at the doctor's office," I said in a soft voice. "He's a local medical examiner."

"What did she die of?" asked Wendell.

I thought that was obvious.

"From the fall, I guess," said Ben.

Percy turned around to face everyone. "I'll notify her parents. We must have their number in our personnel files." He spoke gruffly, as if he wanted the entire conversation to come to an end.

It didn't work.

"I can't believe this," said Bizzy, her voice barely audible. "Was she drunk? Percy, you would know!"

"Me? How would I know?" he retorted.

Kelly looked at her husband. "I didn't know that Dinah had a drinking problem. She had wine with the rest of us at dinner."

"She didn't have an issue with alcohol," said Percy. "Not

that I know of, anyway. But Dinah was very independent. There's probably a lot we don't know about her."

"What's that supposed to mean?" asked Ben.

"Nothing untoward. She always forged ahead with whatever she had in mind," said Percy. "I expect she didn't tell us every detail of her life. Her hobbies and interests, for instance."

Wendell sipped a glass of scotch. "It's like losing a member of the family. Poor Dinah."

"It just goes to show how fast something like this can happen." Kelly snapped her fingers.

Simon raised his glass in a toast. "To Dinah. We will miss her."

One by one, they went up to bed.

When they had all gone to their rooms, I made quick work of stashing the serving cart away before heading up to my bed. But I couldn't sleep. Thoughts of Dinah ran through my head. She had been young. Close to my age. In the prime of her life, really.

Sleep continued to elude me. I tossed and turned. Eventually, I donned my plush Sugar Maple Inn bathrobe and ventured down to the private kitchen through the secret stairs in my dining room. Trixie, Twinkletoes, and Squishy acted as if they were ready for another adventure and bounded down the stairs. Squishy bolted through the dog door in the private kitchen that led to the lobby. Trixie followed along, but Twinkletoes stayed with me. I poured milk into a little pot and placed it on a burner to heat up. I had expected the two of them to return right away. When they didn't, I pulled the sash on my bathrobe tight and peeked in the lobby. I didn't see a soul.

Tiptoeing a little farther, I spotted Squishy in the Dogwood Room. Trixie roamed nearby. It took a moment for me to realize that someone was hugging Squishy. His tail swished back and forth with joy.

"Hello?" I said.

The person's head popped up, a mess of blond hair covering her face. She pushed it back and wiped teary eyes with the backs of her hands. "Oh, hi," said Ella. "I hope I didn't disturb you."

I gazed around. Casey, the night manager, must have gone to the reception lobby. "Not at all."

"I couldn't sleep."

"Me, either. Would you like some warm milk?"

"I don't want to put you to any trouble."

"I was just warming some for myself." I motioned for her to follow me. "I have to hurry so it won't boil over!"

I dashed back to the kitchen and moved the milk off the stove just in the nick of time. The door to the kitchen opened tentatively.

"Come on in," I called.

"This says Private."

"Technically it is. We like to have a little hideaway where we can relax."

"This is nice. Very cozy. Homey. Our kitchen is pretty, but it looks sort of sterile, like no one lives there. Wendell won't let me leave anything out, like a sugar bowl or a bowl of fruit. He always wants it to look like it's ready for a photo shoot."

Squishy remained by her side. Her fingertips brushed the top of his coat. I didn't say anything, but I had worked hard at keeping him away from Ella. She certainly wasn't acting afraid of him now.

"Must be hard to cook in a kitchen like that." I poured her hot chocolate into a mug. "Marshmallows?"

"Of course! I love marshmallows. It's hard to *live* in a house like that."

"Did you know Dinah well?" I asked.

"Not really. She was nice enough, and smart, I guess, but I always got the feeling that she looked down on Kelly and me because we weren't clever lawyers like her."

Oh! That surprised me. I hadn't picked up on that, but then, I'd barely spent any time with Dinah.

"Someone said you were a reporter."

Ella seemed surprised. "That was years ago. Who told you that?"

"Mr. Huckle, who works here. He said he remembered you but didn't know you personally."

"I didn't think anyone here would remember me anymore. That's nice. But I haven't worked in years. I do a lot of volunteering, though. There are so many people in need. Especially around Washington, DC. It feels and looks so prosperous, but you would be amazed at the number of people barely scraping by." She sipped her hot chocolate. "We're surrounded by strangers, walking by them every day without a clue about what they're going through. How they're suffering." She scratched behind Squishy's ears.

I wondered if she might be a candidate to adopt him. She had clearly gotten over her fear of him. But some instinct told me it was too soon to make that suggestion.

"So you grew up around here?" I asked.

"About an hour away. My mom still lives in the same little bungalow on the small farm where I grew up." She lowered her voice to a whisper. "I'm so incredibly lucky to live in a mansion. But I'd trade it any day for a sweet little house with framed cross-stitch on the walls and hand-hooked rugs." She no longer whispered when she said, "I caught the first whiff of early honeysuckle today. Funny how a scent like that sticks with you. If I could, I would plant it all over our backyard. I know it's invasive, but the smell would be worth it. I have honeysuckle-scented French soap in all my bathrooms." She giggled. "Wendell had a fit about it until I told him it was imported from France. Then it was okay! Isn't that ridiculous?"

It was, but I knew people like that. "Wendell must be very upset about Dinah."

"I think the worst day will be when they go back to work and she's not there. The empty office, you know. That's when they'll feel it the most." She rose and went to the sink to wash her mug.

"Thanks, but you don't have to do that. That's my job," I joked. But it was part of my job to clean up after guests.

"I don't mind." She held her hand out for my mug.

"How did you and Wendell meet?" I asked, handing it to her.

"There was a big murder case in Snowball. Wendell represented a friend, Cooper Adams. It seemed like the evidence was stacked against him. Still, Wendell got him a reduced sentence. No one ever thought that would be possible. I was in court every day to report on the case. Wendell flirted with me and sent me flowers. He was very romantic, and things developed from there." She dried her hands, folded the towel carefully, and hung it to dry. "I guess I'd better get some sleep."

"I don't mean to be rude, but are you sleeping in the Dogwood Room?"

Her face flushed red with embarrassment. "Wendell is such a light sleeper. Honestly, I can't cough or turn over or move without waking him. But with my bruises and injuries, I can't lie still all night. I'm much more comfortable dozing off on a sofa for a while and then reading a book until I doze off again. I'm sorry. I guess I shouldn't be sleeping in a public area."

"I wish we had another room for you—"

"Oh no! Don't do that!"

"—but we're booked solid. At least let me get you a blanket and some pillows. You might be more comfortable in the library. Fewer people will be walking by."

Ella followed me to the main-floor storage room. I carried a fluffy blanket and a couple of pillows to the library for her. "When you're up for the day, just leave them here on the window seat. I'll pick them up when I make my morning rounds of the inn."

"Thank you. This is so kind." She slid her hand over Squishy's head.

Squishy wanted to stay with Ella, but I coaxed him to come upstairs with Trixie, Twinkletoes, and me. This time, when I went to bed, exhaustion overwhelmed me, and the next thing I knew, it was morning and a chocolate croissant, under a dome to prevent Trixie from eating it, waited on a tray in my bedroom next to a pot of tea, a china cup, a cat cookie, and two dog biscuits.

The French doors in my bedroom that overlooked Wagtail had been opened and birds chirped outside. I slipped on my fluffy Sugar Maple Inn bathrobe, poured myself a cup of tea, and ventured to my little balcony to see the town coming to life.

Early joggers and walkers, accompanied by dogs and cats, inhaled the spring air as they moved along the sidewalks and the green.

They looked so content. That thought brought the events of the previous night back to me. It had been bad enough, but today everyone would have to face the reality of Dinah's death. I guessed that their entire group would be checking out. It happened from time to time when someone got sick or an incident at home required a sudden departure.

We hadn't known Dinah. While anyone's death was a tragedy, we wouldn't be experiencing the upset and emptiness that her friends and coworkers would feel.

I hopped in the shower while Twinkletoes and the dogs ate their prebreakfast snacks. I blew my hair dry, then slipped on a blue wrap dress with a bold white floral pattern.

The door to my guest room was still closed. I assumed that Ben was sleeping in after our late night. Trixie, Twinkletoes, and Squishy followed me down the grand staircase. I could see Oma eating breakfast.

I took the dogs outside. Twinkletoes sat on the railing of the porch and waited for us to return. Fortunately, Squishy had caught on quickly and knew that breakfast came next. He ran back to the inn at top speed.

Dr. Engelknecht and Officer Dave, who was actually a sergeant but was lovingly nicknamed Officer Dave, were eating breakfast with Oma. I was glad to see one empty chair at their table. "May I join you?"

"Of course," said Oma.

Shelley Dixon, who was sweet on Officer Dave, brought me my usual mug of hot tea without me asking for it. "Is it true?" she whispered.

Officer Dave, who had eyes for Shelley, couldn't help smiling at her. He nodded.

"That's terrible! What a tragedy. Holly, our specials this morning are lemon ricotta pancakes, breakfast tacos, and cloud eggs."

Oma pointed at her plate. "I have tried the cloud eggs and can recommend them."

I had never heard of them. "Okay, I'll take a chance on cloud eggs. How about minced chicken for Twinkletoes and breakfast burgers for the pups?"

"Be right back."

When she left, I said, "While I'm glad to see you here for breakfast, Dr. Engelknecht, I'm guessing your presence has a purpose?"

He sucked in a deep breath and spoke in a low voice so others would not hear. "I can't draw definite conclusions yet. We'll know more after the medical examiner has a look at Dinah. But in general, people who fall tend to land face down. It's an instinct to hold out one's hands to break a fall, which often results in broken arms. I don't see that here. All indications are that Dinah landed on her back, which would indicate that she was pushed."

I knew he was keeping something from us last night, but I never imagined it was anything like this. "I assume she could have fallen backward?"

"Possibly. But no, I don't think that's what happened."

"You're saying Dinah was murdered?" I whispered.

"Yes. That's what her body is telling me. The mortuary van arrived early this morning to transport her to the medical examiner's office in Roanoke. We'll know more by tomorrow, perhaps even today if we're lucky."

I looked at Dave, who said, "Naturally the entire law firm is suspect, including Ben. I'll be asking them to stay, but I can't force them to remain here, and they probably know that."

"Ben?" His name tumbled out and I shook my head. "He has an alibi—me. He was with Zelda and me when we went looking for Trixie because she was barking."

"You were with Ben the entire evening?"

"No. The whole group, including Dinah, sat together at first. Then people got up for drinks and snacks. I wasn't with him then."

Dave shook his head. "Too bad. I was hoping I could scratch one person off my list." His eyes met mine. "I hope he didn't have a motive?"

I didn't say anything for a minute. "Not a particularly good one. He wants the firm to open an office here and he wants to be the attorney at that office. It sounded to me like Dinah wanted that job, too."

"Rivals," muttered Dave.

"This is terrible," said Oma. "The Ben is not my favorite, but he would not do such a thing."

Shelley brought my breakfast, which turned out to be a beautiful soft egg yolk in the center of a baked cloud of egg white. Strawberries and a slice of cantaloupe gave the dish additional color. Two slices of bacon lay next to a serving of crispy country fried potatoes.

The dogs wasted no time digging into their breakfast burgers, which were mixed with egg and a little cheese. Twinkletoes ate her breakfast primly.

Oma mock-cleared her throat, and we turned our attention to Percy, Kelly, and Taffy walking down the grand staircase. Percy spotted us right away and came directly to our table.

"Good morning," said Percy. "I am terribly sorry to leave your charming inn, but in light of the circumstances, our group will be checking out today. Could you see to it that our bill will be ready? I'll be picking up the tab for the entire group."

Officer Dave rose to his feet. "Good morning. Sergeant Dave Quinlan." He held out his hand and shook Percy's. "May I have a word with you, please?"

Dave escorted Percy out to the terrace that overlooked the lake. They returned quickly.

I could imagine Percy being a formidable opponent in court. Tall with a broad chest, he didn't carry much extra weight. I was willing to bet he went to a gym several times a week to stay in shape and had probably played sports in college. But I could see that he was disturbed by the news that Dinah had been murdered. His jaw was tense, and he came straight toward our table. "It appears we will be staying after all."

"We are glad to have you," said Oma. "Please let us know if there is anything we can do for you."

He nodded numbly. "Thank you for your kindness."

He joined Kelly at the table where she sat. I couldn't help watching. Her eyes grew large, and she reached for her husband's hand.

Dr. Engelknecht thanked us for his breakfast and checked the time. "I'd better get going. I have patients to see. Dave, I'll let you know the autopsy results as soon as I hear anything." He took off in a hurry.

"Our office is available to you should you need it to interview anyone, Dave," said Oma. "Holly, will you take care of sending flowers to the family of Dinah?"

"Yes, of course."

Oma gazed around the full tables at our guests eating their breakfasts. "Perhaps we should move into the private kitchen for further discussion. The dining area is filling up."

I topped off my mug with more tea and beckoned to the dogs and Twinkletoes. They followed us into the kitchen, where Oma, Dave, and I sat down at the farmhouse table.

We had barely settled in when the door burst open. Mom and Mr. Huckle walked in.

"I just heard!" said Mom.

Oma brought them up to date on the events of the previous evening while Mom made a pot of strong tea for us.

"Percy gave me the name and number for Dinah's parents." Dave scribbled them on a pad for me. "I'll give you the address when I get it. Man, I hate making these calls. I always think how I would feel if a total stranger called me to say my loved one was dead. Dinah is their daughter. Their baby. She's probably the one who made it big and they're incredibly proud of her. And now, one phone call and all their hopes and dreams will instantly be wiped out."

"I don't know how you can do it. What an awful job," I said. "But I think Percy was going to notify them."

"Comes with the territory," said Dave. "But it's always gut-wrenching for me. I can't imagine what a nightmare it is for them. I promised Percy that I would call them first. Hey, Holly, don't send anything until after I contact them, okay?"

"No problem." The only thing worse than getting a call

from the police about their dead daughter would be getting bereavement flowers from strangers before they knew why.

"Where is the Ben?" whispered Oma.

"Upstairs in bed, I guess."

Dave rubbed his forehead. "It was a late night for everyone. It's probably good that he's not here."

Mom brought the teapot to the table. I added a creamer of milk and a sugar bowl.

"Good. We have much to talk about. Have you made any progress, Dave?" asked Oma.

Dave shook his head. "It's as if Dinah walked up the mountain, sat with her friends, and then vanished." He looked around the table at us. "I think it's safe to assume there is a limited number of people here who know Dinah. Who are they and what do you know about them?"

"Obviously, there's Ben. Then there's Percy—"

Dave interrupted me. "Percy appears to be in charge. Is that right?"

"I would think so. Percy and Bizzy." I watched as he wrote it down. "His name is first in the firm's name, so I would guess that he's the bigwig. His wife, Kelly, is very nice. She dotes on their dachshund and is very concerned about Ella."

Dave nodded and wrote down the names.

"Simon LeFavre strikes me as a little aloof," said Mr. Huckle. "Almost as if he works there but doesn't consider himself part of the group somehow. I know nothing about him, but he's a quiet kind of person. None of the others were palling around with him. Ben says he's a legal whiz of some sort."

"Interesting. Who else?"

"Bizzy Bloom," I said. "I have to hand it to her. She's very stylish. Not runway-model fashionable. More comfortable chic. Her son is Logan Verlice, the bartender over at Tequila Mockingbird."

"Really?" said Oma. "I must meet her. He is a fine young man."

"You mentioned Ella?" said Dave.

"She's married to Wendell Walters," said Mom. "I think she's quite a bit younger than Wendell. She was in a terrible car accident recently and came here to be with her husband directly from the hospital, which I thought sort of odd. If it were me, I would have gone home and told my husband I would see him when he got back."

"Hmm. Some serious devotion there," said Mr. Huckle.

"And she's afraid of big black dogs," I added. "But I think Squishy may have won her over."

Squishy raised his head at the sound of his name.

"Oh!" Oma perked up. "Is she an adoption candidate?"

I shrugged. "Maybe!"

"Is that it?" asked Dave.

"As far as I know."

"So here's my plan. Ben is our best source of information because he's part of this group. He knows them. But—" he raised his forefinger "—Ben has a vested interest, so he's not entirely reliable. And I have to consider him a suspect."

"You mean because he wants them to open an office and give him the job of working here?" asked Mom. "He wouldn't kill anyone for that."

Dave scoffed. "People have murdered for less than that. Holly, I need access to Dinah's room, please. And I need you to hang out with Ben and infiltrate the group."

"Ha ha. Very funny."

"I'm not joking."

"It's not a bad idea," said Mr. Huckle. "Ben is our best route to finding out which one of these people pushed Dinah to her death."

"I'm not *infiltrating* anything."

"Holly, it's not as if one of them will confess to me during an interview. We need to know which ones had motives and which ones have alibis. I can handle the alibis. They'll tell me that in a hurry. But no one is going to tell me how they would benefit from her death. That's what I need you to find out."

"You are aware that I have a job?"

"Maybe go to dinner with them," said Mom. "Hang out with them in the evenings. Cozy up to them and get the scoop. I would put my money on the three women."

"You think one of them murdered her?"

"I don't know. But I think they might talk. And they won't be relaxed around Dave like they would be around you."

"So we're your spies?"

"I wouldn't say that. More like undercover informants," he teased.

"A murder club," said Oma.

# Nine

Before Dave borrowed the inn's office to interview Dinah's friends, I took a few minutes to go over the daily schedule. Nothing stood out, so I phoned the one person who I thought might know something about them.

I had met Sophie Winston when I worked in fundraising. Undoubtedly the best event planner in the Washington, DC, metropolitan area, Sophie and I had a lot in common. For starters, we were both crazy for animals. And we'd both had a few murders to solve.

Sophie answered the phone on the first ring.

"Sophie, hi! It's Holly Miller."

"How nice to hear from you. Are you back in town?"

"I'm afraid not. I'm in Wagtail and we've had an unfortunate death. Dinah Bonetti, a lawyer with Calhoun, Bloom, and Walters. Do you know anything about them?"

"I do. I'm so sorry to hear that Dinah died. That's awful. I've met Dinah. She was recommended to my cxhusband, Mars, when one of his clients had a tax problem. She's supposed to be brilliant with money."

"Is there a reason someone in their group might have a beef with her?"

"Not that I know of. Bizzy Bloom is an amazing woman. She's always on top of things and highly involved in a number of charities. Definitely a socialite but not full of herself. Percy Calhoun seems to be a nice guy. His wife, Kelly, is the outgoing one in that couple. I would call Wendell Walters prim. Like an old maiden aunt. Everything must be just so for him. His wife, Ella, is very nice. Always looks perfect and says the right thing, but I don't know her as well as I know Bizzy. Does that help at all?"

"It gives me someplace to start. No rumors of dissatisfaction in the law firm?"

"Gosh, not that I've heard of. I'm truly sorry to hear about Dinah. She was still so young. When are you coming back for a visit?"

"No plans yet, but I promise I'll call you when I'm in town."

"That would be great! I'd love to get together."

"Thanks for the info."

"I'm glad I could help."

I said goodbye, disconnected the call, turned the room over to Dave, and went on my rounds, thinking about what Sophie had said.

Each morning, I checked all the public spaces to be sure everything was in order. No lightbulbs out. No raincoats, shoes, briefcases, or beloved stuffed animals left behind. Trixie, Squishy, and Twinkletoes followed me. We started on the third floor, where I lived. That never took long. On a rare occasion a lightbulb went out, but most guests never ventured up to the third floor. Half of it was my apartment, and we used the other half as a huge room for storage. Followed by the dogs and Twinkletoes, I walked down the grand staircase to the second floor, where Dave met me and used my passkey to open the door to Dinah's room.

The soft blue of the walls was accented by a set of blue-and-white-checked chairs in front of the window that faced the green. White nightstands and a matching dresser interrupted the blue theme and kept it feeling light and breezy. A white mantel over the fireplace held blue chinoiserie vases.

Dinah wasn't the tidiest person. Or maybe she had been in a hurry. She had flung a sleeveless green silk dress over the duvet on the queen-size bed. A red dress was draped over the back of a chair, and a navy dress lay in a crumpled puddle on the floor where she had probably stepped out of it. I didn't know which dress Dinah had worn to dinner. Dresser drawers hung open. A pair of black sneakers embellished with bling lay on the floor.

"When did she check in?" asked Dave.

"Yesterday."

"So she was in here for probably six, seven hours max?"

"That's a good guess. And she went out to dinner." I peered in the trash can. "Looks like she bought or brought a bag of chips with her."

"And she bought a box of cookies in Wagtail." Dave nodded toward the bed.

I recognized the box immediately.

"Don't touch anything."

"I wouldn't dream of it. I don't need anyone blaming me for her murder. Although my fingerprints are probably in

Splash somewhere." I smiled at the name. When Wagtail went to dogs and cats, Oma had named all the bedrooms after dog and cat activities.

I backed up and glanced in the bathroom. For a woman who didn't wear much makeup, she had brought a lot of lotions and drugstore items with her. Among them, a contact lens case lay on the counter, along with a toothbrush, toothpaste, and a plastic container of powder with sparkles in it.

"Did she bring a briefcase?" I asked Dave.

"I haven't seen one. Why?"

"If I had some kind of beef with someone at work, that's probably where I would stash something about it. Notes or dates or whatever." I heard his camera click.

"It's over here in the closet with towels draped over it as if she meant to hide it."

My eyes met his.

He placed it on the bed and tried to open it. "Locked."

"Check the drawers in the nightstands and the dresser," I suggested.

"That would be an extremely feeble attempt at hiding a key," he muttered as he pulled open drawer after drawer. "Aha! Found it inside a book in the nightstand." He unlocked the briefcase and snapped it open. File folders lay inside. "Looks like mostly case files. I'll ask Percy about them." He snapped it shut. "Would you tell Marina not to clean the room? I'll get someone over here to collect everything and do a proper inventory."

"No problem." We left the room, and I locked the door behind me.

Dave went downstairs, but I spied Marina's cleaning cart in the hallway and went in search of her. Trixie,

Squishy, and Twinkletoes, who had been excluded from Splash so they wouldn't contaminate anything, played happily in Hike. The difference between Dinah's room and the one occupied by Wendell and Ella was remarkable. Hike was pristine. Nothing cluttered the surfaces. There wasn't even a glass or book on the nightstand.

"Good morning, Marina."

"Good morning." She smiled at me.

"Would you skip cleaning Splash for a few days? The police need to collect evidence first."

"Yes, of course. That is where the lady was staying who fell off the cliff?"

"Yes."

"Everyone is talking about it. Do you know anything about the killer, Cooper? I'm nervous to walk around town with him on the loose."

"Why do you think Cooper killed her?"

"That's what everyone is saying. It is just like he did before."

"I don't know much about him, but I don't think you have anything to worry about. Maybe don't go near cliffs?" It was a lousy attempt at calming her nerves, but I honestly didn't know how to respond. "I know for a fact that Dave is just beginning the investigation. Dinah could have been killed by anyone."

"Aha. Or too much to drink, perhaps?"

"Maybe. The autopsy results aren't back yet, so I wouldn't be too worried about a killer on the loose." I was concerned about that myself, but I also thought it was early in the investigation to blame Cooper.

I continued my inspection of the inn. Trixie knew to stop

where the cat wing began. No dogs allowed! Squishy followed her lead and lay down, pawing at Trixie's tail like a bored puppy.

Simon emerged from his room with a good-size Siamese on a leash. Twinkletoes noticed her but minded her own business.

"What a beautiful cat," I said.

"Thank you. I was pleased to be able to bring Blossom here. I hate leaving her home alone. I always hire sitters, of course, but it has been wonderful to have her here with me, and she loves the screened balcony with the tree for her to climb. I'd like to build something like that at home, but I doubt that my condo association would approve it."

"You didn't take her up the mountain last night."

"I was worried that it would be too much too soon. It was a comfort to know I could leave her in the room and no one would be opening the door and accidentally letting her out. I don't know what I would do if she got lost."

"I can relate to that. Is she wearing an AirTag? They're great for tracking cats and they're lighter than most of the GPS systems."

"That's a good idea. I can take her to the dining area, right?"

"Absolutely. And there are some fun things to do with cats in town."

"I was looking through the list on the desk in my room yesterday. We will definitely try some of them if we stay long enough. I fear this sad business with Dinah may have cut our visit to Wagtail short."

"I believe you may be staying a bit longer after all. Percy confirmed that a while ago. How are you holding up?"

"It's a shock, of course. Dinah was a complex woman, but we got along for the most part. I'm terribly sorry that she died. She was so young. The whole thing is a bit odd to me. Why would she have ventured off like that by herself in the dark?"

It was a good question. Why, indeed?

"Hey, I noticed that a lot of people had special backpacks for their cats last night. Can I buy one here?"

"Absolutely. I bought mine at Purrfectly Meowvelous. Be sure to take Blossom with you. She'll love that store."

"Thank you. That's very helpful." He went on his way with Blossom, who explored various scents as they strolled.

I walked through the hallway to the end of the cat wing and back. Trixie knew that we would reappear at the library. Sure enough, Trixie and Squishy wagged and wriggled in greeting at the inn's library. Ella had neatly folded her blanket and placed it in a pile with the pillows. I collected them, intending to put them away.

When we walked by the dining area, Kelly's dachshund recognized her friends from the night before and bolted to the lobby for a game of chase.

Kelly ran after her but then stopped to watch. "Isn't that cute? They're all playing like old friends."

They were adorable, bowing as dogs do to indicate they want to play. All tails wagged. Twinkletoes had no interest in such behavior and leaped to the concierge desk and the safety of Mr. Huckle.

"Have you seen Ella this morning?" I asked Kelly.

"I texted her about joining us for breakfast. She said she was out walking and would grab a bite in town."

"I'm glad to hear that. I think she's on the mend."

"Most definitely," said Kelly. "I'm eager to spend some time in town myself. All those cute stores! I have to bring some things back for the kids."

She whipped out her wallet and proudly showed me photos. "Percy Junior is built like his dad. He loves football, but it scares me to death. It's so easy for boys to be injured. You know?" She flipped the plastic sleeve. "This is my little darling, Naomi. I love her to bits, but the child has so much energy that I can hardly keep up! In a few years she'll be old enough for a driver's license. On the one hand, I'll be glad when she can drive herself, because she is one busy kid. On the other hand, I'm not ready for her to drive yet! My parents are staying with them while we're here." She snapped her wallet shut, crossed her fingers, and held them up. "I hope my parents have the stamina to keep up with those two."

"You're lucky that they can help out. I'm sure the kids love being indulged by them."

"Oh, don't you know it! They'll be impossible when we get back and don't give in to every little thing."

Her children were sweet, but I needed to switch the conversation back to Dinah and the group. "How is everyone else taking Dinah's death?"

"I haven't seen all of them this morning. Simon acts as if nothing happened. Bizzy has been weepy, which I, personally, find more normal than Simon's indifference. Percy is plain gloomy. You know how men try to hide their emotions. Your Ben is worried like my Percy."

I longed to correct her and tell her that he wasn't *my Ben* in any sense of the phrase. But Ben was an important link to these people, and they were more likely to open up to me if they thought I was close to Ben, so I bit back my desire to set that straight. "Why is Percy worried?"

"It upsets the apple cart. They'll have to hire someone to replace Dinah. He says she was very good at her job. And they will have to pick up all her cases, you know. She was up for partner, as well, so things are looking better for your honey!"

"My honey?"

"Ben! I'm thrilled to have you joining our group. To tell the truth, I've never been particularly fond of Wendell. Of course, Percy had to socialize with him. Ella is lovely, which made it more bearable for me. I remember my mom complaining about the men and women splitting up at dinner parties. All the men talked together, and the women gathered in another room. It's a cliché, isn't it? But I never felt as if I had to like Percy's business partners. Lawyers aren't the most interesting people. And when it comes to someone like Dinah, I'm just at a loss. She was so serious. We had absolutely nothing in common."

"Kelly?" Percy beckoned to her.

"It was nice chatting with you, Holly. Taffy! Taffy, come!"

The little dachshund reluctantly left her playmates and returned to Kelly, who placed her hand on my arm. "Don't worry about Ella. I'm going to text her about meeting up for lunch while the others are dealing with all that boring office business."

"She's lucky to have you looking after her."

"That's what friends do."

"Kelly!"

"I'm coming, Percy! Hold your horses!" She swept Taffy

up into her arms and, with a little wave, rushed to join her husband.

That was a lucky break. Kelly liked to talk, and she'd said a few things that caught my attention. Dinah's death probably changed more than I could imagine. Most deaths did.

I heard voices down the hallway where Percy and Kelly had gone. Not yelling, but stern voices. Afraid guests were having some kind of difficulty, I hurried along toward the reception lobby, pausing briefly to stash the pillows and blankets in the storage room in case Ella needed them again.

When I walked into the reception lobby, Zelda was manning the desk and watched wide-eyed as Percy, Kelly, and Officer Dave appeared to be in a standoff.

"What's going on?" I asked.

Dave didn't take his eyes off Percy.

Percy turned to me. "Sergeant Quinlan will not allow me to accompany my wife during her questioning. As far as I'm concerned, I am her attorney and I have every right to be present."

I had to think that through for a moment. He was her attorney? Why would Kelly need an attorney? Did Percy believe that his wife had murdered Dinah? Was there some personal squabble between the two? An affair between Percy and Dinah was the only thing that came to mind.

The corner of Dave's mouth pulled back in annoyance. "Kelly hasn't been accused of anything. I would like to hear what she saw last night." He glared at Percy. "Not what you told her to say."

"She has the right to remain silent, and you're not pushing my hand in this matter."

Wow. Didn't people use the right to remain silent when

they were guilty of something? If Kelly murdered Dinah, she was either a fabulous actress or completely insane. Or both. She had acted totally normal a few minutes ago when I spoke with her. I knew enough to realize that Percy had the upper hand. Everyone had a right to remain silent. Both men were clearly upset. I wasn't sure how to end this stand-off. And I couldn't help wondering what Kelly might say that had Percy so worried. Could he be relying on her as a witness? Had he left her side last night during the eclipse? In that case, Kelly couldn't give her husband an alibi. No wonder Dave was concerned and wanted to talk with her alone. There were endless possibilities, and instead of easing the situation, Percy had managed to elevate it to a point where they looked guilty of something.

I tried my best to speak calmly. "I understand both of your points of view. Dinah was a friend of yours, Percy. I'm sure you have an interest in knowing what happened last night. Kelly is very perceptive. She may have noticed something that you didn't see. Why don't you give Sergeant Quinlan an opportunity to hear what Kelly has to say? If you feel a question is inappropriate, you can tell him so. But Kelly is an important witness and may be able to help with the investigation of the death of your friend."

I felt like I was rambling, but something must have hit home with the two of them. Percy grumbled but nodded and the three of them returned to the office. Before closing the door, Kelly reached her hand out and gave me a thumbs-up.

"Well done!" whispered Zelda. "You showed up just in time. Two more minutes and Percy would have left with his wife. Poor thing. She was stuck in the middle. I could tell *she* wanted to talk with Dave." Zelda leaned toward me across the desk. "What do you think he's afraid of?"

"I wondered the same thing! Have you heard any scuttlebutt about what happened last night?"

"Nothing very interesting. When I came to work this morning, Ella was stepping out. She looked tired, like she hadn't slept, which is to be expected. It's hard when someone dies. It's such a shock. And so many things run through your head. I still don't understand how and why Dinah was in such an odd location."

"I don't, either. They're checking for alcohol or meds in her system. Something that might have caused her to be disoriented."

"Like a roofie? That's the only explanation, isn't it?" Zelda gasped. "Do you think someone slipped Rohypnol into her drink last night?"

"I hadn't considered anything like that. I suppose it's possible." I thought about mentioning what Dr. Engelknecht had said about someone pushing Dinah but thought better of sharing that with Zelda just yet. She blabbed information far too willingly. "We'll know more when the autopsy results are in. Until then, all we can do is wait."

"And pick people's brains. I took a lot of photos last night. I should look through them. Maybe Dinah is in one of them."

"Do you think any of the photos came out okay with the moon so red?"

"I think so. I'll go through them tonight. I bet I'm not the only one who took pictures with my phone. I'll ask around."

"Thanks, Zelda. That could be a big help!"

Because Dave was using our office, I thought I'd check with Shelley to see if she had overheard anything while serving.

I went to the dining area, which had cleared out after the breakfast rush. Shelley was getting the tables ready for the lunch crowd.

I poured myself a fresh mug of tea and one of coffee for Shelley and sat down at a table. She promptly joined me with a grilled ham and cheese sandwich.

"Busy morning," she said. "And just about everybody was talking about the woman who fell off the cliff last night. Do you think Wagtail will be sued?"

"Is that what people were saying?"

"Some of them." She took a bite of her food.

"I certainly hope not. She wandered off the trail. We had guides, and people were cautioned to stay with their groups. I honestly don't know what more could have been done."

"A few people thought someone must have pushed her over."

That didn't take long for people to figure out. "Did they say who would do that?"

Shelley sipped her coffee. "Cooper. All the locals think it was Cooper. You know, the murderer who just moved to town. Personally, I think it could have been him. But this morning one person intimated that Dinah was hard to get along with."

"Did anyone mention other problems with her?"

"Not that I heard. Simon and Bizzy ate breakfast together, and Simon thought Percy was upset about something and it all would have come out at the meeting today."

"I hope Percy wasn't involved," I muttered. But there it

was again. A reason Percy might not want his wife talking to Dave. Was Percy afraid Kelly would blab about his workplace problems? He probably talked about work troubles at home. Everyone did.

Shelley finished her sandwich. "Well, lunch should be easier for me. Ben's lawyer friends are having a catered lunch over at the convention center. I hope the medical examiner says Dinah was drunk and died from an accidental fall. Dave and I are going to the Blue Boar for dinner tonight and I don't want him to have to cancel. That's awfully selfish, isn't it? A woman died and I'm thinking of myself."

"Some special occasion?" I asked. The Blue Boar was the fanciest and most elegant restaurant in town.

"No. I think Dave's romantic side has finally emerged. It just took a while for him to realize that he has one! He was so busy trying to be the tough guy in town so people would respect him that he didn't let his soft side show."

"I'm glad you brought it out."

A woman walked in from the main lobby. "Excuse me. Oh! There he is!" She held her hand out. "Here, boy! Here!"

Trixie ran to her but Squishy stayed put and watched her.

Lanky with short straight hair the color of light brown sugar, she squatted to pet Trixie. "Oh, you're just the sweetest! Is she good at paying attention?"

"Sometimes. How can we help you?" I asked.

"The shelter sent me over here."

# Ten

"I'm looking for a youngish Labrador retriever to compete with in rallies." The woman eyed Squishy.

"Rallies?" asked Shelley.

She strode toward us. "Hi, I'm Becka Bartusek. Rallies are sort of like obedience competitions. It's teamwork between the person and the dog. The shelter sent me over here to see the black Lab."

Her words struck me like a cold knife in my heart. She was here to adopt Squishy! I had known we were only fostering him, but I loved the guy and hadn't thought this day would come so soon. I swallowed hard. For a long moment, no one spoke.

Becka reached toward Squishy. He got to his feet and wagged his tail as she cooed sweet nothings to him.

Meanwhile, I called the shelter, where I was told she had passed their inspection process for adoption and was interested in a Labrador. I had hoped she hadn't been approved yet, but that was not the case.

"Do you live around here?" I asked.

"Gosh no. I saw Squishy's picture on the shelter website and drove hours to come to meet him. He's just darling! Exactly what I was looking for."

Oh no! It got worse by the minute.

"May I take him outside on a leash to see how he does?"

"Yes, of course." Shelley and I exchanged sad looks. I rose to collect a leash and harness from the cloakroom, but Becka whipped exactly what she needed from a tote bag that she carried.

Trixie, Twinkletoes, and I followed the two of them outside. Squishy acted as if he thought he was in the daily parade and walked with his head high and his tail wagging. Trixie tagged along next to him. When Becka said sit, Trixie and Squishy promptly sat. "I'll take both of them!"

"I'm sorry, but the Jack Russell, Trixie, is my dog. She's not up for adoption." I longed to say the same about Squishy. It was hard being a foster mom! I forced myself to think about the wonderful new life he would have being the center of attention and training for rallies.

Reluctantly, I agreed to bring Squishy to the shelter so she could sign the adoption documents and take him with her.

Pushing back tears, I drove him over to the shelter in a golf cart, with Trixie and Twinkletoes along for the ride. I hugged him one last time and told him what a good boy he was. When I handed him over, I left in a hurry and couldn't look back.

We returned to the inn, and now that the office was empty, I busied myself with paperwork so I wouldn't have to think about Squishy.

Dave showed up at four thirty with his white long-haired

dog, Duchess, walked into the office, and plopped down on the sofa. "Dinah's autopsy reveals red wine in her system. According to her friends, she drank two glasses with dinner, but her blood alcohol content was at .18, so she must have consumed more after she reached the plateau on the mountain. Enough to make her woozy and cause serious confusion and disorientation. But the bruises sustained in the fall and the position of the body when found indicate that she fell backward. The official cause of death is homicide."

"So Dr. Engelknecht was right."

"Looks like it. What do you know about Percy?"

"Is he your prime suspect?"

Dave cocked his head. "Didn't you think he was acting very odd this morning?"

"You mean when he was afraid to have Kelly speak with you?"

"Mm. The man is definitely hiding something."

"You don't suppose he was sleeping with Dinah? Kelly is so attractive, and she clearly adores him."

"It wouldn't be the first time two people fell into a relationship at work. Late nights, a few drinks . . . I wish I'd had my eye on that group last night," Dave groaned.

"You couldn't have anticipated something like this. If you had joined us, someone else might have been murdered. Zelda took photos and thinks other people did, too. Maybe you'll see someone following Dinah in one of them."

"I should be so lucky. You were sitting with them, weren't you?"

"Yes, but they all got up to look around and get drinks at about the same time. I didn't notice anything peculiar."

"The thing is," said Dave, "Dinah fell in a location that someone had to direct her to. Let's say she was walking around alone during the eclipse. There isn't a single easy path that would have taken her to that spot. Either she had seen it on a map or someone directed her there. Most people would have balked at going through the woods alone in the dark."

"Unless she knew someone else in Wagtail, your list of suspects will be very short."

Dave inhaled deeply. "Did Oma tell you about Cooper Adams?"

"The convicted murderer?"

"That's the one. Wendell was his lawyer."

I stared at Dave for a long moment while I considered that strange coincidence.

"You think there's a connection between Cooper and the murder? No, no, no." I shook my head. "I don't see how that's possible. Cooper moved here before Wendell arrived. How would he know Wendell was in town? And why would he kill Dinah? It's very tempting to want to see a link between Cooper and Dinah's murder, but that doesn't seem plausible."

"Stranger things have happened. Maybe she knew him. Maybe she was his prison pen pal. Some people become infatuated with prisoners. Have you pumped Ben yet?" asked Dave.

"I haven't even seen Ben today."

No sooner had I said his name than Ben and his work colleagues came through the door of the registration lobby.

Ben burst into the office. "We're going to the Blue Boar tonight. Can you come?"

"Gosh, I'm sorry, but I'm on inn duty tonight." It wasn't completely untrue. Oma was up early, and I was usually available for evening crises.

"You can't always be on inn duty. I need you to help me sell them on Wagtail. You can imagine what they think about Wagtail now that Dinah was murdered. They'll all be inclined to nix the idea of a local office."

I hated for anyone to have a poor impression of Wagtail. And how could they not, given what had happened?

Ben put on his best puppy face. "Holly, this is important to me. I need to make a good impression. They need to see that Wagtail is a stable town with good people and that I fit in and will bring in business."

Dave eyed me and nodded.

I knew Dave didn't care about the law firm coming to town. His only interest was solving the murder. And I would be in a good position to watch the likely suspects interact.

Aargh. I picked up the phone and checked to be sure Oma planned to stay in tonight to watch the inn. Unfortunately for me, she was available. "All right. What time?"

"Our reservation is for seven."

"Okay."

Ben grinned. "I'll meet you there. Maybe put your hair up and wear something nice?"

Eww. There was something I just didn't like about that kind of directive. "I'll think about it."

"How did the meeting go?" asked Dave.

"Dinah's death means we have to make some adjustments and hire someone to replace her. We wasted a lot of time on that. It's all kind of tedious."

"No decision on the new office yet?" asked Dave.

"That was shifted to tomorrow's agenda." Ben frowned at me. "You'd better get dressed for dinner."

I flicked my hand at him as an indication he should leave.

Dave jumped up and closed the door behind him. "This is perfect. Pay attention to what they're discussing. Let me know if someone seems worried or out of sorts."

"Right," I said sarcastically, "because I know them all so well." I rose from my chair and called Trixie and Twinkletoes. "We'll walk you out."

"Where's Squishy?"

I took a deep breath and said very softly, "He was adopted today."

"Oh. Are you okay with that?"

I watched Trixie as she and Duchess sniffed around the grass. "To be perfectly honest, no. It was hard to let him go. I'm not sure I'm cut out to be a foster parent."

He wrapped an arm around my shoulders. "You did a good thing for him."

"I guess so." It didn't feel good, though.

Dave and Duchess left, and I dashed up to my apartment to get dressed. I changed into a strapless dress that reminded me of springtime with splashes of colorful flowers all over it. I had barely known Dinah but still felt very sad about her death. And I worried about Squishy in his new home. Would he have the wonderful life I hoped? The last thing I wanted to do was wear a cheery dress and smile. I stared at myself in the mirror, thinking I must be an awful person because Ben's request that I put my hair up made me want to do the exact opposite! Surely that was some sign of grouchiness on my part or at least a disagreeable character.

But in the end, I rolled it into a chignon at my neck. I dreaded the dinner but cheered myself up a little by imagining that someone might slip up and say something incriminating.

I placed a little faux-flower collar on Trixie and offered one to Twinkletoes, who declined immediately by springing over my hands and making a run for it.

I checked my watch. "All right, Trixie. Let's go." We walked downstairs and out through the main lobby. The Blue Boar was very close to the inn. Twinkletoes decided to come after all but stayed warily away from me lest I try to dress her again. We arrived in mere minutes.

Ben smiled when he saw me. I was still feeling gloomy about Dinah and Squishy, but I held my chin high, determined to make the best of the evening.

When we entered the dining room, I caught a glimpse of Dave, Duchess, and Shelley at a table overlooking the lake.

Ordering took quite a while for such a large group. But it gave me time to observe them. Percy ordered expensive wine for the table and was decisive about his prime rib dinner order. His wife, Kelly, gave him a critical look. Probably worried about his health, I thought.

Bizzy requested a dirty martini, then asked everyone else what they were having.

Simon wanted to know what Twinkletoes recommended on the feline menu. His Siamese cat, Blossom, behaved beautifully on a leash and watched everything wide-eyed. Twinkletoes appeared much more relaxed, having been to the Blue Boar many times before.

Simon ordered roasted pork loin with duchess potatoes and only sparkling water to drink. On my recommendation, he asked for the Salmon Mouse for Blossom. "Are you certain it's not a real mouse?" He wrinkled his nose at the thought.

"It's supposed to be a little play on the word *mousse*. It's a mousse kind of texture shaped like a mouse."

Wendell went with the heart-healthy salmon entrée. Ella did not attend the dinner.

I leaned over toward Kelly and whispered, "Where is Ella?"

"She's not up to dining out yet. Mostly she wants to go home. We're hoping we can leave once the autopsy report is in. Percy says we don't have to stay, legally speaking, but they still have some matters to discuss, so they might as well do it here."

Dinah's name came up repeatedly in conversation throughout our meal. I listened quietly as they reminisced.

Percy held up his wineglass. "To Dinah. May she rest in peace."

The group toasted Dinah with him, and as the appetizers arrived, the conversation turned to Wagtail and how charming the town was.

"There's not much glitz or glamour," said Bizzy, "but I came here years ago, and the changes are simply delightful. Some of the houses are amazing. My son lives in the cutest place with a beamed ceiling and a stone fireplace. It's tiny but enchanting. And I met someone this morning who I wouldn't mind getting to know a whole lot better."

That was interesting. I wondered who she'd met.

"I'm quite smitten with Wagtail," said Simon, gazing down at Blossom, who sat regally and watched the goings-on in the restaurant. "Blossom is having the time of her life here. I should like to be considered for a Wagtail office. I took a walk around town this morning. Everyone was so friendly, saying good morning as if they knew me. At home, everyone is in a big rush. It's peaceful and calm here. I could hear the birds singing, and that park in the center of town had me feeling connected to the earth. Trees and flowers instead of honking horns and gas fumes. I could get used to that."

Ben didn't say anything, but I saw his hand tighten into a fist. That was the position he wanted.

The din in the restaurant died down and everyone looked around to see what was happening. A violinist strode in, positioned himself at the table where Shelley and Dave sat, and played "Clair de Lune." Duchess held a small box in her mouth, which she presented to Shelley. The violinist paused. Dave knelt on one knee before Shelley.

"Shelley Marie Dixon, would you do me the honor of becoming my wife?"

Even from my position, I could see that Dave was nervous. It was sweet and romantic, and I knew that Shelley would be thrilled.

"Yes!" She sang it with conviction, strong and clear, leaving no doubt that she loved Dave.

Many full-time residents of Wagtail were dining there that night, and a roar went up among us. I joined them by standing and applauding, so happy for the two of them.

Servers brought our main course. I sat down, and we began to eat.

"Was it difficult to make the transition from city living when you moved here, Holly?" asked Bizzy.

"Not at all. But I spent my childhood summers here.

And I had relatives in town, so there wasn't an awkward transition where I didn't know anyone."

"This must be a wonderful place for children." Kelly eyed her husband. "I would love to spend summers here. The kids could swim and boat. The town feels quite safe, too. They could run and play on the green with Taffy."

Obviously, she hadn't heard about Cooper Adams.

Percy raised his eyebrows but didn't protest his wife's notion.

The servers cleared our dishes and presented an entire cake to the table. They brought out champagne glasses and several bottles of champagne, which they poured for us. Having eaten there many times, I knew that was the sort of thing they did for a celebration. In light of Dinah's death, I thought it was a little bit out of place, but it was possible that Percy or Bizzy had planned it in advance.

And that was when it happened. The nightmare I never saw coming.

Ben rose from his seat, knelt on one knee beside me, and held out a diamond ring. "Will you marry me, Holly Miller?"

# Eleven

I desperately wanted to wake up from my nightmarish dream. This could *not* be happening to me.

The diamond sparkled and caught the light from the chandeliers above. The entire restaurant had hushed. No one spoke! And all eyes were on me!

*Infiltrate*, Dave had said.

Trixie snarled at Ben and showed her teeth.

Twinkletoes hissed at him.

I was taking too long to respond. If I wanted to marry Ben, I would have already said so. I would have been delighted. But instead, I sat there in horror and didn't know what to do.

If I said no, Ben would be mortified in front of his friends and colleagues. Could I do that to him?

If I said yes, it would be a lie. But it would enable Ben to avoid humiliation, and then all I had to do was break the engagement. But what about Holmes? Wouldn't he be upset? Maybe not if I explained it to him. After all, he liked Ben!

Wouldn't he want me to help Ben save face? Holmes might even get a laugh out of my brief faux engagement to Ben. I would just have to explain it to him as soon as I could so he wouldn't think it was for real. Yes. That would work. That was the easiest way out. Win-win. I didn't have to go through with the engagement or—horrors—the wedding. It was like putting a bookmark in a book. Everything would pause, and then I could come back and finish the story. *Yes! Say yes, Holly. Do it.* It was only one little word. Yes. "Yes," I choked.

The relief on Ben's face made me glad I had managed to utter that word. He slid the ring on my finger and hugged me. Everyone in the restaurant applauded, and I felt as if my face were on fire. It was only an act, I reminded myself. And on the bright side, even though I fully intended to break off the engagement, at least Ben hadn't texted it this time.

Everyone spoke at once. I smiled at them and murmured *thank you* over and over. Champagne bubbled in a glass that was handed to me. Ben clinked his glass against mine. I sipped, glad I didn't have to speak.

The chaos calmed down, but my face burned with heat. Ben babbled about planning the proposal and all the people who were in on it. He was so proud of himself that I almost felt guilty for making my own plans about how to get out of it.

I didn't need to stage a fight. All I had to do was say that I was in love with Holmes. Holmes! Oh no! He was going to hear about this before I had a chance to warn him. I ate my slice of cake in a rush, wishing I could get out of there and let him know before someone else told him.

There was more applause as we left the Blue Boar. Ben kept talking and actually held my hand. What had I done?

I consoled myself by remembering that it was to save Ben from being embarrassed. He kept stalling and speaking to people. All I wanted was to go home and call Holmes.

It was a relief to finally be out in the cool night air. I thought we would head back to the inn, and I could get away from them, but Bizzy said, "I'm going to Tequila Mockingbird, where my son works. Who's coming with me?"

Very quietly, I said to Ben, "I think I'd better get back to the inn."

Ben was not as quiet. "This is our night! Bring on more champagne!"

I considered my options. I had a headache? I had to relieve Oma? Aha! I had it. Speaking louder than before, I announced, "I haven't gotten much sleep the last two nights. I'm afraid I have to bow out, but I'll see you all tomorrow morning!"

Kelly linked her arm through mine. "How can you sleep when you just got engaged? I was so hyper when Percy popped the question that I could hardly sit still for days. Come with us. You'll get a second wind."

Ben shot me a look and whispered, "Please don't do that."

I was being a pushover. I knew it and I didn't like it. What I really needed to do was call Holmes and tell him about the faux engagement before he heard it from somebody else. But I did want to talk with Bizzy's son, and this might just a be a good opportunity. *Infiltrate.* Pretending to be a good sport, I said, "Just for one drink!"

I suspected the crowd at the bar in Tequila Mockingbird exceeded the maximum capacity. Even though I was glad to see a local business thriving, had I arrived with two or three friends, I would have gone elsewhere. In addition to all the voices, a live band played. Bizzy's son, Logan, grabbed a microphone and announced, "My mom is here tonight!"

Everyone cheered and Bizzy took a bow. She looked giddy and very happy as she planted a kiss on Logan's cheek.

I had miscalculated a bit. There wasn't much talking going on because of the noise level. Percy rolled his eyes at me, and I knew he was about as thrilled as I was to be there. When the opportunity arose, I slipped away and wandered outside, planning to call Holmes. Trixie and Twinkletoes followed me. We wandered down some steps that led under the deck that faced the lake.

To my surprise, someone moved in the dark.

"Sorry, Holly, didn't mean to scare you."

I craned my neck a little and could make out Logan's handsome face. "What are you doing down here?"

"I'm on my break. Does me good to get outside." He sat on a stump, his legs stretched out before him. "Some days I think I might be getting too old for this job. I like it, though, and the tips are good."

I perched on a nearby stump, my eyes adjusting to the darkness. "I know what you mean. I used to be in fundraising and spent a lot of late hours at events."

"Cooper and Jeff were friends of mine," he blurted. "That was really tough. I didn't know Dinah. She was part of my group on the moonlight hike." He shrugged. "She seemed okay. I'm a poor judge of character, though. I couldn't believe that Cooper could have thrown Jeff off the cliff. Still can't."

"After all these years you still can't believe he did it?"

"Yeah. What am I supposed to think? I was buddies

with a murderer? I can't believe that Cooper killed Jeff or that Jeff is dead."

"Have you spoken to Cooper since he's been back?"

"I haven't seen him yet. I guess he wouldn't come to Tequila Mockingbird because Jeff's parents own it. I sure wouldn't if I were him."

He looked over at me. "Who do you think killed Dinah?"

"I don't know. Do you have a theory?"

He picked up a twig and toyed with it. "Not really. But I was wrong about Cooper the first time."

"So you're worried that he killed again?"

He nodded.

"Your mom lives in Washington. How did you end up in Wagtail?" I asked.

"My dad's family has a house here. After the divorce they shuffled me back and forth. Mom likes city life better, but Dad used to bring me here. I like the outdoors. You know? I guess I'm more like my dad that way."

"I can relate." I wanted to get back to what he knew about the murder. "I heard Cooper and Jeff had an argument over a girl."

He nodded. "Jenny Pickens. She was pretty and smart and nice to everybody. Cooper and Jeff had too much to drink, and they just acted stupid. Jenny didn't want anything to do with either one of them. Jeff and I were camping up on the mountain that night. I guess he kept drinking and then ran into Cooper, and they went at it, and one of them fell."

"Fell?"

"That's what I prefer to think. I mean, neither of them would ever have done anything like that sober. Jenny left and went home to Wisconsin, so she wasn't really in the equation anymore, you know?"

"So you think there's a connection between Jeff's death and Dinah's death?"

"I don't want to, except the tie to Cooper is so obvious. But why would Cooper kill that woman? He probably never heard of her before. Mom told me that Officer Dave has been interrogating everyone in her law group. The thing is that you'd have to know about that cliff. Right? A lot of locals know about it, but unless one of the members of the law firm has been here before or done some research online about hiking in this area, Cooper's lawyer and my mom are probably the only ones who knew about the cliff."

There were other people in Wagtail who knew about the cliff and what happened there. And at least one other person in the party staying at the inn—Ella, who had been a local reporter. "Thanks, Logan. If you hear any rumors or pick up on anything, let me know?"

"Sure thing, Holly. I'd better get back to work. I'll show you a shortcut."

Logan opened a door that was nearly hidden in the darkness. He flicked a light switch on and both of us shielded our eyes for a moment. We were in a storage room, with tables and extra chairs and an assortment of old restaurant paraphernalia. Stairs led up to the back of the restaurant. Trixie and Twinkletoes raced up them. When Logan opened the door, they darted through.

I followed, and suddenly I was face-to-face with the owner, Harold Harvey. He appeared surprised to see me. I nodded at him. "Hi!"

Harold looked from me to Logan as if he was trying to

figure out what I was doing there. Logan pushed open another door for me and suddenly Trixie, Twinkletoes, and I were back in the noisy bar.

Happily, no one had missed me, and some of Ben's group were ready to return to the inn. I said good night to the others. Several of his colleagues walked back to the inn with us, forcing me to keep up the engagement charade a little bit longer. Ben held my hand the whole way back.

When we entered the main lobby of the inn, Oma and Mr. Huckle awaited us, grim-faced.

I slipped my hand out of Ben's.

Oma swallowed hard. "It is true?"

"How could you possibly know already?" I asked.

"You forget that the owner of the Blue Boar is a dear friend of mine," said Oma.

Mr. Huckle shook Ben's hand. "Congratulations, young man."

Oma's smile verged on a grimace.

"Would you excuse me a moment, please?" I said to Ben.

I signaled Oma with my eyes, hoping she would understand my message to follow me to the private kitchen.

But Ben's colleagues gathered around us.

Kelly kissed me on the cheek. "Congratulations! I'm thrilled to have you as part of our little group." She reached for my hand. "Ohhh! What an engagement ring! I've always wanted one like this. Percy could barely cobble together enough money for a plastic ring when we got engaged. Seriously! Forget diamonds!"

I choked out a thank-you. "Would you excuse me, please? I need to tend to inn business for a moment."

I weaseled my way out of the cluster of people and

marched to the private kitchen without looking back or responding to Ben, who was calling my name.

I banged the swinging door open. Trixie and Twinkletoes dashed inside. I stepped into the kitchen and relished the quiet.

Oma leaned against the island. She did not look happy.

I held up my palms and whispered, "It's not what you think."

"That's good. Because I think you have become engaged to marry the Ben."

"I can see why you would be under that impression. Oma, he proposed in the middle of the Blue Boar."

She walked around the island and put on the kettle.

"What could I do? I couldn't say no in front of all of his colleagues. That would have been a slap in the face."

"And what about Holmes? You don't think this is a slap in his face?"

I froze. I really hadn't thought about it that way. It had all happened so fast. I'd thought Holmes would understand why I had helped Ben. But I hadn't really given much thought to Holmes's feelings. He should have come first. Not Ben. And now the news would be out all over town and people would think I had jilted Holmes. What had I done? I should have considered how Holmes would feel. "I will make it right, Oma. I never meant to hurt him. But he will understand when I explain it to him." At least I hoped he would. "You were present when Dave said to infiltrate them. All I have to do during the next day or two is break off the engagement. Simple as that."

"This is for show only?"

The door whooshed open, and Holmes raced inside. He

strode toward me and picked up my hand to see the ring. "I didn't believe it when they told me." He winced.

"It's not how it looks. Maybe we could speak privately." I glared at Oma.

Hugging me to him, his breath tickled my cheek as he whispered, "I did not see this coming. I thought . . ." He pulled away and shook his head.

"Holmes, please. Just give me a minute to explain."

"Be happy, Holly." He cupped my face in his hands and forced a sad smile at me before fleeing the room.

I chased after him. "Holmes!" I pushed open the door to the lobby, but he was already gone.

"I have warned you about Holmes and the Ben." Oma plunked tea bags into mugs and poured boiling water over them.

"I will find him and explain. Holmes will understand."

"I would not be so sure. Holly, you are usually quite sensible. But the Ben continues to come here and stay with you. Have I overlooked a growing relationship between the two of you?"

"No! Not at all. He's an old friend. That's all. And I have to point out that I don't invite him. I had no idea he would be here this week."

Twinkletoes jumped onto the island, hissed at me, and walked to Oma for comfort.

Trixie watched me with a sad expression.

"I am not marrying Ben. It's a performance for his benefit. Can you imagine how horrible it would have been for him if I had turned him down in public with all those people watching?" No sooner had the words slipped out of my mouth than I realized how painful it would be for Holmes.

All his friends would hear about it. Why had I said yes? I pulled out my phone and tried to call him. He let it roll over to voice mail. "Holmes, I'm so sorry! I've made a huge mistake and I hope you can forgive me. I didn't mean to hurt you. Please call me."

Oma shoved a mug of tea toward me. "I agree. It would have been embarrassing for the Ben. But now you have a big mess to clean up. You may have done it to be kind to him, but you have created a problem for yourself. I hope you are correct and that Holmes will understand."

The door opened again, and Ben walked in. "Everyone is asking for you, Holly. Oma! I'm going to be part of the family!"

Oma shot me a look.

"I'll be right with you, Ben."

I phoned Holmes the second the door closed behind Ben. Holmes didn't answer. I sipped my tea and sank into the cushy chair next to Oma. "He's not answering."

"Would you answer if Holmes's former fiancée came to town and they got engaged?"

"Yes. Yes, I would!"

"I don't think so. You would have been brokenhearted. You may not have been able to bring yourself to speak with him."

I added a lot of milk to cool my tea and downed it. What a mess. But I hadn't actually *married* Ben. It should be a simple matter to get out of. Maybe I would have to stage a fight. A pretend fight. No big deal. It didn't even have to be done in public.

The only problem was Holmes. Why hadn't I realized how it would hurt him? I should have foreseen the impact it would have on him. What if he refused to listen? Or didn't believe me? Had I ruined the trust between us in one stupid move?

I washed my mug and tried phoning Holmes one more time. No response. I considered texting him, but some internal instinct cautioned me about that. It was too cold. Too impersonal. I started for the door. The memory of the expression on his face when he left pained me. How could I have done this to him? I left another voice message. "Holmes, this is all a misunderstanding. Please give me a chance to explain." What if I had lost him forever?

"Holly," said Oma, "you'd better take care of that ring. Ben will need a refund."

The ring. That was the least of my worries. I gazed down at it. It *was* pretty.

Neither Twinkletoes nor Trixie followed me into the Dogwood Room. I felt as if they had abandoned me. Or maybe they thought I was abandoning them!

"There she is!" called Kelly. "Let's have another look at that gorgeous rock!"

I held out my hand.

"Take a good look at this, honey," said Kelly to her husband. "This is what you have to beat."

Percy laughed. "Dream on, baby."

Little did she know he could probably purchase that exact ring in a day or two.

Dave showed up just then. Everyone congratulated him. He and Shelley had left before Ben's proposal, so he probably didn't know about that yet.

He perched on a chair. "I'm sorry to interrupt your festivities, but it's important for you to know that the medical examiner has determined that the cause of Dinah's death is homicide. I planned to tell you tomorrow morning, but it's better that you know tonight."

The group appeared stricken by the news.

Dave continued, "To be honest, there were some irregularities that suggested to our Dr. Engelknecht that Dinah had been murdered, and the medical examiner confirmed that. They are doing further tests. At this time, we know she had quite a bit of alcohol in her system and may have been confused. No narcotics were found."

Bizzy spoke up. "Percy bought wine for the table."

Dave nodded. "Thank you. I need to interview each of you individually again tomorrow, starting at nine in the morning." He pulled a list out of his pocket. "Please come to the registration lobby at the time you are scheduled. If you took any photographs on the night of the eclipse, I would very much appreciate it if you brought them with you. Even if they don't seem important to you. Thank you. I'll see you tomorrow."

"We have a meeting scheduled," said Percy.

Dave squared his shoulders. "Your colleague has been murdered." He scanned their faces. "Likely by one of you. I believe that takes priority. Good night." He left with his head held high, and not one of them objected.

"I think I'll head up to bed," said Bizzy. "It's been quite a day."

Most of them nodded and followed her. Ben glanced at me.

"I have some things to wrap up."

He nodded and followed the others.

Only Simon lingered behind. When they were out of earshot, he picked up Blossom and approached me. Uncomfortably close, he said, "That was quite a clever little display tonight. I didn't think Ben had it in him to scheme like that. But I will never make the mistake of trusting him again."

I stepped back, out of his zone of aggression. "I don't know what you're talking about." I really didn't.

His bitter chuckle echoed up the stairwell. "Playing dumb doesn't become you, Holly. It's obvious that the two of you colluded. If everyone thinks Ben is marrying you, then they will give him the job of running the Wagtail office. It only makes sense to send the happy young groom where he can be with his wife."

He couldn't have shocked me more if he had slapped me.

He plodded toward his room in a huff, leaving me to contemplate Ben's motives.

I had mixed emotions. I didn't plan to marry Ben, so on the one hand, this was great news. If Simon was right and he had planned the proposal solely for the purpose of winning the office in Wagtail, then he would take it well when I broke off the engagement. On the other hand, he had taken a huge risk by proposing. What if I had turned him down? Even worse, what if I really *wanted* to marry him? Then *he* would be in the uncomfortable position of breaking it off.

I found myself smiling at that last thought. It was awfully tempting to go along with it to get even. Did I have the guts to do that? I dashed up the stairs to my quarters.

Ben was already in bed in the guest room with the door closed.

Excellent. That would give me time to consider how to handle this. In the meantime, though, I had to find the man

I really cared about. I changed into jeans and a warm sweater. Then I slipped out of the apartment the back way, down the hidden stairs to the kitchen. Trixie and Twinkletoes ran along ahead of me to the registration lobby.

I grabbed a key to a Sugar Maple Inn golf cart and left through the registration lobby. My two little companions hopped aboard as if our late-night trip were completely normal. I turned up the mountain to Holmes's house, an A-frame secluded in the woods. No lights shone in the house. I knocked on the door, but he didn't answer. He could be asleep, I reasoned. I knocked again. Still no answer.

Luckily, I knew where he kept a key. I retrieved it from under a rock near the firepit and unlocked the door. Trixie and Twinkletoes ran inside.

"Holmes?" I called out as I flicked on the lights. "Holmes?"

I ran up the stairs to his bedroom, but he wasn't there. I checked the time. It was too late for him to be hanging out in a bar. They were closed by now. Would he be at his parents' house? Possibly, but I wasn't going to wake them up.

There was nothing to do but go home. I contemplated leaving a message. What would I say? *I'm not really engaged. Give me a call?* I winced at that idea. *Sorry I missed you?* Weird under the circumstances. No. This had to be done in person.

I called Trixie and Twinkletoes, locked up, and returned the key where it belonged. We drove back to the inn and went up to bed.

I wrenched the ring off my finger and placed it on my nightstand. Oma was right. Ben would have to return it.

# Twelve

Ben woke me earlier than I would have liked. I could hear him banging around in my living room. What was he doing up so early? I longed to close my eyes and not face the predicament I had created.

Twinkletoes pawed at the closed door to my bedroom, and Trixie barked. Reluctantly, I rolled out of bed, pulled on my fluffy bathrobe, and opened my bedroom door for them.

They zoomed out of my room. Suddenly, everything was quiet. They must have left the apartment with Ben. That was odd. Maybe they heard another dog barking downstairs.

My heart pounding, I checked to see if Holmes had contacted me. Nothing. Not a text or an email or a voice mail. I had to find him. The sooner the better. I hated that he was devastated and suffering. I needed to talk with him.

It was Mr. Huckle's day off. Much deserved, but I missed the hot tea and chocolate croissant he usually brought. I showered and dressed in a blouse with a soft ruffle at the V-neckline and a matching skirt printed with a pattern that reminded me of green olives. I wore my hair down. Not that it mattered. I was tempted to leave the ring where I had stashed it the night before, but Kelly was so fixated on it that she would surely notice.

Except it wasn't there! I kneeled on the floor and looked under the bed but didn't find it. Oh no! How could I have lost it? I thought I left it on the nightstand. I looked in the drawers. I checked the vanity in the bathroom. Had it caught on something when I undressed last night? I crawled around the floor of my closet and checked the dress I had worn. It wasn't anywhere. It must have cost a small fortune. I couldn't bear to think about it. It had to be here somewhere. I looked under every piece of furniture in case Trixie or Twinkletoes had played hockey with it, but I still didn't find it. I would have to confess the truth to Ben. He would flip out. I dreaded telling him.

Although it was relatively early, when I walked down the grand staircase to breakfast, Ben's entire group was already eating. Even Ella had shown up. I hoped that meant she was feeling better. But I hid my ring finger and hurried outside to find Trixie and Twinkletoes.

It was a beautiful spring day. I wished the season would last longer. Azaleas bloomed in profusion. Pink and white dogwoods bore their beautiful blooms. Early lilacs scented the air. I found Trixie and Twinkletoes sitting together on the front porch. They watched me carefully.

"What's going on with you two?" I asked. Trixie had dirt on her nose and front paws. And Twinkletoes did, too! They had left a little trail of soil on the porch steps. I followed it until I found a small mess near a purple azalea bush. Someone had scattered the mulch and dug in the soil.

Trixie and Twinkletoes followed me. They watched the little mound of loose dirt. I took in their guilty expressions, found a stick, and dug in the dirt. They took off running.

I looked back at the disturbed soil. The sun gleamed on something. I picked it up. It looked remarkably familiar. I wiped off as much dirt as I could. Sure enough, there was the engagement ring that I had searched for. Those little stinkers stole it and buried it!

Trixie and Twinkletoes waited for me by the door, practicing innocent faces. I rushed straight to the ladies' room to wash off the remaining dirt. Sighing, I slid it on my finger again.

I was reluctant to go to breakfast and face people. I hoped Squishy was happy and living his best life. Trixie and Twinkletoes were certainly unhappy.

I forced myself to return to the dining area but pointedly sat with Oma, Officer Dave, and Duchess as usual instead of with Ben's group. Trixie greeted Duchess and both tails wagged. Gingersnap lounged at Oma's feet.

"Congratulations again!" I said to Dave as I took my seat. "I'm so happy for you two!"

"Thank you. Oma says you're engaged to Ben!"

Oma eyed me.

I flashed the diamond ring at him.

"Wow! That's—" his tone changed and was less enthusiastic "—that's great." He narrowed his eyes and gave me a questioning look.

Shelley hustled to our table. She bent over to hug me and whispered, "We have to talk!"

Aargh. That was turning into a catchphrase. Not surprising, though. Those who knew me would wonder why I had made a sudden about-face where Ben was concerned. They probably even remembered when Ben had texted me that awful proposal. And they knew that I had turned him down for reasons that went far beyond the impersonal proposal.

"Definitely," I murmured, wishing I could spill the truth to everyone. I would tell them as soon as possible. I could trust Oma and probably my mom, but if I told Shelley, half the town and the entire law firm would know by lunchtime. The only one who absolutely needed to know right now was Holmes. And I would make sure he knew what was going on as soon as I could find him.

"Today's specials are banana pancakes, white cheddar and spinach crustless quiche, and country ham with hash browns and fried apples."

"I'll try the banana pancakes. Do you have that in a doggy version?"

"We do! Dogs are snarfing them up!"

"Sounds good. One for Trixie, please."

"Minced chicken for Twinkletoes?"

"Yes, please."

Shelley looked around. "Where's Squishy? Did that woman adopt him?"

"I'm afraid so."

"No!" cried Oma. "He was such a lovely boy. I hope he went to a good home."

"I do, too."

The dismay on Oma's and Shelley's faces was obvious. I felt the way they did.

Shelley walked away and Oma sucked in a deep breath. "It should be a quiet day here."

I nodded. "Dave will be using the office, but I can work up the costs for the Adams family reunion and the Wilkinsons' wedding anniversary."

"Very good. I have much to do planning the July Fourth activities for Wagtail," said Oma.

Shelley arrived with our breakfasts. Trixie danced on her hind legs until her meal was on the ground and she could plant her nose in it. Twinkletoes was far more reserved. She was almost elegant in the way she took a delicate sniff, waited several seconds, and only then deigned to eat.

My pancakes looked heavenly. I added a liberal dose of maple syrup and dug in.

Dave was watching Ben's group. "Which one do you think did it?"

"I don't know. I haven't heard anyone saying they're glad she's gone. But Simon had a little fit with me last night." I kept my voice low. "He thinks Ben set up this engagement so he'll get the job here in Wagtail if they open a branch."

"That's awfully cruel. What a thing to say to you. Does Simon want the Wagtail position?" asked Dave.

"He came right out and said so at dinner last night. Simon has a cat, and I gather the two of them are enjoying Wagtail."

"What will you do if Ben doesn't get the job?" asked Dave.

Dave didn't realize the engagement was fake! I hadn't given that a single thought because it didn't matter. I looked at Oma, who simply raised her eyebrows and sipped her coffee.

What a mess I had created! I desperately wanted to tell

Holmes first. That had been my plan all along. I wanted him to be in on it, and now he was so crushed that he wouldn't even respond to my voice mails or texts.

"Have either of you heard from Holmes?"

Dave had just bitten into a blueberry muffin. I could tell by his expression that he knew something.

I pointed at him. "Spill."

"He just needs some time, Holly."

"Time for what?"

"To come to terms with your feelings for Ben."

Oma nearly choked on her coffee.

Dave tilted his head and pointed at my engagement ring. "What is he supposed to think?"

I lowered my voice to a whisper. "You cannot tell anyone else. Especially not Shelley or Zelda."

Dave frowned and leaned his head closer to mine.

"I only said yes so Ben wouldn't be embarrassed in front of his friends. As soon as they leave, I'll break it off. I never meant to hurt Holmes. I thought I could let him in on it right away, but that part didn't quite work out."

"I told him he needs to talk with you," said Dave. "He thinks you want time alone with Ben."

This time I was the one who almost choked. "You can't be serious. I don't want to lose him over this."

Oma sighed. "I have warned you about this, Holly. What would you think if Holmes's former fiancée came to Wagtail frequently and stayed with Holmes? We would all wonder what was going on. I'm afraid you have pushed Holmes's tolerance too far."

I hated to admit it, but Oma was right. I would not have been understanding if Holmes's spoiled former fiancée came to stay with him. It was all my fault, and now I had to set things right with Holmes—somehow. "I went up to his place last night, but he wasn't there. And he won't take my calls."

Dave's lips tightened. "I think that says it all, doesn't it?"

He was right. Holmes was deeply hurt, and it was all my fault. "Do you know where I might find him?"

"If I see him, I'll let you know. But I'm going to be tied up with these interviews." Dave looked at his watch and said, "Time to talk with Percy again." He rose from his chair, gave a little wave to Shelley, and walked away.

Holmes weighed heavily on my mind. I wouldn't get anything done until I had straightened things out with him. I tried phoning him again, but he still didn't answer.

After breakfast, Zelda offered me cautious congratulations. How was it possible that everyone who knew me well was dubious about the engagement to Ben, yet Holmes, who should know me better than anyone, believed I had dumped him for Ben?

I couldn't tell Zelda the truth, much as I wanted to. Not until Ben's colleagues had left town anyway. I tried phoning Holmes again, but he still didn't pick up. I texted him. He didn't respond. He was ghosting me!

My phone rang quite a bit. My mom couldn't believe it was true that I was engaged to Ben. "Come over when you have a minute so we can talk privately."

Aunt Birdy was glad that I would finally be respectable, but was I sure Ben was the man for me? We "had to talk," but in her case, I knew that meant Birdy wanted to tell me what to do. I *knew* what to do, at least mostly, but I couldn't get through to Holmes.

After my daily inspection of the inn, I told Zelda I would be out for a bit, but I didn't mention Holmes's name. I considered walking over to his parents' house because it wasn't far, but chances were, they would tell me he went home, and it would be much faster to take a golf cart if I had to go to his house.

Trixie and Twinkletoes hopped onto the golf cart as if they expected a fun ride. It probably would be fun for them. I parked in front of his parents' house.

Holmes's mom opened the door before I rang the bell. She looked so sad. "I'm sorry, honey. I think I'm as broken up as Holmes is."

I was thankful that she didn't turn us away. But she didn't invite me back to the kitchen for coffee like she usually did. She patted Trixie and Twinkletoes.

I couldn't share the real details with her, so I fudged. "It's not how it looks."

Her expression brightened. "You're so right. It's *not* how it looks. I'm so glad you appreciate that."

I didn't understand what she meant. Could Oma have called and told her the truth? But what did she mean when she said she was glad that I understood? "I've been trying to reach Holmes, but he won't take my calls."

"He didn't take his phone."

"Take his phone? Where?"

Holmes's father walked into the room. "Grace," he said in a cautioning tone.

Doyle wasn't an angry or sour man. In fact, he was very nice. But today, all he had to do was say Grace's name and she stopped talking. That was odd.

"Where is Holmes?" I asked.

"He went to pick up Rose. She's visiting friends in North Carolina. We thought it best. Some time alone to think will do him good."

I judged both of their faces. Something wasn't right. "I see. He needed to get away from me."

Grace tilted her head as if commiserating with me. "Not from you, honey. But he had to get away."

I left their house with a broken heart. I never anticipated that my gesture for Ben's benefit would result in Holmes leaving town. I thought I would be able to explain everything to him within an hour or so.

I was heading back to the inn, wondering why Grace and Doyle had been acting strange. On a whim, I turned around and drove up the mountain to Holmes's house to see if he was there. Just like the previous night, no one answered the door. I fetched the key and let myself in. Trixie and Twinkletoes ran through the house. If Holmes was there, they would let me know.

Holmes was a fairly tidy person. Not perfect, but neat enough to not leave wet towels lying around or empty snack bags in the kitchen. Yet he had left a pile of cash on the kitchen counter. I picked it up and counted. One thousand dollars in hundred-dollar bills. I was positive that it hadn't been there the night before. Surely I would have noticed. I supposed it could be a deposit on some new project of his. But who left that kind of money lying out where anyone could see it? Of course, it didn't mean Holmes had been there, but someone had. I probably wasn't the only person who knew where he kept the key.

I called Trixie and Twinkletoes, locked up, returned the key to its hiding place, and drove back to the inn, trying to figure out what was going on with Holmes. His parents' strange behavior, the pile of money on the counter, the fact that he hadn't taken his phone when he drove to pick up his grandmother Rose out of state. None of it added up. There was still the possibility that he had his phone but had turned it off or just wasn't answering.

I parked the golf cart and tried to call him one more time. I left a voice mail.

"Holmes, it's Holly. I have to talk with you. Your parents told me that you're out of town, but I have to explain. Please call me. You'll laugh when I tell you. At least I hope you will. Call me!"

# Thirteen

I told Zelda I was back.

"It's been very quiet around here. I sent you the pictures you asked for."

"Thanks. If you hear anything about Holmes, would you let me know?"

Zelda blinked at me. "Holmes? Um, sure."

I collected my laptop from my apartment, retrieved a mug of tea from the dining area, and settled at the desk near the cloakroom in the main lobby, which was usually occupied by Mr. Huckle when he wasn't running errands for guests.

When I opened the laptop, the first thing I saw were the photographs that Zelda had taken on the night of the lunar eclipse. I put off my work and browsed through them. The lighting was odd, probably because it was night, and it likely reflected the strange coloration of the world as Earth crossed the sun. The first group of pictures were mostly of wildflowers on the trail leading up to the plateau.

The next group would be helpful to Dave in terms of identifying who had been there that night. Zelda had captured lots of locals, all grinning and having a good time. She had gotten images of some of the bands and singers. And then I saw Ben's group, which included Holmes and me. They stopped me cold.

Holmes and I were so comfortable together. Someone must have said something funny, because everyone was laughing. In another picture, Ben eyed Holmes and me. I hadn't realized he was watching us. If I didn't know better, I'd have thought Ben appeared envious. In the next photo, Holmes observed Wendell, who was walking away. The following photo showed just me. Holmes had left to talk with Wendell and the rest of the group had gone to check out the drinks and snacks.

I looked through other photos that Zelda had taken. Nothing jumped out at me. Kelly and Percy had stayed together, not venturing far apart. Simon had been a loner. Alone in every photo where I saw him. I thought I had something when I spotted Bizzy coming out of the woods, but then I realized that was the location of the restrooms. Ella was missing entirely. That didn't prove anything, except that she managed not to be in any of the photos. It was a large area. Neither Ben nor I were in many of them, either. Probably because we had been walking around with Zelda.

I wondered if Zelda had sent the photos to Dave. Probably. That's what I would have done.

They didn't mean anything, I told myself. For that matter, there were loads of other people up there that night, many of whom were visitors to Wagtail. Any one of them might have known Dinah and had some kind of beef with her. I clung to that thought.

Trying to shove Holmes out of my mind, I spent the next few hours preparing and sending proposals to the Adamses and Wilkinsons with a number of optional add-ons. Better brands of champagne, open bars, alternative flowers, fancier hors d'oeuvres, and sit-down dinners with servers all added hefty prices to an occasion. Some people opted for all of them, and others wanted none of them. What didn't raise the cost was the presence of their dogs or cats. That was the most crucial thing for many of our guests.

Finished with that, I swung by the desk in the reception lobby.

Whispering, I thanked Zelda for the photos. "Is Dave still in the office?"

Zelda leaned over the desk toward me. In a hushed voice she said, "Kelly went in without her husband! She insisted. Percy was pretty huffy about it and sat out here the whole time! Bizzy was all teary when she emerged, and I heard shouting when Wendell was in there!"

"Wonder what that was about?"

"Couldn't tell you."

"I'm running over to see Mom for a few minutes. Text me if anything comes up."

"Will do!"

I walked toward my mom's house. She had recently moved back to Wagtail after her second divorce. We had spent so many years apart that I'd forgotten what fun she was, and I enjoyed being closer again. Her parents had moved back from California with her and lived in an in-law apartment connected to the house, but they were currently away visiting friends in Maine.

Trixie ran ahead of me with her nose to the sidewalk and occasionally darted off to smell bushes along the way. Twinkletoes would linger over an invisible something and then leap along the sidewalk to catch up. It was a beautiful day. One meant for walking and enjoying warmer weather.

I ambled around the back of Mom's house, appreciating the azaleas that bloomed in pinks and purples with an occasional cluster of bright yellow tulips. I knocked on the back door and tried the knob. It opened easily. Trixie and Twinkletoes ran inside.

"Mom?" I called.

# Fourteen

When Mom didn't respond, I looked for Trixie and Twinkletoes. They would find her with their superior noses and hearing. I trailed along after them to a guest room on the opposite end of the house. But what I saw gave me pause.

Her back to me, Oma sat on a chair, holding binoculars to her eyes. She had positioned them through the slats of a venetian blind. My mother stood next to her, also holding binoculars. She peered through the blinds at a slightly higher level.

I mock coughed to announce my presence.

Mom gasped and swung around. She tapped Oma's shoulder.

Oma waved her away.

"Liesel!" hissed Mom. "Hi, honey, I wasn't expecting you."

Oma turned around and lowered her binoculars. "Lieb-chen! Have you come to join us?"

"Well, I don't know. What are you doing? Has a handsome man moved in?"

Oma waggled her head back and forth. "He is not bad looking. Too young for me, of course."

"You're watching a man? Are you kidding?"

"You make it sound as if we're doing something wrong," said Mom. "We're keeping an eye on things."

"More like four eyes. Please tell me he's dressed."

Oma pulled her head back with indignation. "Ach, really, Holly. We are not voyeurs."

"The poor guy. How would you feel if you moved into a neighborhood and people spied on you?"

"We're not spying," said Mom. "We're being cautious."

I heard footsteps in the hallway. Mr. Huckle appeared carrying a tray with teacups and a platter of cookies. Instead of his waistcoat, he wore gray trousers with a lightweight blue crewneck sweater.

I gasped. "Is this a meeting of the Wagtail Murder Club? You left me out?"

"It's nothing official, sweetheart."

"Who is the poor man who unknowingly moved into your web?" I asked.

Oma returned to gazing out the window.

"It's Cooper Adams." Mom pushed her hair back off her face.

"The murderer?"

"I'm afraid so." Mom gave me a look of resignation. "Before you start, he's free to live anywhere he likes. The Bartoes must have rented their house to him."

She was right about that. He could live anywhere. But why did it have to be across the street from my mother?

"Your parents are away. You're here all alone. Maybe you should stay with me while they're gone."

"I have said the same thing to your mother," I said. Oma didn't look away from Cooper's house for a second. "There is no need for her to be here by herself. We have plenty of room at the inn. My guest room is available."

"Exactly what do you think you're going to see?" I asked.

Mr. Huckle exchanged a look with my mom. "There is a woman who comes to visit him."

"I don't think there's any law against him having company."

"We just want to know who it is," said Mom. "If it's someone local, we should warn her."

I thought about Dinah. She had probably been murdered by someone she knew. But what if she hadn't? I held my hand out to my mom for her binoculars. Sidling up to Oma, I positioned them through the slats of the blinds.

There really wasn't anything interesting to see. "How long have you been doing this? He's not even visible." I returned the binoculars to Mom.

"Congratulations again, Holly! I was most surprised," said Mr. Huckle.

"You didn't tell them?" I asked Oma.

"It is your business, liebchen. I have told you what I think."

"The ring!" Mom cried out. "Oh, my word, Holly. Ben must have dug deep into his wallet for that engagement ring." Mom reached for my hand to examine it. "Well," she said, "it's a very lovely ring, but that's not a good reason to marry someone, unless—you love him?"

"Do you promise you will not blab about this to anyone?"

"You know I wouldn't do that."

"That includes your parents and my dad."

Mom scowled at me. "What is it, Holly?"

I explained that I'd only said yes because Ben had proposed in front of all his colleagues. "I didn't want to embar-
rass him. No one would expect us to marry for months or
a year anyway. As soon they're gone, I can just break off the
engagement and he can save face. But now Holmes thinks
I'm really engaged and has left town. I never meant to hurt
him. I should have thought of Holmes and how he would
feel. And now he's gone and I'm afraid I've lost him forever.
I don't know if he can ever forgive me for this."

"He must be devastated." Mom hugged me. "Your heart
was in the right place to be kind to Ben, but you've certainly
made a mess of things."

"But get this. Simon, an attorney with Ben's group, really
wants the job in Wagtail. He said Ben only proposed to me
because he wants the job in Wagtail, and they'll be more
inclined to give it to *him* so he can be with his wife."

Oma finally stood up. "No! Would the Ben do such a
thing?"

"He might. I was appalled at first, but the more I thought
about it, the more it all fit together. For instance, if you had
just become engaged, would you go up to bed without your
fiancée and close the door to the guest bedroom? Wouldn't
you be excited and want to talk about the wedding or your
future life together? Wouldn't you want to smooch or tell
her a fun story about the ring?"

A look passed among Oma, Mom, and Mr. Huckle.

"I see what you mean," said Mr. Huckle. "And you were nice enough to play along."

"That rat!" Mom held out her hand. "Let me see that ring again."

I held out my hand to her.

"Take it off," she said.

I handed her the ring. Mom turned on a small light and examined it. "I don't know, Holly. I'm no jeweler, but I don't think this is gold. There's no mark on it. Fourteen and eighteen karat jewelry always bears a mark."

A mischievous look came over Oma's face. "Shall we also play along with the wedding in a way that will make the Ben uncomfortable?"

Mom laughed at her suggestion.

Mr. Huckle asked, "If there's nothing between the two of you, why would Ben want to move to Wagtail?"

"He said something about his friends having families now, which I gather means not much time for him. He's lonely, and something fun is usually happening in Wagtail. Besides, you know we would include him in holiday dinners and other events if he were here."

Oma sighed. "Yes, we would. Perhaps it would not be bad to have a lawyer around on whom we could call if necessary."

"Let's give this some thought," said Mom.

Oma peered out the window again. "There he is!"

Mom and I tried to look out of the window surreptitiously.

"He doesn't look like a murderer," I said. "He looks . . . nice." His dark hair hadn't changed much from the photo I had seen of him. Clean-shaven, he wore rectangular wire-rimmed glasses and seemed quite pale, as if he hadn't been in the sun much. He wore a golf shirt and shorts and ambled about the front lawn inspecting the landscaping. He raised his face to the sun and closed his eyes. Taking deep breaths, he smiled, opened his eyes, and went back into the house.

"Nell, if you did not live so close by, I would say maybe we should leave him in peace," said Oma. "But now, with Dinah's death, we must be very cautious."

"I'll second that!" I said, feeling guilty for looking through the slats of the blinds. "He would get upset if he caught you spying on him. But if you ever do this again, you'd better include me."

On that ominous note, I called Trixie and Twinkletoes, and we left the house.

The next thing I knew, I was face-to-face with Cooper Adams.

# Fifteen

I thought it was a coincidence that he was in his yard again. At least I hoped it was. I smiled and said, "Hi."

He pointed at Mom's house and asked, "Do you live there?"

My heart thrummed. He had seen us! "I'm just visiting my mom."

He smiled and held out his hand. "Cooper Adams."

I tried to act natural and shook his hand. Nothing terrible happened. "Holly Miller. Welcome to Wagtail."

"Miller? Are you the mayor?" He bent to pet Twinkletoes and Trixie, who were on their best behavior for once.

They had pretty good taste in people, and I took note that neither of them was backing away from Cooper or acting strange.

I laughed. "No, that would be my grandmother." I took a chance and pretended I hadn't heard anything about him. "Are you visiting, or have you moved here?"

"I'm here for good, I hope. It's a beautiful place. Very peaceful."

"Terrific. I run the Sugar Maple Inn with my grandmother." I waved my hand in the general direction of the inn. "If you need anything, just give me a call."

"That's very kind of you. Thanks."

I gave him a nod and tried not to hurry away. I called Trixie and Twinkletoes, who readily ran along the sidewalk past me. It took every ounce of self-control I could muster not to look back. I felt certain that Oma and Mom had seen our little conversation. I hoped he hadn't spotted them spying.

As I walked, I wondered if it was safe to turn one's back to a killer. How would I know if he had raised an axe and was walking behind me? Why didn't I have a little compact mirror that I could subtly raise to see behind me? Why wasn't I the kind of woman who wore makeup that I needed to check constantly? Maybe I should start carrying a compact. Having managed to frighten myself, I made a pretense of crossing the road, which gave me the opportunity to turn just enough to see Cooper bending to pull up a dandelion.

I felt foolish. Maybe he was as nice as he seemed. Still, I didn't really relax until I was well on my way, reasoning that he had been convicted of murder after all, and no matter how normal he acted, we would all be wise to stay alert around him.

Ben caught up to me as I walked. "Hi!" He rubbed his palms together. "In spite of Dinah's death, Bizzy, Percy, and Wendell love Wagtail! You and Holmes did a great job pitching it at the eclipse. And everyone has been very friendly."

"I'm happy for you." I tried to sound sincere, but it wasn't easy considering the role I had played, which may have cost me the one man I truly loved.

"So, um, I haven't seen much of Holmes. Do you think he could come to dinner or lunch with the firm? Maybe talk up Wagtail a little more?"

"No one knows where he is." I sounded bitter.

"What? Could he have murdered Dinah?"

How could Ben be so clueless? "No."

Ben stopped walking. "Ohhh. He didn't take our engagement well. That's too bad. I should talk to him. Tell him to buck up. He'll find another woman. He's a fairly good-looking guy."

Why had I ever felt sorry for Ben? I desperately wanted to reel in time and go back to the night I had said yes to his proposal. If only I could do that and change my answer. "I don't think he would appreciate that. Maybe you should leave him alone."

At that moment, Kelly yoo-hooed at Ben. He waved at her.

"Excuse me, I need to get back to the inn." I hurried away, mentally kicking myself.

I entered the inn through the registration lobby, glad to be home. "Hi, Zelda. Anything new here?"

Zelda was at the desk, putting on makeup. "Absolutely dull. You know who else wants the job in Wagtail?"

"Simon."

"How did you know?"

"He told me."

"Well, when he was leaving the office, he was cozying up

to Dave and said how great it was getting to know him and that he hoped to be part of the community soon. And then Dave thanked him for the information he shared!"

I made a mental note to have a chat with Simon.

The door to the office opened. Bizzy walked out, her lips mashed as if she was irritated. She appeared tired.

I flashed her what I hoped was a sympathetic smile.

I peeked into the office. Dave was scribbling something in a notebook.

"Any progress?" I asked.

"A little. They're starting to turn on one another. I thought it would happen sooner or later. It just took this bunch some time. Lawyers are used to keeping secrets."

His phone buzzed. "Sergeant Quinlan." He listened for a moment. "Keep everyone calm. I'm on the way." He ended the call, grabbed his pad, and leaped to his feet.

"What's up?"

"Doyle had a heart attack."

"I'm right behind you."

I phoned Oma and could hear her ringtone somewhere nearby.

Oma and Mom had just walked in. Mom carried a little overnight bag.

"You're going to stay here?" I blurted.

"We think it's best under the circumstances." Mom eased the shoulder strap. "What did Cooper say to you?"

"I'll fill you in later. Oma, can you take over here to-night? Holmes's father just had a heart attack. I'm headed to their house."

"Ja, liebchen. You go. Quickly!"

I grabbed a key for a golf cart, which would be faster

than walking. Trixie and Twinkletoes ran out with me, but I quickly ushered them back inside.

"Mom, would you look after Trixie and Twinkletoes? I don't want them getting underfoot."

"My granddog and grandcat! Of course."

I ran outside, hopped on the golf cart, and shot over to Grace and Doyle's house as fast as the golf cart could go.

When I arrived, neighbors had gathered in front of the house. I didn't see Holmes or his mother, or Dave for that matter. I guessed they were still inside. I debated going in. I considered walking in the front door. Maybe I could be of help. But the issue with the phony engagement stopped me from being so obvious. I didn't want to stress anyone more! I could sneak around back to see if one of the doors happened to be open. That seemed like the right thing to do.

Acting as if I belonged, I walked through the side yard. No one stopped me. The family room in the back had a sliding glass door. I tried it and it slid open.

I stepped into the family room and could hear Dr. Engelknecht. "Grace, there's enough room for you to go with Doyle in the ambulance. Holmes, I don't want you driving yourself."

Holmes protested. "Nonsense. I'll be fine."

"I'm sure one of your friends can take you," said Dr. Engelknecht.

I followed the sound of their voices to the foyer. The door was wide open, and I could see Doyle being carried out on a stretcher.

"I'll drive Holmes." I said softly.

The doctor, Grace, and Holmes simultaneously turned to look at me.

"You go ahead, Grace. Holmes and I will lock up the house," I said.

Dr. Engelknecht patted me on the back. "I'm glad you're here." He lifted my hand and looked at the diamond engagement ring but didn't say a thing. He just shook his head.

I hurried to the sliding door and locked it. I checked the kitchen to be sure nothing was cooking. All clear there. And then I slid off the ring and stashed it in my pocket. I found the keys to Holmes's truck on the console in the foyer and walked out to the street, where the Wagtail ambulance was leaving to meet the real ambulance that would transport Doyle to Snowball.

"Do you need to get anything from the house?" I asked Holmes.

"My keys."

I held them up and he reached for them, but I was faster and snatched them away. "I'll drive." I returned to the house and locked the front door.

Neighbors were saying comforting things to Holmes. I walked up beside him.

"Doyle will be all right."

"You know he's strong."

"He'll rally."

Holmes slid his hand into mine. For a moment, I thought he wanted the keys. Without looking at me, he squeezed and held on like I was his life raft.

We walked to the golf cart that way. He didn't let go until we had to climb in. I drove to his truck, which was parked in the lot outside of town, and in minutes, we were on the way to Snowball.

Neither of us spoke. I wanted to reassure him. To tell him his dad would be okay. I finally croaked, "I'm glad Grace is with him. Do you know what happened?"

"I didn't have a chance to ask. But I know it's that guy who wants our land."

"Wendell?"

"Yeah. I never should have left."

"Where have you been?"

"North Carolina. Grandma Rose went to visit some friends and . . . it seemed like a good time to get out of town. I had just arrived back in Wagtail when my phone rang. I thought it was you. I almost didn't answer."

Ouch. He still didn't want to speak to me. But he *was* talking. That was some comfort. "You can't blame yourself."

"Yes, I can. I should have stuck around to deal with Wendell instead of letting him badger my parents."

"You could not have predicted this. You can't protect them all the time."

"Two days ago, everything was perfect. Then that jerk came to town and my life flipped upside down."

I didn't know if he was including our relationship in that statement, but technically that was Ben's fault, not Wendell's.

"Where's the ring?" he asked.

"In my pocket."

"Why?"

"Do you want to talk about this now?"

"No."

I drove in silence for a while.

"I want you to be happy, Holly."

"Thanks, Holmes."

"Just answer one question. Have you been in love with Ben all along?"

It sounded to me like he did want to talk about it. I glanced over at him. "No. Of course not. I'm so sorry, Holmes. I never meant to hurt you. I should have realized how you would feel. I only said yes so Ben wouldn't be embarrassed in front of his colleagues. He proposed in the middle of the restaurant with all of them looking on and a huge cake and champagne on the table. I didn't know what to do, but I didn't want to humiliate him in front of all those people, so I said yes and figured I could break it off as soon as they left town. I should have thought of you instead and how it would impact you."

"Why didn't you tell me that?"

"I've been trying to. I called. I left tons of voice mails. I went to your house twice and to see your parents. But you never responded."

"Because I was hurt. I thought I'd lost you. Then I thought maybe you never loved me at all. How could you switch so fast and suddenly be engaged to him?"

"I see that now. I wanted so much to let you know it was all a fake. But in the heat of the moment, everyone was looking at me. Everyone in the restaurant was waiting for my answer. It was a stupid thing to do. The last thing in the world that I wanted was to hurt you." I reached for his hand and felt the warmth as he wrapped his fingers around mine.

"And now Ben will be hurt."

"I'm not so sure about that. There is a strong possibility that Ben doesn't want to be engaged, either."

"I don't get it. Then why did he propose to you?"

"He wants a job in the new Wagtail office, and it's possible that he thinks he's more likely to get it if he's engaged to someone in Wagtail."

Holmes snorted.

I had known it for a long time, but those difficult moments alone in Holmes's truck, driving in the dark, only confirmed how very much I loved him.

# Sixteen

When I parked the truck, Holmes leaned over for a long kiss. "I've missed you, Holly."

This time I squeezed *his* hand. "I've missed you, too, Holmes."

The next hours were anything but pleasant. We spent them speculating on the cause of the heart attack and what tests would show. Could Grace and Doyle change anything in their lives that would make a difference?

It was after midnight when Holmes insisted Grace go home and relax. I thought Holmes should get some sleep, too.

A bossy nurse finally shooed us out of Doyle's room. "He needs sleep, and you folks do, too. There's not a thing in the world you can do for him right now. Y'all go home. I've got this."

I drove us back to Wagtail. It was a quiet trip. Grace fell asleep on the way.

I took advantage of that to softly ask Holmes, "What's with the thousand dollars in your kitchen?"

He tried to stifle a laugh. "I can't get away with anything," he joked. "It's an anonymous donation to the fund to fix houses for people who can't afford it."

"That's nice. They donated cash? Isn't that a little bit odd?"

"People have their reasons. Sometimes a spouse doesn't agree with the donation. Sometimes they won it in a poker game. I don't usually know why they're donating or how they got the money, but if they're willing to give it, I'm happy to accept it. How did you know about that?"

"Apparently, I am not the only person who knows where you keep your spare house key."

"That's true. Some of my friends know where it is. They're always welcome."

After dropping them off, I drove the golf cart home. In the parking lot, I fished the engagement ring out of my pocket and slipped it onto my finger. Running an inn had taught me to be cautious. I never knew who might be up and wandering around in the middle of the night.

Casey, our night manager, let me in through the front door in the main lobby. Trixie launched herself at me. I caught her in my arms.

"Is that a hug or a snuggle?" asked Casey.

"A huggle!"

Trixie kissed my chin as if I had been gone for a month. In dog time, it probably felt that way.

Twinkletoes approached me demurely and wound around my ankles until I put Trixie down on the floor and picked Twinkletoes up. "Everyone likes a huggle, don't they, Twinkletoes?"

"I heard Doyle Richardson is sick," said Casey.

"I don't think he's out of the woods yet, but we're hoping he can make a full recovery."

I left Casey to handle things and dragged myself upstairs to bed, exhausted.

My internal clock woke me earlier than I'd have liked. Still tired from my late night, I got up anyway, delighted to see a pot of hot tea and goodies left by Mr. Huckle in the wee hours. I poured the tea, which still steamed, and handed Trixie and Twinkletoes their treats. The events of the previous night on my mind, I checked my phone for messages. Nothing. Maybe that was a good sign. I hoped Holmes and his mom were able to sleep longer than me.

After a shower, I dressed in a sleeveless navy-blue dress with white trim and went downstairs with Trixie and Twinkletoes.

Mr. Huckle spotted me in the main lobby and stopped me to ask about Doyle. I didn't have much news.

"Let us hope all goes well for him. Your grandmother has asked me to send you to the private kitchen for breakfast."

Uh-oh. I hoped there wasn't more bad news. Trixie hustled outside to do her business while Twinkletoes and I waited. Trixie didn't dally. She knew that breakfast was next.

Shelley snagged me as I passed the dining area on my

way to the private kitchen. She handed me a mug of tea. "We have got to talk!" She pointed at my ring and then asked about Holmes's father. "I'll bring your breakfast to the private kitchen. Eggs Benedict?"

Shelley knew I found that hard to turn down. "That would be great. Thanks! Tuna for Twinkletoes and a doggy version of eggs Benedict for Trixie?"

"You've got it!" She hustled away.

I pushed open the door to the private kitchen. Oma, Mom, and Mr. Huckle were seated at the table eating their breakfasts. Gingersnap lounged in a cushy armchair.

Aah! Breakfast with the Wagtail Murder Club! "Good morning! What's going on?"

"First, please tell us about Doyle," said Oma.

I filled them in on his condition as of the night before. "I haven't heard anything yet this morning."

Mom headed straight for me and wrapped her arms around me in a hug. "That was a close call yesterday with Cooper. You have to tell us all about it. Oma, Mr. Huckle, and I were holding our breath!"

"We were very relieved to see you walk away from Cooper," said Oma.

Shelley swung the door open and placed my breakfast on the table.

Trixie and Twinkletoes rushed at her, eager to see their breakfasts placed on the floor. They started to eat before I sat down.

Shelley smiled at us. "Y'all need anything?"

They assured her we had everything we needed. I tasted the eggs Benedict. Was there anything better than hollandaise sauce? I didn't think so!

"So spill, Holly," said Mom. "What did Cooper say?"

"Honestly, if I hadn't known he was a convicted felon, I never would have guessed it. He was very polite and asked me if I lived in your house. He introduced himself, and I think I welcomed him to Wagtail and said to contact me if he ever needed anything."

Oma rolled her eyes. "That is all we need. He didn't say anything about seeing us?"

"Not a word."

Oma and Mr. Huckle looked at each other.

"Maybe he didn't see us!" said Mom.

"Did you know Cooper when he murdered Jeff Harvey?" Oma asked Mr. Huckle.

"No. I worked for Mr. Wiggins then. I only know what I read in the newspaper and heard in local gossip. It is my understanding that the cliff where Dinah fell is the exact same cliff where Cooper Adams pushed Jeff Harvey to his death twelve years ago."

"Have any of you heard of a connection between Cooper and Dinah?" I asked.

Mom piped up. "I have been given photos that establish Cooper's presence on the mountain the night of the eclipse. But you were there, too, Holly, as were a lot of other local people. It doesn't link them in any way."

Oma scowled. "It's a bit more than a coincidence that it would happen again a week or two after he was released from prison for pushing someone else over the same cliff."

"Unless someone planned it that way. Someone who knew Dinah and Cooper," said Mom.

"Wendell!" I whispered. "Or Ella. She sat through the

trial. And she grew up around here. Maybe she knew Cooper."

"But why?" asked Mom. "Let's say you're right about Wendell. Why would he murder Dinah? Or Ella, for that matter. Why would she kill Dinah?"

"I don't know." Mr. Huckle refilled their coffee mugs.

The door swung open. I turned around half expecting to see Holmes. But it was Ben.

"There you are! Everyone has been asking for you, Holly. Maybe you could join my friends for a while?"

Ugh. Not that I minded his friends, and come to think of it, I should be chatting them up about Dinah's murder, but I didn't relish playing the fiancée.

"Ben, darling." Mom rose and turned to him with outstretched arms. She hugged him to her, saying, "Welcome to the family!" She pulled out a chair for him and patted it so he would sit down. "We are all so thrilled that the two of you will finally be tying the knot. Especially Holly's father. You know how much he likes you. And he was delighted to hear that you're going to pay for the entire wedding."

Oma nearly choked on her coffee, but I didn't think Ben noticed.

"'A true gentleman' is what he called you." Mom quickly sat down beside Ben.

Ben tried to interrupt her, but Mom rambled on, not letting him get a word in.

"Holly and I have decided on a sit-down dinner for five hundred guests. Or more if need be. We should have given more thought to your side of the family. All those work friends and clients, too."

Oma smiled slyly. "We have agreed that we should use a venue in Washington, DC. That way we can enjoy the celebration and we won't have to work. They have so many beautiful places to wed. We've been going through them on the Internet. We will need a block of rooms at one of the hotels. Holly is familiar with all the best ones from her previous fundraising job. We had better reserve them as soon as possible. I will have relatives coming from Germany just for this occasion."

I watched as Ben's face turned paler than normal. Two circles blazed red on his cheeks, almost like the coloring on a doll.

He opened his mouth to speak, but Mom hopped in again. "We don't want to push you two, but we need a date soon. Maybe you can discuss it while Ben is here? June is the traditional wedding month, so we would have to move very fast for that."

In his current state of panic, I was fairly certain it wouldn't occur to Ben there was no way we could possibly schedule anything by June. We were booked solid with weddings at the inn all the way through August. Not to mention that venues in Washington had to be booked at least a year in advance, but he wouldn't know that.

It was cruel of me, but I rather enjoyed knowing he was squirming inside. Though I was a little concerned that they were going too far and he would catch on.

I joined in. "It all sounds wonderful. Ben, I guess I should go back to DC with you to shop for a dress."

"Not before you have your engagement photo taken," said Mom. "We have to do that first thing."

"Engagement photo?" Ben mumbled. "What for?"

Mom gave Ben a little push on his shoulder. "Oh, you! To announce the engagement, of course. We'll have it published in the *Snowball News*, the *Washington Post*, and online. Ben, I'm sure you brought a nice suit with you." Mom looked over at me. "Or would you prefer something informal? A pose in front of the azaleas, perhaps?"

Ben released a breath in relief. "I like that idea much better. Just tell us when you'd like to take it."

Ah. He thought that would be easy and that it wouldn't cost him anything. "I suppose it depends on when the photographer will be available."

The tension in his face ratcheted up again. "Wouldn't a casual shot be better? One that's not posed? Nell could take it with her phone."

Mom placed a hand on Ben's arm. "That is so sweet of you. I do enjoy photography. But you'll be glad you had a professional picture taken. Especially because you're a bigshot attorney! You don't want clients seeing a blurry photo. What would they think? And what if you're chosen to run the Wagtail office for your firm? You need to put your best possible foot forward to impress future clients!"

My mother's performance blew me away. She should have been an actor!

Ben winced. "You're right, Nell. I hadn't thought about that."

Yikes! The plan was backfiring. He was actually thinking about impressing clients.

I had one more dart to throw his way. I stretched my arm out and let the diamond in the engagement ring catch the light. "I have to remember to get my ring appraised today. I want to be certain this beauty is insured."

Ben frowned at the ring. "No need. I can send you the receipt when I get back to Washington."

I saw right through him. He was buying time. "I wouldn't dream of it. What if something happens to it before then? No, no. I'll get it done today." I held my hand up and wiggled my fingers. The diamond caught the sunlight.

Twinkletoes mewed at the dancing reflection on the ceiling. "Ack, ack, ack. Ack, ack, ack."

I lowered my hand and covered the ring so she wouldn't jump on the table to chase the reflection.

Ben looked miserable. If his proposal had been a scam to get him the position in a Wagtail office, then it served him right. Sweet as syrup, I asked, "When is the vote on the office in Wagtail?"

"Today. Wish me luck!" He took a deep breath. "I better get back to them to make a last pitch."

"Good luck," I said half-heartedly. "I'd better get going. I have a lot to do today."

I piled empty dishes onto a tray and carried them to the commercial kitchen to be washed. When I emerged, Ella was petting Trixie, whose little tail wagged as fast as it could.

"Holly! I thought you must be around here somewhere. Trixie is never far from you. But I don't see Squishy. I didn't see him anywhere yesterday, either."

"Squishy was adopted."

Her smile faded. "Oh. By a big family with kids?"

"By a single woman who wants to train him for rallies."

"What is that? I've never heard of it," she said.

"It's about teamwork between the dog and a person. They work their way through a course together. I haven't seen it done."

She nodded. "Sounds like something I would enjoy. Well . . . I'm glad he found a good home."

"I'm sorry. Were you interested in adopting him?"

She shook her head. "I can't have a dog."

She said it firmly. I didn't push her for explanations. "How are you feeling? You're walking much better."

"I've been getting some sleep, which was what I needed. You know how hospitals are. The noise and all the people coming in and out of the room make it hard to sleep."

"If you don't mind my asking, what happened?"

"A truck slammed into me, causing my car to flip down an embankment. I'm lucky that it wasn't worse."

"Was the truck driver all right?"

"I was unconscious. I didn't see what happened to him, but I guess he was okay, because the cops never found the truck. I don't understand that, because the truck has to have collision damage at the very least. All I can imagine is that he parked it on a farm or in a barn somewhere so he wouldn't get in trouble."

"A drunk driver, maybe?" I asked.

She nodded. "That's my assumption. Drunk or high and didn't want his blood tested."

"I'm very sorry that happened. But you already look better than the day you checked in."

"It's so peaceful here. I've been walking a lot, in town and up the mountain, to regain strength. I didn't think I could do it, but it has been calming for me. Sitting in nature without another human soul around and listening to the birds has allowed me to unwind. Kelly takes me shopping every chance she gets, and she's good for me, too. She's hilarious! I don't have children to buy for like she does, but

I've found some nice gifts for family and friends. For once, I won't be behind at Christmastime."

"I think it's great that you and Kelly are such good friends."

"She's lovely. So is Bizzy. Did you know that she hired someone to come and give me a massage?"

"That was thoughtful!"

"It was wonderful! Wendell says we'll probably check out and go home tomorrow. Frankly, I'll miss Bizzy and Kelly fussing over me!"

"Ella! Ella!" Wendell frowned as he walked toward us. "Hello, Holly. Ella, it's the strangest thing. I sent your mother some flowers to brighten her day, but the delivery man said she's not home and they can't reach her. I'm worried about her."

"She probably went to visit a friend. I'll call her and find out. Nice chatting with you, Holly. I'll let you know about Mom, Wendell. If the two of you will excuse me, I promised I would meet Kelly in five minutes!" Ella threw her shoulders back and walked away in a hurry, showing only the tiniest bit of a hobble.

Wendell watched her, his nostrils flaring.

"I hear today is the big vote on the office in Wagtail," I said to Wendell.

"Yes, indeed. Ben must be anxious."

"A little, I guess. It means a lot to him."

"Just between the two of us, I think your Ben has it in the bag."

# Seventeen

Oh no! I struggled to maintain a pleasant smile. "I won't say a word."

"I look forward to having you join our group as Ben's wife."

"Thank you."

"I'm glad I caught you alone. The black dog you had— did I hear someone call him Squishy?"

"Yes. It's an unusual name."

"Indeed. How did he come by that name?"

"We don't really know. He was found as a stray."

"Really? Hard to believe anyone would part with a handsome fellow like that. I'd like to adopt him. For Ella. She's quite taken with him."

Hadn't he told me he thought Labradors were overrated? "I'm sorry, but he was adopted. There are a lot more dogs in need of homes at the shelter. I'm sure you could find another one she would like."

"I don't think so. Thanks anyway."

As he walked away, I heard him mutter, "Pity."

I watched him, feeling terrible for fooling everyone into thinking I was going to marry Ben. My gaze met Simon's across the lobby. It wasn't fair to him, was it? Maybe I should stage an argument with Ben right that minute so both Ben and Simon would be on equal footing before the vote rolled around. Was that the right thing to do? Or would it only add more fuel to the big mess I had created when I said yes to Ben's proposal?

I crossed the lobby to Simon. "Good morning!"

"Good morning," he said without any joy in his tone.

His cat, Blossom, who was on a leash, mewed a greeting. I bent to pet her. "Is there anything I can do for you?"

"I think you have done quite enough. No, that's not fair. My daughter always tells me I shouldn't blame the clerk."

I peered at him, not understanding what he was trying to say. "Am I the clerk in this scenario?"

For the first time, I saw him laugh. "In a manner of speaking. She means that you shouldn't blame the clerk for the policies or mistakes of someone else. The clerk is just doing their job, so there's no point in yelling or being angry toward the clerk. You don't seem prone to drama. Given the long pause before you accepted Ben's proposal, I would have to guess that you were wavering on your response. So in a manner of speaking, you weren't the person who scored points with Percy, Wendell, and Bizzy. Ben did that all on his own. And I feel that your shock was genuine when I told you why I believe he proposed."

"You're a pretty good sleuth. That's some excellent deducing!"

"Ah, so I was correct. And you are not the hapless clerk. You were aware of Ben's scheme."

"No. I was not."

"Ha!" He said with delight, "You are the hapless clerk who got the blame through no fault of your own. I'm terribly sorry if I offended you or caused you anguish."

I'd had about enough of being called a hapless clerk and tried to steer him in another direction. "How old is your daughter? She sounds like someone I would like."

"Twenty-eight. And she has had many jobs where she was the hapless clerk. My son is in the navy, much as your Officer Dave was."

"I didn't realize that you were married."

"I have been a widower for over twenty years now." He took a deep breath. "I was mom and dad to my children for a long time. Now my son is at sea, but he can't tell me where, and my daughter has moved to Greensboro, not too terribly far from here. I think we would both like to live in a place like this. Peaceful, no cars, lots of animals. It would suit us."

"Then may the best man win."

Simon smiled at me. "My daughter is driving up here tomorrow. I'm taking Blossom and her to tea."

"That will be lovely. But Wendell said something about leaving tomorrow. Will you be with us a few extra days?"

Simon snickered. "I wouldn't go by what Wendell says." He waved and walked away with Blossom.

My phone rang as I was on the way to my office. I answered and was delighted to hear Holmes's voice.

"Holly! Good morning! Did you get any sleep?"

"Not much. How's your dad?"

"The doctor says he should make a full recovery. They're keeping him for a few more days, though. I just need to keep that jerk Wendell away from him."

"Good news, then. Wendell's wife said they're probably checking out tomorrow."

"Not if Dave can help it," said Holmes. "He's convinced that someone in Ben's group murdered Dinah. Oops. There's Mom. I'm driving her over to the hospital. Hey, Holly?"

"Yes?"

"Thanks for helping us yesterday. And for being there for us. Talk to you later."

I disconnected the call and walked into the office to collect my clipboard, determined to make a more thorough check in my rounds. I felt as if I had been giving it short shrift lately, and I didn't want to overlook anything. I began on the third floor as I always did. Everything looked fine.

As I started down the stairs to the second floor, a door opened and Percy peeked out, as if he was making sure no one would see him. I froze in my position on the stairs, still high enough that he might not notice me. I hoped Trixie and Twinkletoes wouldn't give away my presence.

Percy pulled the door closed behind him, straightened the golf shirt he wore, and hurried away. I heard a door close. Probably Chase, where he was staying. I knew perfectly well which room he'd been in, but I looked at the name anyway. *Cuddle.* Bizzy was staying there.

I didn't like to jump to conclusions, but I wondered if something might be going on between them.

By the time I reached the main lobby, I had decided that overall, the inn looked great. I made note of a couple of minor things for Shadow to fix. A leaky faucet in Wendell and Ella's room, which Marina, the housekeeper, told me about, and a flickering lightbulb in the first-floor cat wing hallway. I settled in my office and texted Shadow about the repairs.

After ordering the flowers for Dinah's parents, I began to pay bills.

Ben came in and made himself comfortable on the sofa. "Today's the day!"

"So I heard." I kept on writing checks.

"Have you got some kind of mountain lore about what to do for good luck?"

I looked up at him, tempted to make up some silly thing about hopping backward on one foot. "I'm afraid not. What have you heard about Dinah?"

"That was something else. I mean, she wasn't one of the senior attorneys, but it will be hard to replace her. Her death was so awful. Why would anyone do that?"

I nodded. "Any guess as to who threw her over the cliff?"

Ben's eyes met mine. "I work with all those people. You realize this is like me asking you if you think Oma or Zelda or Mr. Huckle did it?"

Ouch! I had been so busy being annoyed with Ben that I hadn't considered his feelings. The tension in their group must be terrible with each of them suspecting the others.

"Maybe Simon," he said. "He's not very broken up about it."

Now Ben had my full attention. "Would he have a reason to kill Dinah?"

"There were rumors of a little office romance between them a few months ago."

"He's a good bit older than Dinah was," I said. "Not that there's anything wrong with that. I just wouldn't have expected the two of them together. Was it an ugly blowup?"

Ben shrugged. "It was awkward. Lots of glares and 'tell him yourself' from Dinah. Simon just sulked. He's not very talkative. Frankly, I think he would be a terrible choice for a Wagtail office. He's smart and a good lawyer, but he's too socially reserved. Kind of a legal nerd."

"Now that Dinah is dead, you're his only competitor for the job in Wagtail." I watched his reaction.

He sucked in a deep breath. "Are you suggesting that Simon murdered her because he thought she would get the Wagtail job?"

"It's a motive."

Ben's brow furrowed. "What if he comes after me? I hadn't thought about it before you brought it up, but I'm the only one standing in his way!"

"Not the only one," I tried to sooth him. "Don't Percy, Bizzy, and Wendell still have to vote on whether or not to open an office in Wagtail first? That's a major hurdle before they choose the attorney who will be in charge. What other reasons are there for murdering her?"

"A personal spat that no one knows about? Maybe she made an error that put the firm in jeopardy and they were eager to let her go."

"Then they could have just fired her."

"I guess. You're giving me a headache. I think I'm going to take a walk on the green. Want to come? You can protect me from Simon."

"Thanks for the invite, but I have some work to take care of here."

He was still frowning when he stood up and walked to the doorway. He stopped and looked around the reception lobby before venturing into it.

It felt good to think about something else for a while. I focused on business and returned some calls.

Shirley McKendrick from the shelter phoned me. The pitch of her voice was off. I knew something was wrong immediately. "Holly, we have a problem. The woman who adopted Squishy is bringing him back. She's been trying to train him, but he just lies down and rolls over on his back. I tried to talk her into giving him more time. He's hardly had a chance to settle in yet. It's really not fair to Squishy to return him so soon. But she doesn't want him now. According to her, Squishy isn't the dog she had hoped. She's bringing him back today. Can you foster him again?"

I thought of Ella and Wendell right away. "You bet. Squishy will always be welcome here. I might even have a couple interested in him! Let me know when they arrive, and I'll come to pick him up."

There was one bright spot. I knew Ella loved him, and it was kind of Wendell to think about surprising Ella by adopting Squishy.

Dave called to say he had sent two police officers to collect Dinah's belongings. They arrived an hour later, and made relatively quick work of photographing and packing up her room. We didn't have anyone booked, so I figured I would leave it until morning for Marina to clean. I stood outside in the hallway with Trixie and Twinkletoes when the officers emerged and went on their way.

Twinkletoes entered the room cautiously, but Trixie bounded inside. I followed them and took a quick look around. If they had collected fingerprints, there was no sign of it. They had taken the dresses that were strewn about and pulled back the duvet and sheets on the bed. The closet contained the ironing board and iron that we provided for our guests but nothing else. They had removed all the items Dinah had left in the bathroom.

I called Trixie, who came immediately. "Twinkletoes!"

"Ack, ack, ack."

"Twinks?"

"Ack, ack, ack."

I looked at the ceiling. The sun was reflecting on something. I twisted the ring on my hand to hide its stone, but the spot didn't go away.

Trixie ran to the far side of the bed, closest to the window. I followed her.

Twinkletoes stood on her hind legs and pawed at something.

The first thing that came to mind was a snake. If it was one, I hoped Shadow would be able to come remove it. I edged closer and realized it was the corner of some papers that were held together by a large paper clip adorned by a giant rhinestone. Each time Twinkletoes pawed at it, it snapped back up, flickering on the ceiling. It was like a laser toy. No wonder she thought it was fun.

I considered trying to catch the police, but then it dawned on me that it might be something a previous guest had left tucked under the mattress. I fetched a washcloth from the bathroom and used it like a potholder to retrieve the papers without leaving my fingerprints on them.

Twinkletoes mewed a complaint when the spot on the ceiling disappeared for good.

I glanced through the papers, careful not to get my fingerprints on them or smudge anything.

They looked like time sheets from the law firm. Pretty boring. Still, I would hand them over to Dave in case they meant something. After all, either Dinah had hidden them or they had slipped over the side of the bed and were caught there.

Trixie, Twinkletoes, and I returned to the office. I slid the papers into a large manila envelope, wrote Sergeant Dave Quinlan on the top of it, and phoned Dave. He didn't answer my call. I left a message for him about the papers we had found. "They look like time sheets for billing. But they were tucked under the mattress so that your guys missed them. I have them in the inn office."

Not twenty minutes later, Dave called and asked if I could bring the papers over to the convention center. I hadn't eaten dinner yet and had hoped for a quiet evening. But I called Trixie and Twinkletoes, nabbed the envelope for Dave, and took a walk to the convention center, thinking I would check the magic refrigerator on my return.

It was a beautiful evening. The temperate air was perfect. I was glad to get out a bit after all. Streetlights began to glow along the sidewalk.

Holmes had designed and acted as the contractor for the new building. On top of that, it had been named the Liesel Miller Convention Center, after Oma, so it was very dear to me. I walked inside the airy building at the same time as Logan, who carried a large dinner order. The name **Tequila Mockingbird** was plastered on the bags he carried.

"Are you working for a delivery company or looking for your mom?" I asked.

"Mom ordered dinner from the restaurant. I thought I'd
bring it over to her."

"She'll appreciate that."

"Maybe not. She's always pushing me to get what she
calls a 'real job.'"

I nodded. "Parents do that."

I spied Bizzy and Dave in a glass-enclosed conference
room with Percy and pointed at it. The two of us went in
that direction. I had a bad feeling we were interrupting
something.

Logan must not have drawn the same conclusion. He
was bright and cheerful, greeting them all with smiles and
planting a kiss on his mom's cheek. "Our famous chicken
wings, which are really good, and bacon cheeseburgers
with French fries. To top it all off, I stopped by Pupcakes
and got you some vanilla cupcakes, which I happen to know
are Mom's favorite."

The adorable cupcakes were iced to look like cute fuzzy
white dog faces.

"Do you want to stay for dinner?" asked Bizzy. "Wendell isn't here, so we have extra!"

Logan's gaze swept over Dave, and for a moment a grim
look crossed his face. "And talk business? I'll pass. How
about dinner tomorrow night? Just the two of us?"

"It's a date." Bizzy smiled at her son and watched him
leave. When the door had closed, she said, "Jeff, the young
man who died when he fell off the cliff years ago, was a
friend of Logan's. Dinah's death has brought back long-
suppressed memories of that terrible time. It's as though
Logan is reliving it. In fact, I was planning to come see you,
Holly. I don't know when we'll be able to leave, but I would

like to stay on for a few more days if possible. I feel like I should be here for Logan."

"I think we can accommodate you. I'll check when I get back to the inn. I apologize for interrupting your meeting. I assume Ben and Simon aren't here because you're deciding on the local office and who will run it?"

"Yes," said Bizzy. "Wendell was supposed to be here, too. We don't know where he went."

I handed the envelope to Dave. "No one touched it. It was tucked away as if Dinah had hidden it."

Dave slid on gloves, ripped it open, and pulled out the contents. "Do these mean anything to you?"

He spread the pages on the table, well away from the food. Percy and Bizzy looked over them.

Percy's face flushed a dark red. He and Bizzy exchanged a look.

"So it's true," she said.

I wanted to melt into the wall because I knew I would be thrown out any minute and I was itching to know what was true. Whatever it was, it was very upsetting to them.

# Eighteen

"That explains why he didn't show up to our meeting today." Percy turned his back to the room and gazed out the glass walls at the lake. "Dinah told me last week that she had noticed some billing irregularities, but she didn't mention any names. I did some preliminary investigating but didn't find anything. It appears that Wendell has been overcharging clients." He slammed his fist into his hand. "I was afraid of something like this, but I never dreamed it was Wendell."

"What could he have been thinking?" asked Bizzy. "I would never have believed that Wendell would do anything like this. He had to know it would catch up to him. He'll lose his license to practice law!"

Percy whipped around toward us. "It's as if Dinah is speaking from the grave." His deep voice made that observation even creepier. "It's best that we know. We'll put a stop to it immediately, report it to the bar, and refund all overcharges. It's far better to face it and clean it up immediately. Thank goodness for Dinah."

His last sentence hung in the air ominously. I wondered if they were all thinking what I was. Had she approached Wendell about this? Had he known and killed her to stop her from revealing it?

Percy picked up his phone and punched in a number. "Sean, I need you to block Wendell from accessing any files." He listened for a moment. "He's here in Wagtail with us right now, so that shouldn't be a problem, but yes, physical access to the offices will need to be changed as well. Thank you."

He hung up and nodded at Bizzy.

"Eat something, Percy," she said. "This is going to get worse before it gets better. There's plenty of food. Holly, have you eaten?"

"How can you eat?" Percy growled. "This is a disaster."

I gratefully sat down next to Bizzy, snagged the burger meant for Wendell, and shared it with Trixie and Twinkletoes.

Dave swallowed hard and put down his burger. He picked up his phone.

I knew who he was calling. Having to enter and exit Wagtail through the parking lot outside of town could be annoying under some circumstances, but it was helpful when someone was trying to sneak out of town. The people who worked there knew who had been picked up by a cab or a car service.

"He's still here," said Dave.

Percy placed both of his hands on the table and leaned on them. "There's a huge elephant in this room that none of us has mentioned. Did Wendell murder Dinah to prevent her from telling us?"

I swallowed a bite and gazed at Dave, who calmly said, "It's the strongest motive I've heard yet."

I finally piped up. "Would Dinah wander through the woods with Wendell?"

Bizzy gave me a horrified look. "Oh no! Do you think he was pretending to seduce her?"

"Wendell and Dinah?" asked Percy, an appalled look on his face.

"She was rotten drunk, Percy," said Bizzy. "It wouldn't have taken much for her to wander off with someone."

It was only conjecture, but I knew it was plausible.

Dave wiped his mouth with a napkin and reached for his phone again. "Excuse me." He walked away for a moment while he gave instructions to someone. When he returned to the table, he said, "Eat up, Holly. I need you to go back to the inn with me and let me into his room if he doesn't answer the door."

Percy finally sat down. "Okay. Here's the thing. While Wendell obviously knew that Dinah had the goods on him, he doesn't know that *we* know. He clearly wasn't aware that Dinah had documentation, or he would have swiped it. So he may not realize how much we know at this point. It is imperative that no one breathe a word of this. If he gets wind of it, then he'll bolt." He pointed at me. "What did we discuss in here?"

"How good the food in Wagtail is?"

Percy winked at me. "Excellent." He picked up his burger. "Now to find him."

# Nineteen

I walked back to the inn with Dave, keeping an eye out for Wendell. I wanted to think he wasn't a threat to me because he couldn't know about the papers in Dinah's room that Twinkletoes had found. And he probably realized that they wouldn't mean anything to most people anyway. Yet I found myself very much on alert, scanning faces and watching for any stealthy movements. We made it back to the inn without incident.

I unlocked the office to get a key to Wendell's room.

Dave and I walked up to the second floor. In a low voice he said, "I'm putting a couple of cops in the inn to watch for him. They're supposed to tell you or Liesel that they're here."

"Will they arrest him?"

"Unless something changes, no. Not yet. All I have is a motive. But I don't want him to bolt."

He knocked on the door to Hike.

No one answered.

Dave knocked again. "Police, Mr. Walters. Open the door, please."

After a minute, when no one had answered, he nodded and gestured toward the lock. In a low voice he said, "As soon as it's open, I want to you back up off to the side."

I nodded and unlocked the door.

Dave swung it open and entered. He reappeared in a minute. "Their luggage and toiletries are here." He closed the door behind him. "Call me immediately if either of them shows up." Dave tore down the grand staircase.

The next few hours ticked by slowly. I checked in with Holmes to be sure his dad was on the mend. That was going well. Holmes was at the hospital with his mom.

Two police officers in plain clothes let me know when they arrived. Both of them were very young. I double-checked to be sure the reception lobby doors were locked from the outside so they wouldn't have to worry about that entrance. If he was still in the inn somewhere, Wendell could leave that way, but he couldn't enter.

I spied Bizzy in the Dogwood Room all by herself.

"Are you waiting for someone?" I asked.

"Percy and Kelly went up to bed. I was just sitting here thinking that I wished Logan lived closer to me. He brightens my life. Logan is making noises about adopting a dog, so maybe I'll have a granddog soon. Wagtail is charming. I love all the dogs and cats. I'd like to have one, but with my crazy schedule, it wouldn't be fair."

"No thoughts of moving here?"

"My ex-husband's family has a house here. It's a huge place that they call 'the cottage.' When he had visitation, he often brought Logan here for holidays and vacations. I guess in my mind, I always associated it with my ex and never even thought about moving here."

"How are you holding up workwise?"

She heaved a big sigh. "This is a nightmare. When Percy and I brought Wendell on board, he was a brash hotshot lawyer. He had an excellent reputation as a criminal attorney. Sometimes he was a little unusual in the way he handled his cases, but we felt lucky to have landed him. And now—" she gazed out the floor-to-ceiling windows "—I really just want to kick him in the pants. How could he do this? It will ruin our reputation. He's taking all of us down with him."

"Ella says he's very tidy and precise at home. He seems sort of dapper and very conscious of how people perceive him. I find it hard to imagine he would cheat people."

"You're not the only one! It's interesting how different people are. My husband came from a very wealthy family with mansions and trust funds. Not a single one of them drove an expensive or flashy car. They leaned toward practical vehicles. The children often wanted brand-name items, but most of them grew into adults who cared more about quality than designer names. On the other hand, Wendell didn't have an easy life growing up. I understand they moved quite a bit and money was scarce. Yet he has his suits tailored for him. He doesn't buy off the rack. I never see him without a lapel pin. And he always carries a Montblanc pen. I have no issue using a disposable ballpoint pen, but not Wendell. There are certain trappings of wealth that he clings to. He is making a good living, which is why I don't understand his need to swindle people. There's no question that we will make it right with his clients. But we *never* should have been in this position. It infuriates me!"

"Have you told the others yet?"

Her eyes widened. "Ben! Of course. You must want to tell him. But I think it should come from Percy and me. We'll tell them tomorrow morning. Percy and I needed to get our own heads straight about this. I told your grandmother that everyone except me will probably check out tomorrow around noon."

"We'll be sorry to see you go. I guess you haven't seen Wendell?"

"Not a sign of him or Ella. I worry about her."

"She seems to be recovering from her accident nicely."

Her jaw tightened. "Thank heaven for that."

My phone rang, so I excused myself and walked away. "Holly Miller."

"Holly, it's Shirley from the shelter. Poor Squishy has no luck at all."

I felt as if the blood had drained from my face. "Oh no! Is he okay?"

"The woman who adopted him was bringing him back and he got away from her when she let him out of the car. I'm hoping he's trying to find his way to the inn."

"I'll post it online and then go looking for him."

"We're on the alert over here, too. I'll call you if I hear anything."

I retreated to the office and posted a picture of Squishy on the Wagtail social media sites. **Lost dog. Very friendly. Responds to Squishy. Please call the shelter or Holly Miller if you see him.**

I eyed Trixie. "You better not run off."

She beat her tail against the couch where she lay.

Trixie and Twinkletoes accompanied me on a golf cart

ride around Wagtail in search of Squishy. If we hadn't been looking for a beloved lost dog, it would have been nice. The warm air held the promise of summer days ahead. But my stomach was in knots. What if that woman had dumped him somewhere because she didn't want to drive all the way back to Wagtail? What if something terrible had happened to him and she didn't want to admit it? I wanted to give her the benefit of the doubt, but she had rejected Squishy so fast that I didn't trust her. She hadn't really given him a chance. I could understand that Squishy might not have been the right dog for her, but clearly she wasn't the right person for Squishy. Poor fellow. At least it wasn't cold or raining.

It was late enough for the streets to be empty. House lights had been turned off. Wagtail was sleeping, except for a lone woman walking along the street where my mother lived. I turned off the lights on the golf cart and slowed down. The electric motor barely made a sound.

She opened the front door to a house across the street from Mom's. Cooper's house! She looked out at the street briefly as if checking for witnesses before she closed the door.

I thought I saw blond hair as she entered the house. I hoped it wasn't Zelda.

# Twenty

When I rose the next morning, I opened the French doors to my little balcony and searched for any sign of Squishy. There was no shortage of dogs accompanying runners and walkers in the fresh morning air. But Squishy was nowhere to be seen.

I poured my morning tea, savored my chocolate croissant, and handed treats to Trixie and Twinkletoes. This would be a particularly difficult day. I wanted to think that it would be wonderful, but Ben would learn about the disaster that had befallen his firm, and poor Squishy was still out there somewhere in the world all alone.

After a shower, I donned a short-sleeved dress in bright spring colors and slid the engagement ring onto my finger, feeling like a fraud. If Ben and his group were leaving that day, I could give it back to him very soon. I just had to pick the right moment.

The door to my guest room was open, but Ben wasn't

there. Maybe Percy and Bizzy had called an early breakfast to break the news to everyone.

Trixie and Twinkletoes hurried down the grand staircase ahead of me. They stopped at the main entrance to the inn and waited for me to open the door. No sooner had I swung the door open than both of them shot outside.

Ella sprang up the steps as I walked down them.

"You look like you feel much better," I said.

"I do! My bruises are fading and all this walking around Wagtail has done wonders for me. Your Dr. Engelknecht removed the stitches from my eyebrow yesterday. Little steps, but I'm getting there."

I walked leisurely toward the grass meant for dogs to use as a potty area but quickly realized that neither of them was there. "Trixie? Twinkletoes?"

They were gone. Oh great. Now two dogs and a cat were running loose. Maybe they picked up Squishy's scent and ran to him? This wasn't like them. Something was wrong.

I pulled out my phone and looked up Trixie's whereabouts on the GPS locator. She was going toward Mom's house. That was odd. Had Mom's parents come home? Had Mom moved back to her house and they sensed she needed help?

I jogged in that direction, phoning Oma as I walked so she wouldn't worry when we didn't come to breakfast. I explained what had happened.

"But Holly, your mother is here, sitting beside me and eating wonderful waffles with strawberries."

Just about that time, I heard the howl. Trixie's deep, sad song that meant someone was dead. "I'll call you back. I think Trixie may have found some . . . thing."

I hoped it wasn't Squishy. Though, to be honest, Trixie had never yowled that way when a dog died. Probably because most dogs weren't murdered. I picked up my pace and jogged the back way, behind the Blue Boar and Tequila Mockingbird. I emerged at the Davises' house, turned, and headed to Mom's backyard.

But I didn't see Trixie or Twinkletoes anywhere. They certainly weren't in Mom's garden. I heard Trixie again.

Surely, she wasn't across the street. Not in the murderer's yard! Had someone killed Cooper?

I stood across the street from his house but didn't detect any movement. Should I ring the doorbell and tell him I thought my dog was in his backyard? What if Cooper had killed someone? Would he shoot us all? Did he have a gun? He probably wasn't allowed to. But he could kill just as well with a carving knife, and there was no question that I wouldn't be able to overcome him.

Sneaking into his backyard was also an option. But the only difference in that scenario was I wouldn't have told him why I was in his backyard before he killed us all.

I phoned Dave. "I think Trixie and Twinkletoes have found something in the yard behind Cooper's house."

"Something? Like a dead squirrel?"

"I don't know. I can't see why she's howling." As I spoke, she did it again.

Dave groaned. "I know that howl. I'll be right there. Wait for me."

I was torn. I knew I should wait for Dave. But what if Trixie's howling was driving Cooper nuts and he hurt her? Or what if it was Cooper who was dead or dying? What if he was still alive and needed help?

I gazed around. Where was Dave? I should have asked
him how far away he was.

I texted Holmes and Ben.

I'm at Cooper's house, across the street from my mom.
Trixie is howling murder in Cooper's backyard. Could use
some backup.

Ben would be useless, but I figured there was safety in
numbers. I took a deep breath and crossed the street. Trying
to act casual, I walked along the sidewalk, just past the house,
then turned left abruptly and sprinted to the backyard.

It was spacious with neatly cut grass and a large patio.
Trixie and Twinkletoes sat next to a prone figure. If the
killer was in Cooper's house, he could probably see us from
the windows. I bent and scuttled toward them.

A man, I thought, given the brown leather shoes and
trousers neatly pressed with a crease on each leg. I inched
forward on my knees, noting his torn shirt, which was no
longer tucked into his trousers. And then I could see his
face. Wendell's eyes stared at me as though they were accusing me of something. Welts on his cheeks and chin indicated
he had been beaten. A trickle of blood below his nose had
already dried.

I didn't know him well, but I felt pity for him, even if he
had cheated people by overcharging them. He had died a
horrible and painful death.

With a jolt, I remembered Cooper. Where was Dave? I
needed to get out of there. I grabbed Trixie, who fought me,
but that only caused me to tighten my grip. I scooped up
Twinkletoes and ran like the devil was chasing me.

Right into Cooper.

He strode along the sidewalk with shopping bags, as if he hadn't a care in the world. But now he knew I had been in his backyard.

I forced a smile. "Oops. Sorry, these two got away from me."

Trixie kicked me in the ribs. "Ugh. Gotta go." I ran straight to Mom's house. The key was under the front mat. I didn't want him to see that! But I had no choice. She would simply have to find a better hiding place. After all, everyone looked under the front mat.

Kneeling with a squirming Jack Russell and a cat who was wiggling her way out of my grasp wasn't easy.

"Can I give you a hand there?" Cooper was directly behind me.

# Twenty-One

I didn't dare hand either of my precious babies to Cooper. But I struggled to reach the key without loosening my grip on one of them. If I asked him to hand the key to me, all he had to do was unlock the door, push me into the house, and beat me like he had Wendell. My heart pounded as if it were trying to jump up my throat and exit.

*Stay outside, stay outside. Don't let him get you into the house.* The words repeated in my head. And then it occurred to me that being outside hadn't helped Wendell.

Cooper bent next to me and gently plucked Twinkletoes out of my failing grip. "Hey, pretty kitty. What beautiful fur you have. What's her name?"

I could hear her purring! Had she lost her ability to discern good from evil? "Twinkletoes." I slid my free hand far enough under the mat to reach the key. A jolt of euphoria shot through me.

Still clutching Trixie, I staggered to a standing position and unlocked the door.

Cooper leaned over and opened it for me. "I remember this house. Wow. I like what your mom has done with it. The foyer used to be closed off and . . . Hey, how come everything is gray? Your mom's house isn't, but it seems like gray is everywhere. Gray towels, gray walls, gray rugs and sheets. What's up with that?"

Okay, that was a weird thing to bring up. He was a psychopath! He was right, of course. "Gray has been a decorating trend for a long time."

He shook his head. "I don't get that. Green, I understand. Blue, white, yellow. I like colors, the brighter the better. Like your dress."

"Oh! Thank you." I heard footsteps, like someone was running. Did he have an accomplice? I needed to get Twinkletoes and slam the door!

There wasn't enough time. Thankfully, it was Holmes who appeared behind Cooper.

"Holmes!" I shrieked. I tried to gather myself. "Have you met Cooper Adams?"

For a millisecond, Holmes shot me an odd look. Then he held out his hand to Cooper. "Holmes Richardson. Welcome to Wagtail."

"Thanks."

Holmes reached out for Twinkletoes, and Cooper handed her over. The purring commenced again.

My entire body relaxed. I could feel the tension ebbing away. "Thank you for helping me, Cooper."

"Anytime. See you around." He ambled toward the sidewalk just in time for three golf carts to pull up in front of his house. Dave and a handful of uniformed police officers jumped out of them.

"Hello, Cooper," said Dave.

"Is there a problem?" asked Cooper, picking up the shopping bags he had dropped in order to help me.

I reached for Twinkletoes and placed her inside of Mom's house with Trixie. I stepped outside and closed the door behind me.

Holmes whispered, "I don't see a body."

"In his backyard," I whispered.

"We'd like to have a look around," said Dave.

I could see the concern on Cooper's face. He shrugged as if it weren't a big deal. "Okay. I thought no one would be checking up on me."

"We received a report."

Cooper looked back at me. I could imagine what he was thinking. I hadn't had a free hand to phone anyone. "What did they report?"

"There's something in your backyard."

Holmes and I walked across the street, careful to keep our distance.

"There's nothing back there but a shovel. I was planning to start a vegetable garden. I asked the owners if that was all right. They know about my . . ." He paused as if searching for the right word. ". . . history."

Except for the incriminating mention of a shovel, he sounded ever so innocent. How many times had he practiced saying that part about the shovel? He had to come up with a reason if there was going to be a big grave in the backyard. A garden was exactly the right cover. But why hadn't he covered Wendell with a tarp or a blanket before he left the house?

And then the cops saw Wendell. Boots pounded the grass as the officers ran toward him.

Cooper dropped the bags he carried and ran behind them. He stopped and stared, open-mouthed. "Who is that?" He held his palms up in protest. "I had nothing to do with this. It's the first time I've seen anything out here except for squirrels."

Dave kneeled and tried to find a pulse. He punched a number on his phone. "Engelknecht? We have a deceased man across the street from Nell Goodwin's house." After a short silence, he said, "Okay," and ended the call.

"Do you recognize this man?" Dave asked.

Cooper inched closer as if he was reluctant to see the person. "That's my lawyer!"

Dave beckoned one of the officers. "Take Cooper to Snowball. I'll be there as soon as I get the medical examiner here."

Cooper backed up with his palms in the air again. "Hey, I had nothing to do with this. I swear he wasn't here when I left this morning. Actually, I . . . I didn't even look out at the backyard. I made a cup of coffee, but the kitchen window looks out on the front yard. Then I went to buy some supplies and doughnuts. I swear I don't know anything about this."

"But you do know the deceased."

"Well, yeah. But why would I kill my own lawyer? The man helped me!"

"I'll talk to you about this in Snowball." Dave left no room for doubt about what was coming.

"Not again. Am I going to be questioned every time someone dies in this town? You already took me to Wagtail for questioning about that woman who fell off the cliff. A woman I never met before in my life."

Dave stared at him. "He's in your backyard."

"Am I under arrest?"

Dave considered for a moment before responding. "Not yet. But it doesn't look good."

"What if this guy—" Cooper peered at the officer's name "—Dombrowski, comes inside with me. I'm not going anywhere." His eyes met Dave's. Cooper held out his open hands. "I've got nowhere to go and no way to get there. No car, no golf cart, not even a skateboard."

I seriously questioned my sanity. Minutes ago, I had been afraid of Cooper, and now I felt incredibly sorry for him. "I'll make some coffee," I said.

Dave sighed and cocked his head at Dombrowski, who followed Cooper inside.

Holmes reached for my hand and squeezed it. "I'm coming, too. I haven't had any coffee yet this morning."

The interior of Cooper's house had clearly been renovated. The kitchen, family room, and dining room were one large open area. A cozy stone fireplace was flanked by tall windows that looked out on the backyard. A large-screen TV was mounted above the fireplace, and cushy light brown leather couches picked up the color in the stones. The kitchen portion, as he had said, overlooked the front yard and Mom's house.

I moved back and forth, trying to see Wendell through the rear windows. They overlooked a patio and trees beyond it. Wendell's body really wasn't visible from Cooper's family room.

"Nice place," said Holmes.

Cooper nodded. He sat down in a dining chair and rubbed his face vigorously. "I can't believe this is happening to me again."

Dombrowski leaned against a wall with his arms crossed and watched him.

Holmes and I unloaded Cooper's shopping bags. He'd bought a box of fresh doughnuts, a loaf of locally made bread, a jar of local blackberry jam, apples, red and orange peppers, a package of ground beef, and four boxes of giant black trash bags.

I put on a pot of coffee.

"You might as well help yourself to the doughnuts," said Cooper. "I guess I won't be around to eat them."

Holmes held out the opened box to him.

Cooper selected a chocolate iced doughnut. "I'm beginning to think I'm cursed. I know how crazy that sounds, but there's no other explanation for the things that have happened to me." He looked up at Holmes and me. "I was just released after twelve years in prison for a murder that I didn't commit."

Dombrowski's expression didn't change. I wondered if he'd heard that claim a lot.

"Rumor has it you fought over some girl that night," I said.

Cooper nodded. "Young stupid bucks is what we were. Add too many drinks and punches fly. I was camping on the mountain. I went back to my campsite and conked out. Dead to the world, you know?"

"Did you black out?" asked Holmes.

"I don't think so. I was just drunk. The next day I was planning to do some fishing when a couple of cops took me in for questioning. It went downhill from there."

Holmes frowned at him. "Seriously? You have absolutely no recollection of murdering anyone?"

Cooper shook his head.

"So you're claiming that you wandered around the mountain in some kind of drunken stupor?" asked Dombrowski with a snort.

"Wendell, the dead guy out back, argued that as my attorney. I don't recall going to the cliff or seeing Jeff again after our brawl."

"I heard there were witnesses," I said cautiously, hoping I wouldn't upset him.

He nodded. "People who saw us fighting. I admit to that. I've got an ugly scar on my arm from it." He rolled back his left sleeve to show us a two-inch-long scar. "And people saw us on the mountain." He held up his forefinger as if he was cautioning us. "But not together. Not one person could put either of us at the cliff or even together on the mountain. Not one! But they convicted me anyway."

Cooper looked tired and defeated. I felt for him.

"This is the beginning of another round. I can tell. This is how it started last time. I got blamed for something I didn't do and ended up in the slammer. Oh man! I cannot believe it's happening to me again."

We heard a door close. A minute later, Dave walked in. After inspecting the black trash bags on the countertop, he pulled out a chair and placed a small black audio recorder on the table. He faced Cooper. "Want to tell me what happened?"

Cooper shrugged. "I didn't do it. I watched the basketball playoffs on TV last night and went to bed around one."

"Were you expecting Wendell?"

"No. Definitely not."

"Did you see anyone or hear anything?"

"No."

"Talk to anyone?"

"No."

"Text or email anyone?"

"I don't have a computer or a cell phone." He pointed at the kitchen wall. "All I have is that phone."

"Did you call anyone?"

Cooper paused for a split second before answering. "No."

"Were you drinking?"

Cooper took a deep breath. "I haven't had so much as a sip of alcohol since the day I was taken into custody over twelve years ago. Not even a drop. Doubt that I ever will again."

"Check the trash, Dombrowski," said Dave.

We waited in silence as Dombrowski used a fork to lift the lid of a kitchen trash can.

"No sir. Looks like a couple of empty cans of ginger ale and an empty jar of mayo."

I didn't know what Dave was thinking, but I couldn't help considering the fact that it would have been easy for Cooper to throw empty bottles away when he went shopping. But just because he drank alcohol didn't mean he was guilty of murder.

"You said you don't have anywhere else to go. What about your parents?"

"My dad died while I was in prison. I couldn't go to the hospital to see him one last time, tell him I was sorry I had caused him so much pain. They wouldn't let me go to the funeral, either."

"And your mom?"

"I don't know that this is any of your business, but after

my dad died, she moved into a fifty-five-plus community. Kids, even grown ones, can't stay there for more than three days. She likes it there. Has friends, goes on bus trips. She doesn't need her felon son showing up and ruining her life. They wouldn't be too happy about that, and I'd hate to see her lose the support of that community. She's been through enough."

"Pretty nice rental," observed Dave.

"A charity paid the rent for the first couple of months, and I've been doing yardwork for people to make some money. Cleaning out brush. That kind of thing. I don't make much, but I don't have a lot of expenses, either. If I'm careful about what I spend, I think I can swing the rent."

"What are the black bags for?"

"I just told you. I've been doing yardwork."

Dave tilted his head as if he didn't believe him.

"I need them for rubbish. Plus I read that you can speed up vegetable growth by putting black plastic on the ground, piercing it, and planting seeds in the holes. It's supposed to warm up the soil."

"Also mighty handy for getting rid of bodies." Dave mashed his lips together. "I'm going to take you in to get your official statement. You have the right to remain silent . . ."

I wasn't going to jail or being questioned, but I felt queasy just hearing Dave tell Cooper his rights.

Cooper bowed his head like he felt defeated. He seemed almost resigned to what might happen.

"Wait!" I said. "There *was* someone else here last night. A blond woman."

# Twenty-Two

Cooper gazed at me, his eyes wide. "You must be mistaken."

"No. I'm not. I was out late looking for a lost dog when I came down this street in my golf cart. She entered this house. I'm sure of it."

"I wish you were right. It must have been another house."

"No," I persisted. "It was directly across the street from Mom's house. I know this street."

"Thanks for trying to help, Holly." He held out his hands for handcuffs.

"I don't think that will be necessary," said Dave.

When we left the house, Dombrowski and two other police officers took off with Cooper. The last thing he said to me was, "I was thinking of adopting a dog. I guess it's a good thing I didn't."

Dr. Engelknecht emerged from the backyard. "Holly, Holmes! I didn't realize that you were here. Holly, you can tell your grandmother that Wendell suffered serious blows to the head and torso. It was a vicious attack from the rear. I'm willing to bet the person who did this to him doesn't have more than a scratch or two."

I thanked him and retrieved Trixie and Twinkletoes. They were overjoyed to see us. We walked back to the inn.

"Do you believe him?" asked Holmes.

"I did until he denied that a blonde visited him last night."

"He seemed very credible up to that point."

"I thought so, too," I said. "Why would he deny that?"

Holmes stopped walking, pulled me to him, and wrapped his arms around me. He whispered, "Because he loves her and he's protecting her. Either she murdered Wendell, or they did it together. He doesn't want her involved. I would do that for you."

Trixie placed her paws on our legs and yelped for attention. Holmes and I laughed at her, and I swung her up into my arms for a hug.

Twinkletoes was already far ahead of us. She stopped and looked back, her tail swishing with annoyance.

"They haven't had breakfast."

Holmes looked at his watch. "Good grief! It's past one. I was supposed to drive Mom to the hospital. Will you be okay from here? My mom must be swishing her tail like Twinkletoes."

"Go on. We'll be fine."

He kissed me full on the lips and took off at a jog.

We entered the inn through the reception lobby. I marched up to Zelda. "What is the name of the new man you've been seeing?"

"Oh no. Please don't tell me something awful about him."

"What is his name?"

"Lars Norberg," she muttered.

To be on the safe side, I asked where he lived.

"On Pine Street?" she said hesitantly.

"You weren't over near Mom's house last night, were you?"

"No."

"Can't wait to meet him."

She sagged with relief.

The sliding doors opened, and Dave strode in. I knew he didn't plan to stay long, because his golf cart remained in the porte cochere. "Hi, Zelda. I need to speak to Ella Walters."

"Everybody is in the Dogwood Room. They can't find Wendell."

Dave and I found them there. Zelda was right. They had all gathered in the Dogwood Room. Oma and Mom and the entire law firm group, including Ella.

"I'd like to speak with Ella, please," said Dave.

She rose and followed him.

Rats. I was going to have to break the news to everyone else. "I'm so sorry to have to tell you that Wendell has passed away."

A collective gasp filled the air. Then there was silence.

And then they all asked questions at once. At first, I wasn't sure how much I should say, but the nature of their questions told me that they would find out eventually. It might as well be now.

"Dr. Engelknecht says he was beaten. Hit with something most likely. He was found in a backyard, lying in the grass. I'm so sorry. I know you were close to him, and this must be hard for you."

I watched their reactions. Oma and Mom appeared appropriately horrified. Percy looked out the window with his back to everyone again. Bizzy seemed stunned. Kelly clasped a hand to her chest and looked around, probably for Ella. Simon stroked his cat.

Ben reminded me of Cooper. He had a defeated expression. I guessed he was thinking of himself. This probably put a quick end to the entire proposition of a Wagtail office. In fact, I thought there was a good chance that the law firm had probably just imploded.

Oma and Mom left to bring in food and beverages, and I went to the private kitchen with Trixie and Twinkletoes for brunch.

Trixie snarfed turkey and sweet potatoes. Twinkletoes was happy with tuna, one of her favorites, and I was thrilled to find egg salad and chocolate pudding, which were an odd selection but creamy and comforting, which I needed.

The door banged open. Dave walked in, followed by Oma and Mom.

"Ella took the news remarkably well. Some people are in shock when they receive this sort of news, and I think she might be that type," said Oma.

Mom offered Dave some of the egg salad.

"I don't have time for lunch," he said, "but I'm starved. That would be great." He ate standing up as if it would speed up the process. "I have asked them all to stay. I'll need to get statements from them." He glanced at his watch.

"You believe that Cooper killed him?" asked Oma. "Why would he want to kill his lawyer, who was on his side?"

"Because he didn't get him off? Cooper spent twelve years in prison. He had plenty of time to think about his case and how he landed there."

"And it's logical to blame it on the lawyer," I said. "Who else would you blame?"

"He died in Cooper's backyard. I have officers combing the crime scene. But the only real evidence against him other than the location are the black trash bags he bought. Those yard-size ones are huge. I've used them myself. Definitely suspicious."

"But he uses them for work," I reminded him.

"A little too convenient, don't you think? I'm more interested in the woman you saw at his house. She must know something. Are you absolutely certain you had the right house, Holly? Would you testify to that?"

"Yes."

"It must be the same woman we saw," Oma said to Mom.

"Do you know who she is?" asked Dave.

"We could spy on her and let you know when she comes," said Oma.

"That would work, but I don't want either of you taking things into your own hands. Call me. Understood? Do not approach them. Look what happened to Wendell. They could be very dangerous."

Dave plopped his plate on the counter. "One other thing. Holly, were you with Holmes during the night?"

Really? He was asking things like that in front of my mother and grandmother? I shot him an annoyed look.

"Can you give him an alibi?"

"You're accusing Holmes of something?"

"We know he blames his father's heart attack on Wendell. Do you know where he was during the night?"

Holmes a murderer? How could I ever think that? Holmes

was kind and intelligent, not a brute. But it didn't look good. The pieces of the puzzle were coming together in a way that I didn't like. Holmes had said he would lie to protect me. Was I letting him down if I told the truth? "No."

"That's too bad," said Dave. "I'm sorry, but I have to run. Thanks for lunch. See you later."

The atmosphere at the inn was glum that afternoon. I was tempted to break off my engagement to Ben, but it wasn't the right time considering all his group had been through.

I was making myself a mug of tea when I spied Ella sitting on the terrace, staring at the lake.

I made a mug for her, too, and brought it out on a tray with sugar, cream, and lemon, along with a platter of cookies baked fresh that day in the inn's kitchen. I set the tray on a table beside her and sat down.

"How are you holding up?"

Ella was completely dry-eyed. She didn't hold a tissue, and her eyes weren't rimmed with red. She smiled at me. "Thank you, Holly. Everyone is being so kind. I'm fine, but shocked. There's a great deal to do, of course, but honestly, I'm sort of glad that Dave has asked us to remain in Wagtail. It allows me to put everything off for a bit. And it helps that Wendell's partners are here. I don't have to notify them. Percy has recommended a funeral home that he has used in the past. Bizzy suggested a florist." She picked up a chocolate chip cookie and bit into it. "Mm. Good! I love it when they're chewy."

"Let me know if there's anything we can do to help you."

"Thank you, Holly."

As I walked toward the office, a local florist was delivering a beautiful spring arrangement for Ella. I thanked him, carried it upstairs to Hike, and let myself in with my passkey. The previously immaculate room had changed. A pair of Ella's shoes lay on the floor. A dress had been tossed over the back of a chair. A bag of chips sat on the dresser, and a few of the crushed ones had fallen out. It wasn't as though the room was a wreck, but it looked different. Placing the flowers on the side of the dresser, I scooped up the crumbs and threw them out, then scooted the arrangement to where it wasn't likely to be knocked off.

Trixie and Twinkletoes sniffed around. If they found anything of interest, they didn't tell me.

At five o'clock, people and their pets gathered for the daily parade, most of them tourists who were surely unaware of what had transpired.

Kelly and her dachshund joined in. Taffy wore a darling pink dress, sunglasses, and faux pearls.

I couldn't help smiling. Kelly had caught Wagtail fever. I had a strong hunch that she and her husband would be back with Taffy and their children.

Suddenly, a black dog raced to join the parade.

# Twenty-Three

Trixie and Twinkletoes zoomed toward him. From my spot on the porch, I could tell the black dog was Squishy. He appeared to have been in the woods. Twigs and dirt clung to his fur. I dashed to get a leash, then ran out to him.

"Squishy! I'm so happy to see you!" I hugged him, dirt and all, and snapped the leash on him lest he run off again. I wished he could tell me what had happened. He looked okay, though. I didn't see any wounds. He wagged his tail and turned those puppy eyes toward me, obviously thrilled to be back.

Trixie and Twinkletoes sniffed him thoroughly to be sure he was the Squishy they knew. I wished they could tell me more about what they smelled on him.

When the parade ended, I took Squishy inside, assuming he must be hungry. And he desperately needed a bath.

Squishy sniffed the floor, not raising his head until he heard his name.

"Squishy?"

He ran to Ella, who fell to her knees and hugged him. Her tears finally flowed, and she buried her face in Squishy's fur.

Kelly burst into tears as well, kneeled beside Ella, and placed an arm around her. Percy looked on, and a couple of tears ran down his masculine cheeks.

Ella raised her head. "Oh, Squishy! You smell like rotten eggs! Where have you been?"

"Yuck," said Kelly. "He does stink." She stood and gazed at Squishy. Then she looked at Ella. Her eyes narrowed. "Could Ella and I take Squishy to the Dog Wash?" She sidled over to me and in a hushed voice said, "It might be good for her to take her mind off Wendell."

It might at that. "As long as you don't let him run off." I worried a little, but Kelly was very good with Taffy, and some dog therapy would probably help Ella cope with her loss.

Kelly held her hand out to Ella. "Let's clean him up and then we can all go out for a nice dinner. On the law firm in remembrance of Wendell."

Percy didn't object. The three of them and the two dogs left for the Dog Wash, where people could wash and dry their dogs for a fee without all the mess at home. I phoned Shirley at the shelter to let her know that Squishy was back.

Given my late lunch, I shouldn't have been hungry, but when Mom texted me, I returned to the private kitchen in search of food anyway. Trixie and Twinkletoes needed a decent dinner, too.

I found the members of the Wagtail Murder Club there,

eating a lasagna they had reheated, spinach salad, and Italian garlic bread.

The magic refrigerator yielded something called **Italian Dinner for Dogs**, which turned out to be macaroni with chunks of ground beef, zucchini, and sweet potatoes.

I also found a small dish labeled **Rodeo Dreams for Twinkletoes**. Beef with tiny bits of pork in aspic? Whatever it was, it was met with her approval.

I poured myself a tall glass of iced tea and joined the club.

"Do you think the same person murdered Dinah and Wendell?" asked Oma.

I hadn't given that any thought yet. "Maybe." I savored a forkful of the lasagna. Delicious!

"Two people murdered from the same law firm points a finger in their direction," said Mr. Huckle. "There's no question in my mind that it has to be one of them. Who seems the most nervous and uncomfortable?"

"I'm not sure you can go by that," said Oma. "Everyone reacts to death differently. Some may feel guilty that they were not closer to the deceased. Or that they said ugly things to the dead person before the murder. Some may not be close at all."

"Like Simon?" I asked.

"A very good example," said Mom. "I have tried to talk with him, but he's rather uncommunicative. Not a chatty sort at all. He could be the type of person who would kill without any remorse."

"Not being friendly to strangers hardly makes a person a psycho killer, Mom."

"On the other hand, what about Kelly? She is very outgoing. A cover-up perhaps?" asked Mr. Huckle.

"I'm not sure that there's a killer personality," I said. "Maybe we should focus on motive? Plus, there's something you should know. Dave is aware of it, but we should probably keep it quiet while the firm straightens it all out. Wendell was overbilling his clients."

"No!" said Oma.

"There's more. Dinah had the goods on him. Twinkletoes located some paperwork that Dinah brought with her, ostensibly to show Percy. She had told Percy she'd found billing irregularities. I suspect that's what he's been so nervous about."

"So Wendell probably killed Dinah!" Mom exclaimed. "And then Percy, angry with Wendell, knocks him off!"

I nodded. "That's the presumption. I don't know of any concrete evidence tying Wendell to Dinah's murder, but that's a major motive, for sure."

"I wonder how he found out that she knew," said Mom.

"Good question. We might never know." I poured more iced tea for all of us.

"I did not think Kelly was involved in this," said Oma. "But she would know who was causing problems for her husband. A good wife always sees these things."

"You are so right, Liesel. I understand why Kelly would have knocked off Wendell." Mom sipped her tea. "He put the firm in jeopardy. That would impact her husband and her entire family."

"We must consider those who had the most to lose." Mr. Huckle helped himself to a slice of the bread. "Percy and Bizzy. What kind of name is Bizzy anyway?"

Mom laughed and got up to look in the refrigerator. "I asked her! Apparently, her brother was a year older and couldn't say Betsy. He said Bizzy. And it stuck. Cupcakes!" shrieked Mom. "I need these." She left them on a cake stand on the counter to come to room temperature.

"Very sweet," said Oma. "Older siblings are often the cause of these peculiar names. I think Bizzy is one tough lady. I admire that and would very much dislike to imagine her killing anyone. She is rather cultured and elegant."

Mom snorted. "Like that ever stopped anyone. From a practical standpoint, though, Percy is much stronger and more likely to have had the strength to attack Wendell."

I hated to agree, because I liked Percy, but it was true that he was larger than Bizzy or Kelly and could have overcome Wendell more easily.

"Is it possible that Percy was also overcharging clients like Wendell was?" asked Oma. "Maybe Dinah confronted him about it. The only way to save himself would have been to eliminate both of them."

My heart sank. Mr. Huckle was right. The problems in that law firm might go much deeper than any of us realized. Poor Ben.

I told them about the woman I had seen at Cooper's house the previous night. "It was late. Well after dark."

Mr. Huckle almost dropped his cupcake. "Then we need to watch the house again. She may not have stayed long, or she could have been there all night."

"I agree," said Mom. "We need to watch for her and find out who she is."

Thus it was agreed that I would call Casey to come in early to watch the inn while the four members of the Wagtail

Murder Club spied on Cooper's house. Before dark, Oma and Mom would take a golf cart over to Mom's house to set up their spying operation. They would park in Mom's garage so the golf cart wouldn't give away their presence. Mr. Huckle would walk over in the dark. I would remain at the inn until Casey showed up.

Under normal circumstances, we didn't provide evening snacks or desserts to our guests. But Ben's law firm members had been through so much that we thought they might feel like talking and consoling one another. Not to mention the possibility that they might reveal information. I set up an informal bar in the Dogwood Room with after-dinner drinks, bowls of nuts and grapes, a cheesecake, cream puffs, and a platter of brownies so they could help themselves.

Mom, Oma, and I mingled with them. We hadn't been there long when a breathless Ella joined them with Squishy.

"I have to see him," she blurted. "I have to see Wendell. Where is he? In a morgue?"

"He has been taken to Dr. Engelknecht's office," I said. "Maybe it would be better to wait until morning?"

"Yes, of course," she said softly. But after only seconds had passed, she said in a loud and panicky tone, "No! I have to see him now. I won't be able to sleep a wink if I don't! I have to see him!"

I couldn't blame her. If it had been someone close to me, I would have felt the same way. It was late and I was tired, but I knew I had to do the right thing. "I'll call Dr. Engelknecht and see if we can go over there now."

"Thank you," she said in a more measured tone.

I made the call and Dr. Engelknecht, while clearly not

thrilled, acquiesced. "I expected this. It's a typical reaction, although most people wait until morning."

I took Trixie and Squishy up to my apartment. They settled quickly after a crunchy biscuit. I closed the door softly behind me and locked it. Curiously, Twinkletoes waited at the top of the stairs. She followed me down but made no effort to go with Ella and me.

Ben and Percy waited with Ella.

"We're coming, too," said Percy.

"What about Kelly?" I asked.

"She declined," he said in a hasty manner that led me to believe she didn't relish seeing a dead man.

The four of us climbed into a golf cart and drove to Dr. Engelknecht's office.

Lights blazed in the big house he had converted into an office downstairs and a residence upstairs.

Inside, it was eerily quiet. We solemnly followed him into a cold room where Wendell lay on his back. His head showed bruises and a long scratch. His eyes were closed, which made him seem peaceful.

Ella gasped.

# Twenty-Four

Ella's hand shook slightly as she held it over her mouth. She walked toward Wendell slowly, then reached out to touch his hand, which I imagined to be very cold. "His head—" she said softly "—is this normal from a fight?"

Dr. Engelknecht spoke gently. "Most people who die this way do show some contusions."

"When Dave said he was gone, I didn't believe it. Wendell was indestructible. And now, a simple walk in the dark of night has ended his life." Ella couldn't take her eyes off him. Her heart pounded visibly in her chest.

Percy walked around to the other side of Wendell's body. His eyes narrowed as he examined his friend.

"It's hard to believe, isn't it?" asked Ella. "I expect him to stand up and make fun of us for thinking that he died." Then she withdrew a compact from her pocket, opened it, and held the mirror under his nose.

I looked at Dr. Engelknecht, who shrugged.

Ella snapped her compact shut and put it away. She turned to Dr. Engelknecht. "I'll text you the name of a funeral home where we live so he can be transported."

"Actually, he'll be going to the medical examiner in Roanoke first. But I appreciate your offer. I can send that information to them so they can transport him home when they're done."

"The medical examiner?" asked Ella. "What for?"

"State law primarily. Unless he was under the care of a physician for a terminal condition, they're required to do an autopsy. And there's clearly enough here to warrant that in any event."

Percy's head snapped up. "What do you mean?"

Dr. Engelknecht paused. Speaking slowly, he said, "He was clearly murdered. He didn't just stagger around under the influence of alcohol or some kind of drug and fall. Though it is possible he was drunk or high and unable to defend himself or run from his attacker."

"I can assure you . . ." Percy's voice faded off. He met the doctor's gaze. "No. I can't assure you of anything anymore."

Ella thanked Dr. Engelknecht for allowing her to see Wendell, and we left. No one said a word on the drive home.

Back at the inn, Percy and Ella thanked me for taking them to see Wendell. Percy said good night and plodded up the grand staircase looking like he carried the weight of the world on his shoulders.

Ella looked out the window at the lights of Wagtail.

"Would you like some hot chocolate?" I asked.

She turned slowly. "I would love that." She followed me

into the private kitchen and watched as I poured milk into a small pot.

"Would you like marshmallows?"

"Oh my gosh, yes!"

While I heated the milk, Ella asked, "Do you do this for every guest?"

"No. It's not a regular thing. But you've been through a lot today."

"Kelly says it's too soon to make any decisions except about Wendell's funeral, but I'm pretty sure that I'll be selling the house."

My eyes met hers.

"It was too big for the two of us anyway. I would just ramble around in there remembering bad times. Though I may cook one really big dinner in it and make a mess just because I can."

Oh! That was an interesting response to the death of her husband. An unhappy marriage?

"That's childish of me, isn't it?" Nevertheless, she smiled at the thought. "But I'll probably do it anyway. There would be so much satisfaction in it. Or I might just sell everything and never go back into the house. There's not much there that I want."

I was getting the feeling that Wendell might have bossed her around. Or at least had certain expectations of her that she resented.

I handed her a mug and gestured toward the two cozy chairs. Ella shed her shoes and curled up in one of them, holding the mug as if she wanted it to warm her hands. "Can I adopt Squishy?"

"I thought you were afraid of big black dogs."

"Not him. He's so comforting."

"Have you ever had a dog?"

"Oh, lots. I grew up in the country a little bit north of here. Wendell liked to call me a country bumpkin."

Ouch! "How did you feel about that?"

"I think it was ignorant and demeaning. He never lived in the country. We met when I reported on Cooper's trial. I know country life isn't for everyone, but city life isn't always so great, either."

She had a point. One that I understood very well, having lived in both places. Each had its drawbacks and benefits. "If you're serious about adopting Squishy, you will have to go to the shelter tomorrow morning and fill out an application."

She nodded. "I'll do that first thing!"

"I'm sorry about Wendell."

She shook her head slowly. "I never imagined anything like this would happen. It's so hard to believe. I keep thinking he'll walk in here. That's why I wanted to see him. I'm twelve years younger than he was, but he wasn't old, and he was neurotic about eating right and working out. You saw him, not an ounce of fat."

"How do you feel? After your accident, I mean."

"Oh, much better. *So* much better." She closed her eyes briefly. "It was a nightmare. I still can't believe that it happened."

"I'm glad you're on the mend. Are you still a reporter? That must be an interesting job."

"No. I might go back to it, though, now that Wendall is gone."

And then Ella asked, "Could Squishy spend the night with me?"

She was going to adopt him! I could feel it. What a lucky break that it hadn't worked out with the other woman. "Sure. Would you like a dog bed for him?"

"No, thanks. He can sleep on my bed."

"Wait here." I ran up the hidden staircase to my apartment and called the dogs. As soon as they saw the open door, they ran down to the kitchen. I could hear Ella cooing to Squishy before I reached the main floor.

We took the dogs outside so they could use the doggy bathroom. The air had turned brisk, and we hurried back inside. Squishy readily followed Ella upstairs to her room. She was a much better match for him than the other woman.

Casey had cleared away the food and drinks in the Dogwood Room.

"Thanks for cleaning up."

"No problem. Is there anything I should know?" he asked.

"Like what?"

"Is there someone I should avoid? Be on the lookout for?"

"Both of the victims worked for the same law firm. So I don't think you have anything to worry about."

"No? All the same, I won't be napping tonight. That's for sure! Do you think the killer is staying here in the inn?"

I hated to admit it, but I had to be honest with him. "Yes. I believe that's quite likely."

I hurried upstairs to change clothes. Ben sat in my living room watching TV. Twinkletoes glared at him as if he were an intruder. Her tail twitched like she was annoyed by his presence.

"Hi. What are you doing up?"

"Can't sleep. My life is falling apart and there's not a single thing I can do to stop it."

"I'm sorry everything turned out this way." I twisted the ring off my finger and handed it to him. "You gave it your best shot."

"Thanks. You know me so well."

"Actually, it was Simon who figured it out. You took a big chance. What if I wanted to marry you?"

"Oma and your mom gave it away. They terrified me at first, but then they kept going with all those things I was supposed to pay for and I realized they were having fun with me."

"Is it real?" I asked.

"The ring? Really? You know me better than that. Do you think I would waste thousands of dollars on a chunk of carbon? I have to admit, though, that I was beginning to like the idea of being married and living in a cozy place in Wagtail. That's not anything I ever thought I would want in my life. I thought I would be like Wendell or Percy, with a big house in DC or one of the suburbs. But things haven't worked out for me that way. And now I don't know that there will even be a Calhoun, Bloom, and Walters tomorrow."

I couldn't help thinking that the tables had turned. When I decided to move to Wagtail, I had lost my job and life wasn't going as I had expected.

"I'm sorry, Ben. Maybe Percy and Bizzy will pick up the pieces and start fresh. You know they would hire you."

"I think they would. But neither of them has pulled me aside to reassure me of that. And now I don't know if that's even what I want anymore. I didn't expect Dinah or Wendell to die. Much less be murdered. What if I die tomorrow? What if I'm the next one? What if I die in a month? In a year? Is this how I want to live the rest of my life?"

I sat down next to him. "I doubt that you'll be next." But I had nothing to back that up. I rambled on, trying to help him feel better. "You should look at this as an opportunity for a new beginning. Not everyone has a chance to reassess life and make a change. This could be a new start for you. Maybe that's not a bad thing."

"The rainbow after the storm, so to speak," he said. "I'll tell you one thing—I'm not going anywhere alone in Wagtail. Not even with a couple of people from my firm. They say there's safety in numbers, but not when one of your colleagues has been murdering other colleagues."

"Do you suspect one or two of them?"

"I suspect all of them!"

"That can't be. There isn't one you trust? That would be a sad state of affairs."

"If someone was knocking off Sugar Maple Inn employees, wouldn't you be a little bit nervous?" he asked.

"Of course. But you can't distrust them all. Ben, I think you need to get some sleep. Maybe you'll think more clearly in the morning."

He nodded. "If you hear anything in the middle of the night, will you come save me even though we're not getting married?"

"I'll come save you *because* we're not getting married."

I waited until I heard the door to the guest room close, then I slipped quietly into my bedroom and changed into jeans and a black top. I put leashes on Twinkletoes and Trixie and slipped out through the hidden staircase that led to the private kitchen. I left through the main lobby, prepared to tell anyone I might encounter that Trixie needed to potty before bed.

As it happened, I didn't see or hear anyone. Not even Casey, who was watching the inn. We avoided streets as much as possible, cutting behind the Blue Boar and emerging near Mom's house. I used my key to let us in through a back door and released Trixie and Twinkletoes so they could run loose in the house. Gingersnap came to greet us. Not a single light glowed inside.

"Holly?" Mom called in a low voice.

I found Mom, Oma, and Mr. Huckle in the dark guest room. Oma looked through binoculars wedged between slats in the blinds.

"We're taking turns," said Mom. "Was he released? Brought back from the police station? Does anyone know?"

"I spoke with Dave," said Oma. "He gave them a statement, but he continued to deny that anyone else had been at the house last night. They released him."

"I've gone over Cooper's court transcript," said Mr. Huckle. "Wendell never put Cooper on the stand. That's their choice, of course, but Cooper might have wanted to testify. Could have been the wrong call to keep him off the stand. Maybe he spent twelve years dwelling on it and it festered in his mind. People obsess about things like that."

Mom switched places with Oma, who said, "What I find interesting is how Wendell's body lay. He was parallel to Cooper's house, with his head near the patio. If he was running away from Cooper, wouldn't he have been facing in the other direction?"

"Oma, you're brilliant!" Mom took her eyes off her

binoculars for a moment. "You're right. He was running toward the house, not away from it!"

I could barely make out Mr. Huckle in the darkness, but I thought he appeared to be considering that. "In a fight, things can turn around quite quickly. But I'm told most of the contusions were on Wendell's back. I think you might have something there, Liesel."

"She's here!" Mom hissed.

Everyone grabbed their binoculars and gazed out the windows.

A slender woman walked along the sidewalk with . . .

"What is that?" asked Mom.

It was big and dark. Only when she turned toward the house and opened the door did I realize what we were watching. "It's Squishy!"

# Twenty-Five

"The dog?" asked Oma. "Our Squishy?"

"He turned up this afternoon. I think Ella might want to adopt him. A couple of days ago she said she couldn't have a dog, but today she asked if he could stay with her overnight."

The woman going into Cooper's house was unquestionably Ella, the new widow.

"Let me get this straight," said Mom. "A murderer moves to Wagtail. A man is murdered in Wagtail. And now the known killer appears to be in cahoots with the dead man's wife?"

"*Cahoots* might be a strong word. We don't know that. But it's certainly a little bit suspicious that she's going to a killer's house late at night," I said.

"A *little* bit suspicious?" Oma shook her head.

"And here's another odd twist. She met Wendell because he was representing Cooper in his murder trial."

"Should we keep an eye on Ella?" asked Mom. "That

could be me thinking he's a perfectly nice man and not believing that he was guilty."

"We cannot watch her twenty-four hours a day," Oma pointed out. "But you are correct. It could be any of us falling for a man and ignoring his history. On the other hand, if she hired him or they are a couple, then we could be putting ourselves in danger. It may not be wise to tell her what we know."

Stunned, I watched the house for a few minutes. She had been notably absent since her arrival in Wagtail. She didn't eat at the inn often, nor did she join the law firm for most meals. She said Kelly, who was presumably her friend, had taken her shopping on more than one occasion. And now, at an hour when most people were in bed, she was sneaking into a house. She hadn't paused to unlock the door, suggesting that it was unlocked and Cooper was expecting her.

I wasn't sure what that meant, except that Cooper was planning to see her.

"Poor Squishy," said Mom. "Now a murderer wants to adopt him. That poor fellow has had nothing but bad luck."

"So," said Mr. Huckle. "The wife of the murder victim conspired with the killer. This changes everything." He returned to his chair and massaged his forehead. "I confess, I never saw this coming. I was so sure the murderer was one of the lawyers. But this is difficult to overlook. The victim's wife is seeing a man who killed someone before? It puts a whole new light on finding Wendell in Cooper's backyard. No wonder he didn't want to admit that Ella had been there."

Oma put her binoculars down on the nightstand. "This makes no sense to me. Ella is delicate and sweet. Does this mean that she hired Cooper to kill her husband?"

"Hired or seduced," said Mr. Huckle.

"Maybe he was protecting her. He didn't want anyone to think that Ella was involved. But she wasn't sleeping in her room at the inn," I said.

They all looked at me. "I brought her pillows and a blanket because I found her trying to sleep in the Dogwood Room late one night. She said Wendell was a light sleeper and with her injuries, she had to toss and turn and didn't want to keep him up all night."

Oma and Mom exchanged a look.

"Or Wendell told her to get out." Mom's mouth skewed to the side in dismay. "When you have an argument with your husband, it's not unusual for one of you to sleep on a sofa. It happens."

I peered out the window.

"Or she wanted to get away from him," said Oma. "She seemed rather stiff and quiet in his presence."

"Someone else is there now." I watched as a man walked up to the front door. "Wait! There are more of them."

Oma, Mom, and Mr. Huckle hustled to the window.

The porch light turned on.

"It's the police!" exclaimed Mr. Huckle.

A uniformed officer emerged from the house with Squishy. But Squishy immediately lay down and rolled onto his back. The poor officer tried hard to get him up, but Squishy wasn't going anywhere. He lay there like a beached seal.

It wasn't good timing, but we couldn't help giggling a little bit about Squishy's performance. He did not want to go anywhere. The officer leaned inside the doorway. We could hear him calling for help.

I ran down the hallway and out the front door into the night.

Dave emerged to look at Squishy.

I ran across the street. "Squishy, what are you doing?" I reached down to tickle his tummy.

He gazed up at me and bounced to his feet.

I took the leash from the officer. "And what are you doing?" I asked Dave.

"We're taking them in for questioning."

"Because?"

"Because sweet Ella is in this up to her ears. She has been sneaking out every night to sleep with Cooper. Oh man! We think Wendell was onto her. He grew suspicious and followed her." Dave rubbed his eyes as if he'd had a long day and was tired. "This may turn out to be a domestic spat that ended in the death of a jealous husband."

"But that doesn't explain who murdered Dinah," I said.

Dave sighed. "In light of the evidence that Dinah planned to share with Percy, I think Wendell killed her."

I walked Squishy across the street to Mom's house. He was more than willing to come and was excited when he saw Oma and Mom.

They stood on the stoop with Mr. Huckle and watched as Ella and Cooper were escorted out.

"Does anyone else feel guilty about this?" I asked.

"I do," said Oma.

"Me, too." Mom wrapped an arm around me.

We watched as the police departed with Ella and Cooper.

"Oma, I appreciate you putting up with me, but I'm going to sleep in my own bed tonight." Mom beamed at her.

"Are you certain about this?" asked Oma.

"Absolutely. In the first place, I have nothing to do with Ben's law firm, so I'm in the clear there. And secondly, Cooper and Ella will be tied up all night at the jail in Snowball."

"That reminds me," I said, "Cooper helped me reach the key under your doormat. You need to find a new hiding place for it."

"Thanks for letting me know. I wouldn't want him walking in! I'll see you two tomorrow morning at the inn." She saw us out the door and we heard it latch behind us.

"Mom! The key!" I bent over and picked it up.

Mom opened the door and snatched it out of my hand. "Thank you." She shut the door again.

Oma shook her head. "I see where you get your stubbornness from."

"Hah! It was inevitable. You're not exactly a pushover. I inherited it from both sides of the family."

Oma and I gave Mr. Huckle a ride home.

When we arrived at the inn, it was so quiet that we would have heard a mouse skitter across the floor. Casey assured us that nothing of interest had happened in our absence.

We said good night and walked up to our respective quarters.

I was glad that Ben was asleep. I was too exhausted to stay up talking about his future.


I slept later than I should have. I rushed through a shower and dressed quickly in a white skort and coral short-sleeve top. While I didn't like keeping Squishy on a leash, I thought it best for the time being, lest he get lost again. I took him out with Trixie while Twinkletoes yawned and waited inside.

When we returned, Shelley steered me to the terrace, where I joined Dave and Oma at their table. Gingersnap and Duchess had finished their breakfasts and were sprawled in the warm morning sun.

Shelley returned quickly with a mug of tea for me. "Squishy's back! Hi, sweetie," she cooed. "I heard about last night! The next time you spy on someone, I want to be included!"

Dave groaned, but then he said, "No wonder I love you."

She laughed at him. "Today's specials are whole grain French toast, two fried eggs with bacon or ham, your choice, and a pancake with maple syrup or a berry yogurt bowl."

I knew the berry yogurt bowl would be the healthiest, but I dared to try the whole grain French toast. "Flaked salmon for Twinkletoes, please, and how about hard-boiled eggs and hamburger for the dogs?"

When she left, I asked, "How did it go at the police station last night?"

Dave set his coffee down. "According to them, they're old friends who knew each other before Cooper was convicted of murder and before Ella married Wendell. She insists that Wendell didn't know she was visiting Cooper at night."

"How could she know that?" asked Mom. "Maybe he followed her there every night."

"That's what I think," said Dave. "Cooper didn't want her to be involved in the murder, which was sort of chivalrous on his part, but everything comes out eventually. It was folly that they imagined they could get away with this."

"So they're in jail now?" I asked.

"Nope. They both bonded out. I gather that Ella is a rather wealthy woman. She paid their bonds." He took a deep breath. "May I borrow your office again today? I feel like I just went through this with the same group of witnesses, but I'm afraid I have to find out what Wendell's colleagues knew about Ella and her relationship with Cooper. I'm hoping Wendell might have confided something to Percy."

The door burst open. "Squishy!" Ella held out her arms and he ran to her, dragging his leash, his tail wagging like crazy. She hugged him and scratched under his chin. "I hope you don't mind. Shelley told me you were out here."

An awkward silence followed. "Have you eaten breakfast?" I asked.

"I don't want to interrupt anything," Ella said.

"Nonsense." My mother had walked out on the terrace just in time to hear her. "Shelley is bringing me breakfast. Come sit with us."

Dave rose and politely said, "Good morning, Ella. I'm afraid duty calls. Thank you for breakfast, Liesel."

Ella swallowed hard when he walked past her. "Are you sure you want me to join you? I can eat alone." She raised her eyebrows. "Or maybe Kelly is still talking to me."

"Of course you are welcome here," said Oma. "You must be exhausted."

"I am. But I'm thrilled to see Squishy." Ella took a seat. Squishy sat beside her and gazed at her with adoring eyes.

Shelley brought breakfast for us and took Ella's order of a country breakfast with fried eggs, hash browns, and Virginia ham.

When she left, Ella said, "Just so you know, I did *not* murder Wendell. You don't have to be afraid of me. Cooper didn't murder him, either. You're not supposed to have to prove your innocence, but it appears that's exactly what we have to do."

"You were at Cooper's house the night Wendell died, yes?" asked Oma.

"Yes, I was. Cooper is an old friend. I knew him before Jeff was murdered. I know it looks bad because my husband died in his yard, but I know Cooper didn't kill him."

"He could have done it before you arrived," said Mom.

Ella shook her head. "Not a chance. You don't know Cooper. He doesn't even want to kill bees if they swarm around his head. He's so gentle and kind. He doesn't have it in him to murder anyone."

And yet he had been convicted of murder once before, I mused.

"Did you come to Wagtail to see him?" asked Oma.

"No. I didn't want to come here at all. After the accident, I needed rest and sleep. But Wendell insisted I travel to Wagtail."

"And then you looked up Cooper?" I asked.

"Yes. I knew he was getting out of prison. As his attorney, Wendell had received notice of his release. I wanted to see how he was doing."

Shelley arrived with the giant breakfast for Ella. She freshened our coffee and tea, pausing to look curiously at my bare ring finger before disappearing inside again.

Ella buttered her toast. "I always knew he wasn't guilty. He didn't kill Jeff, but I couldn't prove it. I sat through the entire trial, but I was unable to pinpoint anything that would exonerate him. I was a reporter. Digging deeper into stories was what I did. It broke my heart that I couldn't help him."

Ella ate her hash browns as if she was hungry. "This is so good. Wendell always wants . . . wanted to go to fancy restaurants in Washington. They're good, too, but they don't know how to make a hearty country breakfast."

She put her fork down and drained half her mug of coffee. "Look, Wendell is dead, so I don't have to sugarcoat the truth anymore. We had a terrible marriage. I know I shouldn't have fallen for Cooper and stolen away in the dark of night to see him. We've both been through a lot in the recent past and it was just so comforting to see an old friend. Honestly, I don't know what Wendell was doing at Cooper's house. Holly can tell you that I wasn't sleeping in my room, but I never thought that Wendell was onto me."

"I've certainly been through my own marital problems, so I understand how that is. But it just looks so bad," said Mom.

"I know! I fear your police were quite upset with me last night. I wasn't a bit of help to them."

"Do you know what time Wendell died?" I asked.

"Based on the questions your sergeant asked me, I gather they think Wendell died around midnight. We're not kids who stay up all night. By that time, Cooper and I had been asleep for a couple of hours in the master bedroom on the other end of the house."

"Aha!" said Oma. "If you were asleep then you could not know where Cooper was."

"That's true." Ella frowned and nibbled on a piece of toast.

"Those bruises were horrific," I said. "There's no way he didn't cry out. He must have yelled at his attacker or screamed in pain."

Ella shuddered. She gazed at Mom. "You live across the street. Why didn't you hear him?"

"No one was at my house. My parents were away, and I slept here at the inn."

Ella winced. "You can't imagine how demoralized Cooper is. He hasn't done anything wrong. This is like history repeating itself. First Dinah fell exactly where Jeff did, leading the police straight back to Cooper. And then Wendell was murdered in his yard. He didn't kill either one of them. He's convinced that he's going back to prison. He might even get the death penalty this time." Her face wrinkled up in pain. "I feel so helpless."

"It is interesting," said Oma, "that both the victims worked for the same law firm."

Ella nodded. "You think someone in the law firm murdered them? Someone like Percy or—" she turned to look at me "—Ben. Where was he that night? Did he get out of bed and leave the inn? Do you know where *he* was?"

# Twenty-Six

Having the tables turned on me gave me new insight to Ella's situation. I had no idea where Ben might have been. In fact, *I* was the one who had been slipping out after *he* went to bed. But when Ella asked me if I knew where Ben was at night, my first instinct was to defend him, just as she had defended Cooper. And I wasn't in love with Ben like she probably was with Cooper. I gazed at her. She waited for my response. "I assume he slept through the night, but I don't know that."

"So he doesn't have an alibi, either." Ella tilted her head. "Your ring! Where is your beautiful engagement ring?"

"We broke off the engagement last night."

Ella eyed me like a cat studying a mouse. "Are you afraid of him?"

"No! Nothing like that."

Ella reached out and patted my hand. "That was what I always said, too."

Oma's eyes grew large. "Wendell hurt you?"

Ella's face grew tense. "Not physically. Oh no. He would never leave a mark on me. It was all psychological. Threats and warnings. Blaming me for things I didn't do. Twisting my words and being suspicious. It all started out well, but Wendell was controlling. And I learned that I would pay for it if I didn't do as he said."

"Ella," said Oma in a soothing voice, "I am sorry that you suffered in this way. How horrible for you."

Ella smiled. "It's all over now." She polished off her last bite of ham.

Her words echoed in my mind. If her story was true, then she had more reason than anyone to murder him. Had she seduced Cooper and convinced him to rid her of her husband? It was a horrible scenario. A young wife convinces her ex-con boyfriend to murder her husband, who defended him in a previous murder.

"Is that why you held the mirror up to his nose?" I asked.

"You cannot imagine what it was like for me to live with him. When Dave told me Wendell was dead, I was in shock at first. Then it dawned on me that my nightmare was over. But years of torment aren't washed away in a couple of hours. I started doing things I knew he wouldn't like. It was an uncontrollable urge. A sort of celebration that I was still alive and I could do what I wanted. But as the sun set, I realized that I hadn't seen Wendell. I only had the word of other people that he was dead. That was when I asked you to take me to him, Holly. I had to see for myself to erase the fear. To know that it truly was over. It would be just like him to fake his death. I had read somewhere that a mirror held up close to the mouth and nose would cloud up if someone was still breathing. I had to know. Otherwise, Wendell would haunt my dreams and my life. I wouldn't feel free until I saw for myself and knew it was actually Wendell and that he truly was dead. I don't know who killed him, but they released me from a nightmare."

The door swung open, and a stream of guests filled the tables, exclaiming about the view and the warm sunshine.

Oma smiled. "Good luck to you, Ella. I hope you will excuse me. I must get to work."

On that cue, we all rose to free up the table. Shelley was already busy taking breakfast orders.

"May I take Squishy with me?" asked Ella. "I put in an adoption request yesterday. I know it hasn't been accepted yet, but I would love to spend time with him."

As if he understood, Squishy turned his gaze to me. If she was approved, the shelter would allow her to spend some time with him before making her decision. But would they approve a murder suspect? I doubted it. Her future was entirely too unclear, and what would happen to Squishy then? I honestly didn't know what to say. "As long as you stay around the inn."

Mom went to work at the check-in desk, and I started my morning rounds.

I had barely finished when my phone rang.

Shirley was calling from the shelter. "Great news, Holly! We have two people interested in adopting Squishy. A man from Greensboro will be coming up here tomorrow to have a look at him. And the other one is a guest at the Sugar Maple Inn, Ella Walters. Do you know her?"

"I do. Did she put in an application for him?"

"She did. I'm checking her references now. What do you

think of her? I'm trying to be careful after the last disastrous match."

"Squishy loves her. If only she weren't a murder suspect."

"What? Are you serious?"

"I'm afraid so. I'm letting her hang out with him as long as she stays around the inn."

"Holly," Shirley groaned, "are you out of your mind? Make up an excuse and get him back. That's an instant disqualification as far as I'm concerned."

Poor Squishy. I gazed around the main lobby but there was no sight of Ella or Squishy.

"Shirley, you should see them together. Squishy loves her."

"Is this about the guy who was killed in Wagtail?"

"Yes. She was his wife."

"It's a flat no, Holly. What if she's convicted? What would happen to poor Squishy then? We place dogs and cats in secure homes where they will be well cared for and their people aren't heading to prison. Get him back, Holly." Shirley ended the call.

Simon was saying rather loudly to Kelly, "I'm absolutely furious with Dinah and Wendell for getting themselves killed. Never in my wildest dreams did I imagine that we would be the suspects in a murder. At least you have Percy to validate your whereabouts. Blossom can't tell them anything about where I was."

"Keep this under your hat," muttered Kelly. "Wendell murdered Dinah. Didn't Percy and Bizzy fill you in this morning? It's pretty obvious."

"Kelly! That cop has been questioning you because he

thinks *you* could have murdered them. I swear I might make something up just so they'll leave me alone."

It appeared to me that Kelly's cheerfulness and evidently clear conscience annoyed Simon.

"They're not interested in me," he said. "I had nothing to do with murder. I don't practice criminal law like Wendell." He mashed his lips together. "I can't say I'm sorry to see him gone. I don't care for techniques that skirt the law. Wendell was shrewd, I'll give him that. But—" he paused and finally looked at me "—I didn't trust him. Everyone acted like he was some kind of legal genius, when he was actually underhanded."

Kelly gasped.

I wondered if that was a prevailing sentiment among them. So he hadn't liked the way Wendell conducted his cases. I had a feeling he was the type who would come right out and say that to an officer of the law. But I would let Dave know anyway. Just in case he clammed up around him.

"How can you be so naive?" asked Simon. "You're Percy's wife. You had a lot to gain. Percy will definitely benefit from Wendell being gone. We know that Wendell was cooking the books, so his death is almost a lucky break. Or was Percy in on it with him? I wouldn't be so sure that Wendell murdered Dinah. Percy could have been overcharging with Wendell."

I went to the desk where Mr. Huckle usually sat and pretended to be busy so I could listen without being too obvious.

Kelly whispered, but I was close enough to hear. "Excuse me! Are you accusing my husband of fraud and murder?"

Simon tsked at her. "You are a loyal wife, but you'd better wake up and see what's happening, because your life is about to fall apart. A law firm is a business, much like any other, but we're more constricted because of ethical considerations. When the bar finds out about this, it will be curtains for all of us. Even the innocent will suffer. Who would hire me after what has happened?"

"Isn't there a law that says wives don't have to testify against their husbands?"

Simon snickered. "So you do know something."

"No! Of course not. Shh. Here he comes."

Percy greeted them with a forced smile. "I hope the local sheriff is finished with all of us and we can finally go home."

Simon scowled at him. "It's nothing to joke about. He thinks one of us killed Wendell and Dinah. I don't know about you, but I do not want to be next."

Kelly gasped. "Why would there be another murder? Oh, Percy! I think we should leave immediately."

Percy wrapped his arm around Kelly's shoulders. "No one else is going to be murdered, honey. One of us must remember something that would be helpful in the investigation. Did you notice anything unusual, Simon?"

"I've been trying to remember if I saw Wendell or Dinah browsing among the vendors on the mountain."

Percy nodded. "I know what you mean. I was so engaged looking at the food and drinks, not to mention looking up at the moon every few minutes and dancing a little, that I didn't pay any attention to where the members of our group were."

"Percy," said Kelly. "Let's take Taffy for a walk. I need some air."

"Shall I meet you for dinner?" asked Simon.

"By all means," said Percy. "I think our entire group should dine together tonight. Where shall we go?" He spied me at the desk. "Holly? What is your favorite restaurant in Wagtail?"

"Trixie's and my favorite is Hot Hog."

Trixie woofed and danced in a circle.

"She recommends the pulled chicken platter for Taffy."

Taffy wriggled in Kelly's arms. Kelly set her on the floor, and she immediately romped wildly with Trixie.

"It's a barbecue place," I added.

"Oh! That's perfect. Percy loves good barbecue," said Kelly. "We have to try it."

I gave them directions. After Percy texted the rest of the gang about it, they left without another mention of murder. I was willing to bet Kelly would raise the subject while they walked, though.

"That was awful," said Bizzy.

I hadn't realized she was nearby.

"We're all turning on one another now. I feel like a bomb hit the law firm and now I'm watching the bits and pieces collapse into ashes in slow motion."

"I'm sorry, Bizzy. It must be very difficult for you."

"It is. Percy and I worked hard. In the beginning it was just the two of us. We were never a large firm, but we had a solid reputation, and now it's beyond repair. Two attorneys murdered. We won't even be able to replace Dinah. Who would join a firm with that kind of distinction?" Bizzy forced a grim smile. "I'd like to place a bouquet of flowers at the bottom of the cliff where Dinah died. It's not much, but I think of her constantly. Could you recommend a florist?"

"I think that's a lovely idea. Not only can I recommend one, I'll go with you."

"Do you know how to get there? Is it far?"

"It's a bit of a walk." I peered at her shoes. "Definitely not a high heel excursion."

She nodded. "I'll go change and meet you back here."

That was perfect timing. I had an excuse to retrieve Squishy from Ella. I dashed up the grand staircase. Trixie and Twinkletoes shot ahead of me. A little out of breath, I knocked on the door of Hike.

Ella opened it and Squishy ran into the hallway to greet his friends. "Holly! Is everything okay?"

"Yes, everything is fine. Bizzy and I are taking a little walk to lay some flowers where Dinah died, and I thought Squishy might want to come along. It would be good for him to get out."

"May I come, too?"

"Sure. Meet us in the main lobby."

I swung by the reception lobby where Mom was working. "I'm going to take Bizzy and Ella to the spot where Dinah died. Bizzy would like to lay some flowers there."

"That's so thoughtful."

"Do you need anything before I go?"

"No. We're good. It's very quiet today."

I collected a long leash for Squishy and met the others in the main lobby. We walked to Catnip and Bark, where Bizzy selected a charming bouquet of tulips, roses, ranunculus, asters, and daisies.

Bizzy and Ella looked around the shop while Jen Baldwin wrapped up the flowers and tied a beautiful bow on them.

Jen leaned over the counter and whispered, "Did that girl sell drugs?"

"Girl?" I didn't know what she was talking about.

"The one who died like Jeff did."

"Dinah! I don't think so."

"Don't be so sure. I know you're not supposed to speak ill of the dead, but if Jeff hadn't died, my nephew Tom wouldn't be alive today."

I looked at Bizzy and Ella, who were carrying cute gift-type items and still browsing. "Are you saying that Jeff sold drugs to your nephew?"

"He was Harold and Jean's boy, and I know they loved him, but he was a troublemaker. Don't let them tell you otherwise. I'm not the only one who didn't cry when he met his death. It was bound to happen. He was bad news carrying on with the worst sort of people."

"Your nephew's drug supply dried up when Jeff died?"

"Exactly. Thank heaven for that. You can ask him. I'm not making this up. Tom—he works over at Kitty Games. Or Marci at Wagtail Realty. They'll confirm it."

Ella joined us, unloaded an armful of items on the counter, and insisted on paying for the flowers, saying, "There's nothing else I can do for her now."

When Bizzy brought her items to the counter, Jen offered to have them delivered to the inn, which suited us fine. I was anxious to talk with Tom, but had agreed to show Bizzy the way to the site where Dinah died.

We walked up the mountain on a back trail. It was a gorgeous day, sunny and not at all humid. The path was wide and the slope mild since we weren't going very high. Trixie and Twinkletoes ran ahead as always. But Ella kept

Squishy on the long leash. He had room to roam, but he wouldn't be able to get away from us.

"How are you feeling?" Bizzy asked Ella.

"Well, if we could find Wendell's killer, I would be great." She stretched her arms out and lifted her face to the sun. "I feel free again. It's an awful thing to say, but it's true."

She looked so happy. Maybe she was being honest about her husband being cruel to her.

Squishy ran back to her, the happiest dog ever.

The trail grew narrower and steeper.

"Ella, I thought you couldn't have a dog," I said.

"Squishy is my dog."

Did she mean that literally or metaphorically? "You said you were afraid of big black dogs."

"I'm sorry, Holly. I was overjoyed when I saw Squishy at the inn. You can't imagine what a surprise it was to see him there. He was safe and happy. But he kept running up to me. I had to say something so you would keep him away from me and Wendell wouldn't realize that he was my Squishy."

"I don't understand. Are you the person who left him in a crate near the highway?"

"The day of my accident, I was running away from Wendell. I couldn't take it anymore. I was afraid to move or to speak in my own home. He was domineering and I was scared. I couldn't keep living that way. Bizzy was helping me. I wasn't one of her clients, but she represents a lot of battered women, so she knows how dangerous it is to leave controlling men. She called me when I'd been on the road about half an hour and said that Wendell had abruptly canceled his appointments for the day and left the office. The only thing we could imagine was that he had a tracker on me. But I didn't know where. On the car? In the car? In my purse? My wallet? My overnight bag? I can only guess, but I think it triggered when I got about twenty miles outside of the Washington, DC, Beltway. He didn't trust me. He knew he was abusing me mentally and was afraid I would run."

"You took Squishy with you."

"There are only two things on this earth that I care about, my mother and Squishy. Wendell destroyed my shoes and purses and jewelry, but I didn't care. Eventually he realized that he could control me by threatening Mom or Squishy. On that day, as soon as he left for work, I packed Squishy into the car and drove toward my mom's house. I thought I would pick her up and the three of us would drive far, far away and be safe. That was my dream. I was near Wagtail when Wendell texted me. He knew exactly where I was! I'm so stupid. It never occurred to me that he would put a tracker on my car. I didn't know where it was or what it looked like. And I didn't know where *he* was. Only that he was already on my trail. I had to save Squishy. It's a good thing that I left him where I did, where I could go back and get him, or at least someone who loved animals would see him and take him to Wagtail. I couldn't drive him up to Wagtail because Wendell would have seen that on the tracker and known where Squishy was. I can't tell you how it broke my heart to leave Squishy, but it would have been so much worse if Wendell had found him. I don't know what he might have done. I thought I could pick up my mom and then return for Squishy in the dark of night after I figured out where the tracker was. That way, if Wendell

caught up to me, Squishy wouldn't be with me. I drove toward my mom's house to take her somewhere safe before he
could get to her. I was bawling. You can't imagine how it
tore my heart to leave him. But Wendell was awful to my
poor baby. I had to save him, even if it meant giving him
up!" Tears ran down her face.

"Where's your mom?"

"I didn't make it there. When I didn't show up as planned,
she got worried and went stay with a friend, someone Wendell didn't know. She knew about my plan and had her
things packed and ready to go. I was running behind because I stopped at a gas station and asked if they could locate the tracker on my car. I went through my things but
couldn't find it. Neither could the guys in the gas station.
Not ten minutes after I left the gas station, a truck plowed
into me. My car flipped over a couple of times and landed
in a streambed upside down. I was unconscious. I don't remember anything until I woke up in the hospital. To this
day I'm so glad Squishy wasn't in the car with me. He would
have died."

"Why did you come here and pretend to be the dutiful
wife? Why didn't you leave him then?"

"I begged him to just leave me in peace. He said I
wouldn't get a cent in the divorce. I told him he could have
everything. I didn't care. But he threatened to find my
mother. To have her declared incompetent and put her in a
facility. He would have done it, too, if he had found her."

"But he wanted to send her flowers."

"He was trying to find her! That was how he did things.
It always looked like some generous, thoughtful gesture.
But it never was. It was always a scheme. There was no way

I was giving him the name of her friend." She pulled out a tissue and wiped her tears. "He would have had her locked up so she couldn't enjoy her life and her home. He could do that. He could talk people into anything. That's what made him a good lawyer. I wasn't going to let that happen, but I could hardly walk. I know what you're thinking. That I have more reason than almost anyone to kill Wendell. But I didn't do it. I wish I had been brave enough, strong enough to do it myself. But I didn't. I don't know who did. And the terrible thing is that I feel happy! I'm finally free. I'm not one bit sad that he's gone because it's such a relief! Only my mom and Bizzy can begin to understand that Wendell's death was a gift to me."

"He said he wanted to adopt Squishy as a surprise for you."

Ella gasped. "He knew. Thank heaven he was never able to do that."

# Twenty-Seven

"Wendell heard us calling him Squishy," I said to Ella. "It's an unusual name."

Ella nodded. "In the beginning he mentioned the black dog that looked like Squishy, and I wanted to imagine that he just thought dogs look alike. But if he heard someone say Squishy, he would have known instantly. I never should have left his name on that note. When that woman adopted him, it broke my heart. But I was relieved to know that Squishy was out of Wendell's reach. I was serious when I told you I couldn't have a dog. I couldn't have anything I cared about without endangering it. But now—" she bent to pet Squishy, who kissed her nose "—I can adopt him and make sure no harm ever comes to him again."

"Adopt him?" asked Bizzy. "You're his rightful owner. Can't you just claim him?"

"Of course! Why didn't I think of that?" said Ella with a bright grin.

But I didn't know if the shelter would let her have him

back after she'd abandoned him by the side of the highway, not to mention that she was suspected in her husband's murder.

The path narrowed substantially, and we had to turn off it to reach the spot where Dinah died. The brush and trees became more challenging, but we persevered. The area where she had landed had fewer trees. It was off the beaten path. We finally reached it. There hadn't been any rain, so the paint Dr. Engelknecht had sprayed was largely intact.

Bizzy laid the flowers in the middle of the paint markings. "I should have watched out for you that night, Dinah. I'm so sorry that I didn't. I wish I could have saved you."

Squishy sniffed around with Trixie, who was digging a hole. Twinkletoes soaked up sunshine on a warm rock.

"Percy thinks Wendell killed her," said Ella.

I didn't respond. I was more interested in what they thought. After all, they knew the people most likely involved.

Bizzy sat down beside the flowers and touched the ground as if she was remembering Dinah. "Did Wendell tell you anything about Dinah? I know she and Simon had a little fling that didn't work out. She wasn't seeing anyone else, was she?"

"You mean like Percy?" asked Ella.

"For example. Or Ben. Maybe Ben didn't want Holly to know about a former relationship with Dinah."

Ben! He wouldn't murder anyone. He was far too strait-laced. He had complained when we trudged through the woods in search of Trixie. Then again, pushing someone off a cliff would be his style of murder. It was almost hands-off. But I knew him too well. "Even if there was something between Ben and Dinah, I can't see him murdering her or anyone else. He doesn't have it in him."

"What happened to your beautiful engagement ring?" asked Bizzy.

I gave our breakup the best twist I could. "We decided we're not ready for that." There! I was pleased with myself. I hadn't assigned blame to either one of us. It sounded like a mutual decision.

"I'm sorry to hear that," said Bizzy.

Trixie ran over to her carrying a dirty stick in her mouth.

"Do you want me to throw this for you?" She took the stick from Trixie. But when she lifted her hand to toss it, she said, "I don't think this is a stick, Trixie." Bizzy held it away from her and flicked dirt off it. "It's a pen."

I reached out a hand to help her to her feet.

Bizzy blew on the pen. "I think it's even engraved." She wiped dirt off it. "Good grief! Someone must have been upset about losing this. It's a Montblanc."

Ella frowned and took a closer look. "Wendell always carried one. They're ridiculously expensive."

Bizzy rubbed it again. "W. W. Walters."

"That's Wendell's!" said Ella. "Wendell Wayne Walters."

Bizzy and I exchanged a horrified look.

"Are you sure?" I asked. "That would mean Wendell was here. It could tie him to Dinah's murder."

I walked over to the hole where Trixie had found it. It was hard to tell exactly how deep the pen had been buried, but the hole was at least eight inches deep. The pen had been covered with dirt, which wouldn't have happened right away unless someone buried it.

"I don't recall this pen, though," said Ella. "He lost one

once after we had been married for several years, and I thought he would lose his mind over it."

"I would!" said Bizzy. "I lose pens on a regular basis. If I had a Montblanc, I think I would reserve it for use at home."

I took a picture of the hole, and then backed up a bit so the hole could be seen relative to where Dinah had landed, then one more of the pen itself, and texted them all to Dave and the members of the Wagtail Murder Club.

Ella held Squishy's leash so tightly that her knuckles turned white. "Wendell was horrible to me. But I never imagined that he was a murderer. Dear heaven. I married a killer." Her knees buckled and she collapsed into a heap on the ground.

Squishy licked her face as Bizzy and I rushed to her side.

"Ella!" exclaimed Bizzy. "Are you all right?"

She nodded and inhaled a jerky breath. "I'll be okay. He must have killed Dinah."

"Not necessarily," said Bizzy. "He could have simply lost the pen here. But it would indicate that he had been here before, if it's really his."

"That's true. Or someone could have found it and then lost it here," I said. "Besides, it was buried. I don't know how that would have happened in just a matter of days."

"Someone might have thrown it over the cliff in revenge," said Ella flatly. "I thought about doing something like that myself."

"Maybe we'd better get you back," said Bizzy.

"Do you need help walking?" I asked, helping her to a standing position.

"I think I'll be all right. It's horrible to imagine him

throwing poor Dinah over the cliff." She looked up at the ledge from which Dinah had fallen.

We started back. I had no idea what Bizzy was thinking, but as far as I was concerned, that pen could place Wendell at the cliff. But surely he would have visited the cliff when he was representing Cooper. It was a very legitimate reason for him to be there. Had he lost his pen then? Had he gone back for it? Or maybe he didn't realize that was where he lost it and it lay there for years.

Back at the inn, Bizzy saw Ella up to bed. I knew Shirley would be upset with me, but I let her take Squishy to her room.

Shortly after that, Cooper showed up at the registration desk. "Hi. Can you tell me what room Ella Walters is in?"

Mom shot a look at me. Sweet as honey, she asked, "Is she expecting you?"

"Yes, ma'am. I believe she took a fall earlier?"

Mom picked up the house phone and pressed in a number. "Mrs. Walters? A Mr. Adams is here to see you." She listened for a moment. "Very well. I'm sending him up." Mom nodded at me.

"This way, please." I led him to the elevator. Twinkletoes walked into it, but Trixie raced for the stairs. She absolutely would not get into the elevator under any circumstances. I attributed her refusal to having been locked up in a small space before I found her.

"Did Ella tell you about the pen we found?" I pulled out my phone and showed him the photo I had taken. "Do you recognize it?"

"Can't say that I do. Mr. Walters always used those Montblanc pens, though. At my trial, he waved that thing in the air every chance he got. Used it as a pointer on exhibits and twirled it in his fingers."

"It wasn't this one?"

"No. That one is blue and silver. The one he flashed around at my trial was black and gold."

"You're sure?"

"Positive."

The elevator came to a halt and we stepped out.

"It was found where Jeff died," I said.

He blinked hard before looking me in the eyes. "So he dropped his pen. I don't know what you're getting at, but I'm not going to badmouth Mr. Walters. He stepped up and helped me when no one else did."

"Oh? I didn't know that."

"Do you know what a good criminal attorney costs? My life was on the line and the court-appointed lawyer bought his weed from Jeff, the guy I was accused of murdering! My folks weren't poor, but I couldn't ask them to take out another mortgage on their house to pay for my lawyer. And *I* sure didn't have any money to speak of. Mr. Walters came to me and said he would represent me for free. Pro bono, I think they call it. Sure, he got some publicity out of it, but he deserved anything he got. He didn't charge me one cent. I'll always be grateful for that."

Not so grateful that he wouldn't sleep with Wendell's wife, though. "Here you go. She's in Hike."

"Thanks." He knocked on the door and I walked away. After Ella's description of her marriage, I had thought quite poorly of Wendell. But offering to represent Cooper for free gave me pause. The two descriptions of Wendell's behavior didn't mesh for me.

# Twenty-Eight

I returned to the office and found Oma working on the computer. She looked up at me. "I love having a full house, but if Ben's friends don't leave in the next few days, we'll have to see if we can shift some of our reservations to the Wagtail Springs Hotel."

I plopped into a chair. "Oma, do you remember Wagtail having a drug problem?"

"I think everyplace does now. If you know the right people, you can probably find drugs anywhere."

"What about ten or twelve years ago?"

"Does this have something to do with the murders?"

"Maybe. Jen over at Catnip and Bark said Jeff Harvey was a drug dealer."

Oma sat back in her chair. "I wasn't mayor then, so I wasn't as knowledgeable as I am now about the less savory goings-on in town. But it's possible."

That wasn't much help. "Will you be around awhile? I'd like to run over to Kitty Games."

"Yes, of course. Twinkletoes will enjoy that."

"Thanks."

Trixie stayed with Oma when I left the inn with Twinkletoes. We crossed the green to Kitty Games, and when I opened the door, Twinkletoes shot inside and raced to her favorite game.

The receptionist chuckled. "Do you need any help, Holly?"

I paid for her visit. "Is Tom in?"

"Oh sure. I'll send him right over."

I walked to the back where Twinkletoes waited for me on a table that at first glance looked like a billiard table. But it had been retrofitted so that one could pull a handle that would shoot a light plastic ball skittering across the table. Twinkletoes crouched, eager for a ball to shoot out.

I couldn't help smiling. She loved the game so much. "Ready?" I pulled a handle and she pounced on the ball that rolled toward her. I moved around the table and shot another one from a different direction. She batted it back at me.

"Hi! Looks like you've done this before."

A tall man, who I gauged to be in his late twenties, joined us. "Are you Tom?"

"I am. I think I've seen you in here before?"

"Probably. Twinkletoes can't get enough of this."

"It's terrific exercise for cats."

"Your aunt Jen sent me over here."

"That was nice of her."

"She said you knew Jeff Harvey."

He took a deep breath and blew it out of his mouth, then shot another ball across the table. Twinkletoes batted it into a hole and stretched her arm into the hole in search of it.

"Everybody is talking about him again because of that woman who fell off the cliff like he did."

"Fell off? You don't think she was murdered?"

"I guess she was. It's weird that she was up there."

"So how did you know Jeff?"

Tom studied me. "Are you a cop? I thought you ran the inn."

"I do run the inn. I'm just following up on something someone said."

"I see. When I was much younger and a lot more stupid, I thought it was cool to smoke weed." He snorted. "It wasn't like it is now. These days, seems like nobody cares."

"Who did you buy it from?"

"Jeff was my go-to guy for it. But you had to pay him. He was like his dad, you know? If you made him mad, he'd get right up in your face. Punch you, even. I guess you know that. Everyone knows he got in a fight with Cooper over that girl."

"Were you there?"

"I sure was. A crowd formed around them. Cooper never had a chance. Jeff nailed him. All Cooper did was flirt with her. But Jeff must have outweighed him by forty pounds. Cooper was kind of slim."

"How did it end?"

"Jeff was on top of Cooper, punching him. It was getting ugly. A bunch of guys pulled Jeff off of Cooper. The girl, whoever she was, called them both idiots and walked away. She didn't want anything to do with either one of them."

"Sounds like it would have been Cooper who went over the cliff."

He shot another ball for Twinkletoes and then gave me

a funny look. "Yeah, you'd think so, wouldn't you? Maybe Cooper outsmarted him. Jeff wasn't the brightest bulb."

I let Twinkletoes play to the end of her session. She had so much fun! I decided I ought to bring her to Kitty Games more often.

On our return to the inn, Twinkletoes was exhausted and Trixie seemed relieved that we were back. I took care of business until dinnertime, but Cooper and Jeff were never far from my thoughts. If what Tom said was true, then there were any number of people who might have had a tussle with Jeff. Maybe Cooper wasn't lying after all and never should have been convicted.

I hustled to the private kitchen and began looking through the magic refrigerator. A small bowl of fish stew carried Twinkletoes's name. A larger container was marked **Tasty Turkey for Dogs.**

The door swung open. Dave walked in and plopped into a chair.

Oma, Mom, Mr. Huckle, and Gingersnap joined us.

"I'm making no progress. None at all," moaned Dave.

"I thought they were beginning to rat on each other." I poured him a glass of iced tea. "Would you prefer something stronger?"

"No thanks. I need to keep my wits about me." He drank half the iced tea. "They *are* starting to break, but I don't have anything that ties together. No one saw Dinah. No one saw Wendell. It's as though no one saw anything in Wagtail."

"That cannot be," said Oma. "Someone must know something."

"Did Cook leave us any of the cheese and spinach quiche?" asked Mom. "It looked so good."

I checked the refrigerator. "Found it. And there's leftover shrimp!"

While Mom reheated the quiche, I popped a loaf of sourdough bread in the oven to warm up and set the table for the five of us.

Dave ate a shrimp before speaking again. "There's a bigger problem, Holly. You're not going to like it. Was Holmes with you the night Wendell died?"

"Holmes? He's been running back and forth to Snowball to be with his dad."

"He doesn't come back and sleep here at the inn?"

"I'm sure he goes home like any normal person would." Dave was right. I didn't like where this was going.

"Ben reminded me that Holmes was angry with Wendell because he pressured Holmes's parents. He thinks that brought on his dad's heart attack."

I seethed. After what I had gone through for Ben, he would point a finger at Holmes?

"Is this true?" Oma looked at me.

"Yes," I said reluctantly. "Holmes has been very open about it. Wendell wanted to buy their property, but when Holmes refused to sell, apparently Wendell went to Holmes's parents' house and was quite ugly toward them."

Dave spoke softly. "He threatened them."

"What kind of person does business like that?" asked Oma.

"The kind who ends up dead." Dave dug into the savory quiche.

"That's horrible." Mom put her fork down. "Who did he think he was, making that kind of threat to a nice couple like the Richardsons?"

"He didn't just threaten them," said Dave. "He went out and told people they were building a strip club on the land."

"Ohhh," said Oma. "So that's how that rumor got started."

"Oma, you didn't tell me," I complained.

"I don't tell you everything. Besides, it was ridiculous. I was certain there must be a mistake."

"Now *I'm* furious that Wendell had the nerve to spread that kind of gossip. Holmes's parents were unbelievably upset. And Doyle has that heart problem," I said.

"I know Holmes isn't a killer, but we all have a limit in terms of what we can take. Push someone far enough and they'll lash out." Dave helped himself to more salad.

"That doesn't mean Holmes beat him to death," I protested.

"It also doesn't mean that I can ignore the fact that Holmes has no alibi."

Unfortunately, Dave was right. It took my breath away that Holmes was a suspect. Why hadn't I insisted Holmes stay at the inn? Why hadn't I stayed at Holmes's house?

Mom blurted, "Now that her husband has been murdered, Ella is shacking up with Cooper. Am I the only one who thinks that's too weird? The two of them have to be involved in Wendell's murder. That's the only explanation."

I realized that she was trying to change the topic of conversation and move away from the Holmes-must-be-the-killer theory. I shot her a grateful smile.

Dave's eyes narrowed. "I keep coming back to that. The autopsy didn't turn up any drugs in Wendell's system, so his wife wasn't giving him sleeping pills. Yet she managed to sneak out to be with Cooper at least two nights that we can document, probably more. I'm still of the belief that Ella persuaded him to kill Wendell."

"She did have a terrible marriage. She told me quite a bit about it. Wendell had her scared to bits. On the day of her accident, she was running away from him."

"This is very sad," said Mr. Huckle. "He may have brought on his own death."

I rose to put on tea and decaf coffee. "Dave, you said you read Cooper's trial transcript. Was there any mention of drugs or drug dealing?"

"I don't think so."

"Tom at Kitty Games told me that Jeff Harvey was a local weed dealer before his death."

Dave sat back in his chair. "I'll have to check, but I don't remember anything along those lines."

Mr. Huckle fetched a platter of pastries and brought them to the table.

Dave rose and carried his dishes to the sink, then returned to the table and selected an iced chocolate eclair.

"Obviously, I'm not a lawyer," I said, "but if the victim, in this case Jeff, was a drug dealer, wouldn't that open up a whole bunch of possible suspects? Maybe Cooper really didn't see Jeff on the mountain that night. Maybe he went to bed in his tent, just like he said. Meanwhile, someone who wanted drugs but had no money or a rival dealer or someone who thought he got shortchanged could have murdered Jeff. Something else people have pointed out is that Jeff was a big guy, like his dad. But Cooper is a slim fellow. How did Cooper overcome Jeff and push him over the cliff? They had both been drinking, but in most matchups, Jeff would always win over Cooper by sheer size."

"Even if Cooper didn't murder Jeff," said Mom, "why would that matter now? Shouldn't we focus on who killed Wendell?"

Oma piped up. "Nell, if Cooper spent twelve years in prison for a murder that someone else committed, he might blame the lawyer who didn't defend him adequately, namely Wendell."

"Ohhh! I get it now," said Mom. "But that sort of thing must have been ruled out twelve years ago at the trial. Right, Dave?"

He frowned at me. "One would hope so."

# Twenty-Nine

That night turned out to be very calm at the inn. Holmes's dad had finally come home from the hospital. I walked to their house with Trixie and Twinkletoes.

Holmes opened the door. I could tell immediately that he felt much better. He hugged me for the longest time. Actually, until his mother yelled, "You two close the door before neighbors start coming around to see what you're doing."

Doyle sat in the kitchen, as though nothing had happened to him.

"How are you feeling?" I asked.

"One hundred percent better now that I'm home."

"The doctor said he still has to take it easy." Grace smiled at her husband. "But he should be right as rain."

Holmes scowled at her. "You're leaving out the important part."

"Holmes, don't start."

I gazed at Holmes, confused.

"He should be fine as long as he doesn't get upset. It's a

good thing that Wendell can't come around here bothering him anymore."

"Holmes Richardson! What a thing to say. I brought you up better than that." Grace looked at me. "We're very sorry that Wendell passed. Even Holmes. How is Wendell's wife doing?"

"Funny thing. He was not a nice man. Not even to his wife." I stopped short of mentioning that she was already involved with Cooper. They would hear that tidbit soon enough. "So she's not terribly upset."

"I've never heard of such a thing." She placed her hand over Doyle's. "I can't imagine feeling that way. What a shame." She gazed at my hand. "Holmes told us about the fake engagement. We laughed and laughed about it. I was so upset when I thought you really were going to marry Ben. He's nice enough, but . . . And then when we learned the truth, we just couldn't stop laughing. I guess you had a fake fight?"

"I'm not sure what Ben told his friends, but it didn't take a fight. He's feeling down, but not because of the phony engagement and breakup. With two dead lawyers and some internal problems in his law firm, they're sifting through ashes at this point. He doesn't think anything will be left, which means he'll be unemployed."

"That's a pity. But he'll land on his feet. He's a smart fellow," said Grace.

Doyle was doing his best to sit up straight and join in, but I could tell he needed rest. I pecked him on the cheek. "I'd better go. Call me if you need anything."

Holmes accompanied me to the door. "I'll walk you home."

"Stay with your dad. Your mom must be worn-out. She needs your help right now."

"No way. The killer is still out there. I thought I'd lost you to Ben. I'm not taking any chances that someone thinks you know too much."

"I really don't think that's necessary, but if you feel like some fresh air, then that's okay."

He closed the door behind him and slid his hand over mine. As we walked, I brought him up to date on the murders. "There's a good chance that Wendell killed Dinah to keep her quiet about him overcharging clients. Did I tell you that Trixie found an old pen with the inscription 'W. W. Walters' on it? She dug it up near the spot where Dinah landed. I'm not sure what to make of it, unless he dropped it there sometime in the past. After all, he was here for Cooper's trial, though Cooper said he had a different pen at the trial."

"So it might have fallen out of his pocket earlier than that? If I had been Cooper's lawyer, I would have visited the scene of the crime. I'm sure Wendell must have, but now he's dead, so I guess we'll never know."

"You're probably right about him visiting the scene of the crime. There are some things that bother me, though."

Holmes stopped walking. "Holly, I know you too well to tell you to stop looking into this. But please promise me you'll be careful and won't take any risks."

"Oh, Holmes! All I do is ask a few questions. I'll be fine."

We arrived at the inn. "Do you want to come in and have a nightcap?" I asked.

"I would like nothing more, but I think I'd better get

back to help Mom. If Dad falls, she won't be able to pick him up. He's still pretty weak from being laid up in bed."

Holmes kissed me and I wrapped my arms around his neck. "Good night," I whispered before going inside.

In the morning, I enjoyed the tea and chocolate croissant that Mr. Huckle had left. Trixie and Twinkletoes made quick work of their treats. Dressed in a turquoise sheath, I took Trixie outside. We didn't linger over breakfast. I had a bowl of oatmeal with brown sugar and fresh raspberries. Trixie also ate oatmeal for breakfast, but hers had a few bits of bacon mixed into it. Twinkletoes preferred chicken.

Ella and Squishy weren't up yet. Or weren't back from Cooper's house yet. I didn't know how I was going to convince her to give Squishy back to me. But the murders took priority. At least Squishy was safe and happy.

I skipped my regular rounds and left Oma in charge of the inn. Trixie, Twinkletoes, and I hurried to Wagtail Realty.

Marci, the receptionist, greeted us when we walked in. "Good morning! What can I do for you, Holly?"

Trixie ran behind her desk for petting. Twinkletoes jumped up on the desk and surveyed the office.

"Jen suggested I talk to you about Jeff Harvey."

Marci's jaw tightened. "He's been dead for a long time."

"Is it true that he was a drug dealer?"

She nodded. "Not like really big-time or anything. But all the kids knew he was the guy to go to."

"Do you think someone might have killed him because of that? Was anyone angry with Jeff?"

"A lot of us speculated about it when he died. But then people came forward and said they saw Jeff fighting with

Cooper and everything, and it was obvious that Cooper had killed him. Why are you asking?"

"No good reason, really. I just wondered if it was possible that Cooper wasn't the killer. He still claims that he's innocent."

Marci leaned forward. "Oh, he's not innocent." Her voice changed to a whisper even though no one else was in the office. "You know that house he's living in? Who do you think rented it for him? Ella Walters."

# Thirty

"Are you sure?" I asked Marci. "I was told it was rented by some kind of charity that helps ex-cons get a fresh start."

"I saw the check she wrote. And the lease is in her name."

"Have you told anyone else about this?" I asked. "Like maybe her husband?"

"No! And don't you dare tell anyone where you heard about it. I would lose my job. But seeing how it's you, I don't mind sharing. Those two have planned Wendell's murder for months. Mark my word. They'd have been smarter to wait a year or two. Then it wouldn't have been as obvious. But murderers are stupid. It seems like they never think things through."

But Ella had thought things through, hadn't she? And Wendell was a lawyer. He would certainly have thought things through. "Thanks, Marci." I called Trixie and Twinkle- toes and hurried back to the inn thinking about how precise lawyers had to be. A lawyer would know how to commit a crime and get away with it.

Of course, Ella wasn't a lawyer. But maybe I had been wrong about her. She had certainly laid her plans well. The car collision must have been an accident. No one would arrange that! It hadn't been fake. I saw her up close. Those bruises and stitches were the real thing, not some stage makeup. But what if Ella or Wendell weren't what they seemed to be? After all, we knew for certain that Wendell had been cheating his clients.

Back at the inn, I was getting a mug of tea when I ran into Ella.

"Hi!" she said.

I spotted an empty table on the terrace. "Join me for a few minutes?"

"I'd love that."

She might change her mind when she knew why I wanted to talk. We sat down outside.

"Cooper said that his rental house was being paid for by a charity."

Ella looked at me as if she hadn't a care in the world. "Uh-huh."

"It appears that *you* are paying his rent."

"I am. But it's charitable on my part. Here's the thing— I didn't want Cooper to know that I was doing this. Cooper and I were friends when I lived here. Naturally I was shocked when he was arrested for Jeff's murder. I knew Jeff, too, so it was heartbreaking. But I never imagined that Cooper would go to prison. I never believed he murdered Jeff. Ever. I felt just awful about it. For years I pondered what I could do to make his life better. When Wendell told me Cooper was being released, I started wondering where he would go. What would he do? And that was when it came to me. I could pay his rent until he was back up on his feet. It was really the least I could do. I knew Cooper wouldn't accept money from me, so I told the rental agent that the funds were actually coming from a charity, and they selected that house. It's nice, isn't it?"

"He's lucky to have a friend like you. Did Wendell know you were doing that?"

She snorted. "Good heavens, no! I opened a separate bank account just for the rental payments."

When we finished our beverages, she went on her way and I took another mug of hot tea with me to the office. Zelda was working at the registration desk.

I settled in front of the computer and tried to make sense of the facts. When Jeff was murdered, the Wagtail Springs Hotel had been uninhabitable. If Wendell stayed in Wagtail at that time, it would have been at a rental property or the Sugar Maple Inn. I should have asked Marci to look up his name in their rental file while I was at the real estate office.

Instead of doing inn work like I should have, I pulled up the name *Walters* on the computer. Aargh. There were a lot of them. I typed in *Ella Walters*. The current registration flashed onto the screen. It had been made six months before. So both Ella and Ben had known about this trip that long ago.

Ben wasn't really relevant because I didn't think he would murder anyone, but he'd certainly had enough advance knowledge to have called or texted me that he was coming.

I pushed annoying thoughts of Ben out of my head and

concentrated on Wendell. He had been in Wagtail before. He'd probably stayed in Snowball for Cooper's trial so he would be close to the courthouse. Nevertheless, I tried searching for *Wendell Walters*. Bingo! Not only had he stayed at the inn before, but he had checked in the day before Jeff died. And he'd checked out the day after Jeff died.

That didn't really mean anything. I was willing to bet that other people had checked in and out around that time, too. Still . . .

My head spun with thoughts. I was overreacting and reaching for explanations. I tried to jot down some of the possibilities to make more sense of them.

Wendell checked in, murdered Jeff, and left town.
Ella said she met Wendell during the trial. True or a lie?

Maybe she'd met him long before the trial.

What if Ella murdered Jeff?
Could Ella and Wendell have killed Jeff together for some reason?

I had to get a grip. Wendell's presence in Wagtail on the night Jeff was murdered was surely only a coincidence. There were probably a lot of visitors in town on that night. They didn't all murder Jeff. And yet Wendell was also here the night Dinah died in the very same spot and the very same way.

We knew that Wendell had a strong motive to get rid of Dinah. Had he also had a reason to eliminate Jeff?

How long had he suspected Dinah was onto him? He

certainly knew where Jeff had been murdered, and even better, he knew that Cooper was being released from prison. It was all perfect timing for him. Wendell could push Dinah off the cliff. With Dinah gone, no one would be the wiser about him cheating clients. Cooper would be blamed for her death, and Wendell would get away free.

But maybe I was falling down rabbit holes. Ella could be lying about her husband. Cooper thought he had been great and kind to represent him free of charge at his murder trial.

And then it hit me. What a perfect setup! Wendell could have murdered Jeff and then offered to represent Cooper at trial so that he could ensure a guilty verdict and the case would be closed. That couldn't be true, though. It was just a ridiculous notion. That was the work of a madman.

But what if that was what really happened? Then who murdered Wendell? Surely Ella wasn't as wicked as her husband. Or was she?

She'd known Cooper would be getting out of prison and had rented a nice house for him. A really nice house! Had Wendell known about that? Had they planned this together? Was that why Wendell insisted she come directly from the hospital to the inn? Did he need her as an alibi? Could Ella have been waiting for Wendell at Cooper's house the night Wendell was murdered? Was she waiting for Wendell to come murder Cooper? But Cooper spotted him in the yard and knocked Wendell off?

Or had shrewd Ella turned the tables on Wendell by sneaking off to be with Cooper? Had she manufactured her story of woe so Cooper would feel sorry for her and murder her husband? She was a wealthy woman now that he was dead. She wouldn't be the first woman to trick a boyfriend into killing her husband.

I had bought into her story. I saw how Ella acted around Wendell, quiet and almost shy. After his death, she'd become much more open and outgoing. Almost carefree. I couldn't imagine living with someone who punished me for slights or perceived transgressions by destroying things he thought I cherished. I didn't think I would have lasted in that marriage as long as she did, but it was hard to tell how we might respond if we were in someone else's situation. The pieces fit together. She knew about Squishy. She tried to protect Squishy by acting as if she didn't know him. Poor Squishy must have been very confused. And right in front of me, Wendell had pretended to be worried about Ella's mother when he couldn't reach her. Ella hadn't been a bit distressed. She'd had a calm expression as she blew off his concern because she knew exactly where her mother was.

Was that a big act? Or had it been real? Either way, it didn't really matter, because she still could have conned Cooper into murdering Wendell.

In any event, I thought Mom ought to come stay at the inn again. At least until we knew who killed Wendell. I knew I wouldn't be able to talk Mom into coming back to the inn over the phone.

I stepped out to the registration desk. "Zelda, I need to go out for a bit. Would you rather take your lunch break now or later?"

"Now would be great," she said.

I was tidying the inn's gift shop when Dave stopped by.

"Am I glad to see you! I was wondering if you could send me a transcript of Cooper's trial."

"What for?"

"Curiosity. I thought it might be interesting." I hoped I didn't sound too coy.

"Sure. You do know how it ends, right?"

I knew I was asking for a lecture about how that was in the past and I couldn't change it. "You're very funny. I don't think I've read a trial transcript before."

"This is what comes of being surrounded by lawyers all week." He grinned at me. "Actually, I came to tell Percy and the group that the medical examiner has confirmed that Wendell's death was a homicide and declared it to be death by blunt force trauma. Probably a bat."

"A bat? Like a baseball bat?"

"Right. Why do you sound surprised?"

"Well, if it was one of our guests, Marina, who cleans rooms, might have noticed a bat. There are only so many places you could hide a bat in a guest room unless you have a suitcase large enough for it."

"There's a good chance that the killer disposed of it. Threw it into the lake most likely. But it wouldn't hurt to ask Marina to keep an eye out for one."

"Thanks for keeping me in the loop. Is there any chance Ella or Cooper bought a bat?"

"I've already checked that out. No stores in Wagtail sold baseball bats in the last couple of weeks. But that doesn't exclude stealing one or buying one at a yard sale."

"So many possibilities," I said.

"One other thing." He reached for his phone and pulled up a photograph. "Does this look familiar to you?"

I peered at a picture of a knife. A huge knife. The kind that Cook used to cut meat. In fact, it looked exactly like the large knives in our commercial kitchen. "It looks very familiar. Where did you find it?"

"It was under Wendell when he died. Had his fingerprints on it."

"It looks a lot like the ones Cook uses here."

"I'll need to get some photos of your knives for comparison. He obviously was up to no good that night. See you later, Holly."

I continued straightening things until Zelda returned. "I won't be far away, just running over to Mom's. Call me if you need me."

Trixie and Twinkletoes were glad to get out for a bit. I took the shortcut behind the Blue Boar again. When they neared Tequila Mockingbird, Trixie and Twinkletoes stopped to greet someone. As I drew closer, I recognized Bizzy's son, Logan.

"Hi, Logan."

He looked up. "Hi. I knew you had to be close by if these two were here."

"Taking a break?"

"Yeah. I pulled a long day today. But I don't mind. Did my mom send you over to tell me I should go to law school?"

"Actually, she did not. I'm on my way to my own mom's house. Are you thinking about law school?"

"No way! But she has it on the brain. I'm feeling pressured to choose some kind of career other than pouring drinks."

"What would you like to do?"

"If I knew that, I'd be doing it."

"What do you like to do on your days off?"

"I love hiking, dogs, and nature, but I also like interacting with people. You know? I don't think I'd be a good forest ranger. They're alone all the time."

"You did a great job leading us up the mountain the night of the eclipse. Why don't you start your own guided hike or camp-with-your-dog company? You know your way around, and it wouldn't require too much start-up money."

He tilted his head. "That never occurred to me."

"I hope you don't mind, but I think you might be able to answer a few questions that I have."

"Sure! Ask away."

"Your mom told us that you were good friends with Jeff."

He nodded.

"Even though he was a drug dealer."

Logan's eyes widened. "When you say it like that it sounds really bad. Jeff was real low-key. He only sold pot, not any of the pills and stuff they have today. It wasn't like he was a junkie or anything like that. Drank too much, that's for sure. But we all did back then. You know that guy who was murdered? He used to sell pot to Jeff. We thought that was hilarious. A lawyer selling pot."

"Did you tell your mother that?"

"No. It was back before he was a big shot, you know? He didn't realize that we knew, of course. Jeff swore us to secrecy. He was afraid if Wendell found out he blabbed, Wendell would cut him off. We thought Wendell was really cool."

Also really breaking the law! I was willing to bet a lawyer would be disbarred for that. But it was exactly what had been missing from my theory about Wendell having murdered Jeff. I finally had a motive.

"Who sells pot around here now?"

"Beats me. I'm not in that crowd anymore. I've heard you have to drive over to Snowball for it. Some people grow it themselves now that it's legal to do that."

"You don't smoke anymore?"

"Ironic, huh? Now that they've made it legal to have a little, I'm not interested. Uh, I'd appreciate it if you didn't mention this conversation to my mom."

"I'll do my best."

After thanking him, I set out for my mom's house and cut through the backyard. The sun gleamed on something. I bent to pick it up. It was a key chain with a silver-colored marijuana leaf on it. An inscription read, **All I need is my dog and my weed.**

I knocked on the back door and Mom opened it. "Holly! What are you doing here?"

Trixie and Twinkletoes ran inside and were immediately showered with affection.

I dangled the key chain in the air. "Uh, Mom? Is there something you'd like to tell me?"

"Oh, Holly! I asked Oma not to say anything to you yet. Your dad will be spending some time here this summer. He'll be arriving in a couple of weeks." She watched my reaction carefully.

"Why would you hide that from me?"

"Oh!" She paused like she had to search for a reason. "You poor thing. We put you through our awful divorce. I know you'll say that you're fine, but it's hard on children."

"I'm an adult now, Mom. I think I've gotten over it. It will be fun to have Dad around. Why exactly is he coming?"

"He enjoyed his visit last year so much. Lucy is living in

a dorm, and his wife is now officially his ex-wife, so he thought he might relocate. He's coming here to see how it goes."

"Is that just a very long way of saying you and Dad are going to see if you should be together again?"

Mom blushed. "Maybe that was how it was always meant to be, honey."

I hugged her. "I think that would be great."

"So what's that thing you were waving at me?"

"A key chain. Please tell me it's not yours." I handed it to her. "It was in your garden."

She read the inscription and burst out laughing. "It's definitely not mine. I've never seen it before."

"That's odd. Why would it be in your backyard?"

Mom shrugged. "Maybe it was covered by leaves and the wind blew them away?"

I didn't think so. It wasn't dirty as if it had been out there for a long time. I tucked it in my pocket. "The reason I came here is to convince you that you need to come back to the inn until we catch the killer."

"Nonsense, Holly."

"Mom, I have sort of a new theory and I'm very concerned that the killer might have been Cooper."

"A crazy theory?"

I heard doubt in her tone. "Please? I would come spend the night with you, but you know Oma depends on me to handle nighttime problems at the inn."

"I'll come back as long as Oma doesn't mind. I'd hate to be dead before your dad came to visit."

"Thanks, Mom. Do you need help loading your golf cart?"

"I'm not that old! But you could carry this box out to the golf cart for me."

I picked up the box. "Good grief! What's in here? Bricks?"

"Books! I have my book club this afternoon."

"Don't you read one book at a time?"

"Holly, why must you question everything? There are multiple copies of the same book. Each member gets one."

I shifted the box and carried it outside, where I very nearly dropped it. Standing in Cooper's yard was a man who looked exactly like Wendell from the back.

# Thirty-One

I blinked hard and hurried to place the box in the golf cart. When I looked again, the man had turned around. It was only Cooper.

"Hi, Holly." He crossed the street and pointed to the box. "I hope your mom isn't moving out because of me."

I tried to laugh, which probably sounded totally fake. "They're books for her book club."

"That sounds like something I might like to join. I read as much as I could to pass the time in prison. I was always waiting for the book cart to come around. In the beginning, I was picky. But as time went on, I really didn't care. I wouldn't admit it to many people, but I have read a lot of romance novels." His laugh was genuine. "I've been going to every yard sale in Wagtail in search of books to read."

"I'll let her know that you might be interested."

When I returned to the house, I said, "The strangest thing just happened. I could have sworn I saw Wendell in

Cooper's yard. It turned out to be Cooper, but for a minute, I really thought I saw Wendell."

"I've read about that. Sometimes when you expect to see something, you think you see it for a moment. I had that once with my grandfather after he died. I would have sworn he was there, but as soon as I blinked, he was gone. It happens when your brain is on overload."

Oh great. Now I was imagining things. "See you at dinner, Mom."

Trixie and Twinkletoes scampered out the back way and I was right behind them. Logan was gone when we walked by Tequila Mockingbird.

I checked in with Zelda, then paid a visit to the commercial kitchen, where Cook was busy with lunch. Initially I thought it very rude to call him Cook, but it turned out that his last name was Cook! I helped myself to a roast beef sandwich, French fries, and roast beef lunches for Trixie and Twinkletoes. I eyed gorgeous cupcakes but decided to come back for one later in the afternoon. A peek outside confirmed that the terrace was full. I loaded our lunches, a pot of tea, and water bowls for Trixie and Twinkletoes onto a cart and rolled it down to the office and onto the small terrace outside.

It was a gorgeous day. Birds sang and the sky was a brilliant blue without a single cloud. I placed lunch for Trixie and Twinkletoes on the stone patio, then checked my laptop for the trial transcript Dave had sent and opened it to read while I ate.

Trixie and Twinkletoes watched me, their eyes following my every movement. "Okay, one bite of my roast beef. But just to be clear, this is mine. You already inhaled yours."

They expected more, but I showed them my empty hands and they knew what that meant.

I savored the French fries while I read what had happened at Cooper's trial. It was shorter than I expected. In my opinion, Wendell did a lousy job for Cooper. The evidence against him was what we already knew. A couple of people testified about the fight between Cooper and Jeff and said they had both been drinking. A couple more people testified to seeing Cooper and Jeff on the mountain later on that night. Wendell asked if they had seen Cooper and Jeff together, and both witnesses said no. As Mr. Huckle had said, Cooper did not testify on his own behalf. In fact, Wendell didn't call any witnesses at all! His entire defense of Cooper rested on the fact that no one had seen him with Jeff on the mountain. I wasn't convinced that Cooper had murdered Jeff. For that matter, one of the people who testified to seeing Cooper and Jeff on the mountain that night could have been the murderer. What happened to reasonable doubt? I had plenty of it after reading the transcript.

"Holly?" Shadow called to me from the office.

His bloodhound, Elvis, found me right away. He lifted his nose and sniffed the empty plate where my lunch had been. I patted his saggy shoulder. "Out here, Shadow!"

"I need some parts to fix the toilet in Purr. Okay if I charge them at Shutter Dog?"

"Sure. Have them put it on our account. Hey, Shadow, did you ever hang with the pot crowd in Wagtail?"

"No. That was never my thing. Did someone make a complaint about me or something?"

I always forgot how sensitive he was. "No, no. Nothing like that." I smiled at him and pulled out the key chain I had found. "Does this look familiar to you?"

He took it from my hand and read the inscription. For a long moment, he froze. "Uh, no."

It wasn't like Shadow to lie to me. "You're saying *no*, but your expression is telling me something else."

"You'll think I'm nuts."

"I seriously doubt that."

He swallowed hard. "This is really creepy. And it's crazy. Never mind."

"Shadow! I found it in my mom's garden. What do you know about it?"

"That's even worse! Do you believe in ghosts?"

"Ghosts? I don't think they need key chains. They go straight through walls. What are you talking about?"

"Jeff Harvey used to have one like that. I wouldn't have remembered, except for the inscription about the dog. But he's been dead for a long time."

A shiver ran along my spine. I tried to be reasonable about it. "Must belong to someone else, then."

Shadow nodded. "I'll be back soon."

They probably made thousands of those key chains. And there were probably more than an average number in Wagtail, where so many people adored their dogs.

I tried hard to put it out of my mind. I let Trixie and Twinkletoes nap outside in the sunshine, but I returned to the desk and put together an advertisement for our special mother-daughter tea on Mother's Day in May. I was almost done with it when Shadow stopped by the office again just after four.

"The toilet in Purr is working like new."

"Great! Thanks, Shadow. I don't know what we would do without you."

He smiled bashfully, but I knew that he thrived on praise. "Uh, when I was at Shutter Dog, I asked if anyone had come in to make keys." He frowned and hesitantly said, "Mr. Harvey, Jeff's father, lost his key chain. They remembered because he told them it had belonged to Jeff, and he felt really sentimental about it."

A shiver ran through me top to bottom. "Thank you. That's very helpful."

"I'll see you tomorrow, Holly."

"Have a good evening," I said, forcing a smile.

What was Harold Harvey doing in my mother's backyard?

I didn't have time to think about it, because Zelda poked her head into the office. "Ben and the gang are checking out."

I rose from my seat and walked into the registration lobby.

Percy was charging their bill on a credit card.

Kelly and Bizzy hugged.

Simon asked if Zelda had called Wagtail taxis.

Bizzy came over to me. "Sergeant Dave is letting us go. They're pretty sure Cooper killed Wendell. I have mixed feelings about leaving. I'll miss you and Oma and, of course, my son. But it's time to go home and try to pick up the pieces."

"What will happen to Calhoun, Bloom, and Walters?"

She twisted the ring on her hand. "It's dissolving. Dead in the water." She took a deep breath. "After everything that has happened—Wendell's fraud, Dinah's and Wendell's murders—we knew there wasn't a path back to what we were."

"What will you do?" I asked.

"I've been working from my room and making some inquiries. I may open a legal clinic for battered women. It's a matter of getting enough donations, but I think I can do it."

"I hope so. That would be terrific."

"And I wanted to thank you for putting that great idea in Logan's head. I don't know why I didn't think of that. He could make something of a hike-and-camp-with-your-dog program. It would be perfect for him. So he won't go to law school. That was my dream, not his. I feel like we're both beginning something new and wonderful."

She leaned toward me and kissed the air over my shoulder. "If you ever need anything, please don't hesitate to reach out to me."

Kelly waved at me. "Thanks for everything! Percy! We're going to miss our flight."

"Hold your horses. We'll get there on time." He shook my hand. "Thank you for your hospitality. I'm sorry that we brought our chaos with us. I was very worried when Dinah came to me about irregularities. Fraud like that can kill a firm, and I didn't want it getting out until we knew if it existed and what we were dealing with. I apologize if I seemed evasive at times."

"I'm sure you did what you thought was best. It was our pleasure having you here. Good luck to you."

"Percy! Did you remember to pack Taffy's dinosaur?"

"Yes, Kelly. You reminded me a dozen times."

"Well, I'm just checking. I don't want to turn around halfway to the airport."

"If you left anything, I'm sure they can ship it to us."

They continued fussing at each other as they walked out the door.

I had never seen Ben look so glum. "Are you okay?" I asked.

"No. I'm going back to see what I can piece together from the shards of my life."

"Percy didn't make you an offer?"

"Percy doesn't have anything to offer. He's considering a position with another law firm. Bizzy is starting some new project. Simon's daughter wants him to move to North Carolina. And I'm standing all by myself, out in the cold, with no place to go."

"I'm sorry it turned out this way, Ben."

"I had such high hopes when I arrived here. I really thought I might move. But now an income takes precedence. I still need to pay the mortgage on my condo. This isn't where I planned to be at this point in my life. I feel like I have to start over again."

"I'm sure you'll do fine. Once word gets out that you're available, I bet someone snaps you up. Or you could open your own firm."

"And deal with people like Wendell working for me? I don't think so." He waved and trudged toward the door to catch a Wagtail taxi.

"It's almost five, so I'm taking off," said Zelda. "Okay? Oh! And Percy paid for Ella's room. She said she'd be here tonight to pick up her stuff."

"Okay. You've got another date tonight?" I asked.

"Yes! And I think this one is a keeper!" She grinned and hustled out the door.

I returned to the office and finished up the advertisement. My thoughts went back to the key chain. Why would it have turned up in Mom's garden? Harold Harvey must have been there. Apparently, I wasn't the only person who used that back path to get to Mom's house. But why had he been going to Mom's house?

Unless he hadn't. I had gone that way, passing Tequila

Mockingbird, the day Trixie and Twinkletoes found Wendell's body. Harold must have used that path to . . . go to Cooper's house! It would have been in the middle of the night, and he must not have noticed that the keys fell out of his pocket. Or maybe they fell out on his way back, after he had beaten Wendell with the bat. That path was perfect for sneaking around. No one would have seen him. And if someone had, he could easily say he was cutting through to get to his restaurant because of an emergency.

I picked up the phone and called Dave. His voice mail answered. Just my luck.

"Dave, this is Holly. I found a key chain in Mom's backyard that apparently belongs to Harold Harvey. I have a bad feeling that he went that way to kill Wendell."

I hung up and immediately felt like a fool. What motive would Harvey have to murder Wendell? And why would he expect to find Wendell in Cooper's yard? Unless . . . he went there to murder Cooper for killing his son, Jeff.

Could he have mistaken Wendell for Cooper? They were about the same size and would be easy to confuse in the dark. That would also explain what had bothered Oma. Wendell had been going toward Cooper's house, not running away from the house, when he was killed. When Harold showed up and chased Wendell, he ran toward Cooper's house for help. Harold killed the wrong man!

I phoned Dave again and got his voice mail. Why wasn't he answering his phone? I left another message. "Dave, it's Holly again. Call me ASAP. Cooper didn't kill Wendell. It was Harold Harvey!"

# Thirty-Two

I hurried out to call Trixie and Twinkletoes inside after trying to reach Dave. They wasted no time dashing into the office and out the door to the registration lobby.

I locked the French doors of the office and followed them to lock the sliding glass doors so guests could leave but couldn't come in that way. Trixie and Twinkletoes watched me from the hallway that led toward the main lobby. The second they heard the clink of the lock on the gift shop door, they raced down the hall. They weren't fooling me. They knew it was dinnertime.

The inn was blissfully quiet. I didn't see my two rascals anywhere, but I had a hunch they were waiting for their dinners to be served. I pushed open the door to the private kitchen and found them with the Wagtail Murder Club.

"Liebling! I hope you do not mind that we started eating without you. The pork roast and mashed potatoes were too tempting."

"I don't mind one bit. I think I know who killed Wendell."

"Who?" Oma demanded.

"Give me a second and I'll explain."

I searched the magic refrigerator for dog and cat meals and found turkey and macaroni for Trixie and chicken chowder for Twinkletoes. When they were eating, I poured iced tea for myself and refreshed everyone else's.

"Oma has agreed to let me stay over," said Mom.

"That's great. Ben has left, so my guest room is available again."

"That was an interesting group of people," said Mr. Huckle. "It's a pity that Wendell destroyed them. The havoc that one person can wreak on those around him is astonishing." He helped himself to salad. "Shadow said you found a key chain that belongs to Harold Harvey?"

Uh-oh. It was getting around already. I hoped Harold wouldn't hear that I had it in my possession. "I believe that Harold left his restaurant and snuck out the back way to Cooper's house the night Wendell was murdered. Either on his way there or on his way back he lost his key chain in Mom's backyard."

"Why would Harold kill Wendell?" asked Oma.

"Because he mistook him for Cooper. Remember how angry he was that Cooper had come to live here? I think he meant to kill Cooper that night."

"The two gentlemen *are* about the same size. In the dark one could make that mistake," said Mr. Huckle.

"That would explain why Wendell was running toward Cooper's house instead of away from it when he was attacked." Oma nodded.

"Rather ironic, don't you think, that it was all about

Wendell?" Mr. Huckle helped himself to more mashed potatoes.

"I must be missing something," said Mom. "Harold isn't involved with pot. Why would he have a key chain like that?"

"It belonged to his son, Jeff. I think the entire story began with Wendell." I sipped my tea. "According to Bizzy, Wendell had a difficult childhood. He passed the bar, but I have it on good authority that he sold marijuana. I can only speculate that he wasn't making much money yet as a lawyer and that was an easy way for him to supplement his income. One of his buyers was Jeff Harvey, who in turn sold it to people in Wagtail."

"Well, that's stupid. Wendell must have realized that he would lose his license to practice law for that." Mom shook her head.

"Exactly! Now, this is speculation on my part. We'll never be able to prove it because they're both dead—"

Oma piped up. "They argued and Jeff threatened to report Wendell for selling pot. Wendell couldn't let that get out because he would lose his law license."

"So it was Wendell who knocked Jeff over the cliff to his death," said Mr. Huckle. "The Montblanc pen Trixie uncovered in the dirt must have fallen when Jeff fell."

"Cooper had nothing to do with Jeff's death. Yet he was convicted," said Oma.

"It gets worse. Wendell offered to represent Cooper in court for free, which Cooper thought was very generous of him. But his interest wasn't altruistic. Wendell wanted to be certain that Cooper would be convicted so that Wendell would go free for a murder *Wendell* had committed. I read the transcript. Clearly, I'm not an expert, but Wendell did next to nothing to defend Cooper. He was convicted, and Wendell went on his merry way, eventually becoming a partner in Calhoun, Bloom, and Walters. He even married beautiful Ella."

Mom rose and fetched a spice cake that I had noticed in the refrigerator. She cut slices and brought one to each of us.

Oma sighed. "He was a horrible man. Wendell lived a life of luxury and wealth. But no amount of income was enough for him, so he overcharged his clients."

"He was greedy," said Mr. Huckle.

"As far as I can tell," I said, "he stayed away from Wagtail for about twelve years. But then he received notice that Cooper was being released from prison and that he intended to live in Wagtail."

"Ja, ja," said Oma. "This outraged Jeff's father, Harold. He felt Cooper didn't do enough time in prison and that he should not be allowed to return to live in Wagtail."

"Around the same time, Ben was pushing for the firm of Calhoun, Bloom, and Walters to open an office in Wagtail. They planned a meeting here during the continuing legal education program that was going on. At some point, Wendell learned that Dinah was checking up on his billing and would realize that he was overcharging his clients."

"So now Wendell had to get rid of Dinah before she spilled the beans," said Mom. "Does anyone want hot coffee or tea with dessert?"

We all wanted tea. She put the kettle on.

"How fortuitous for Wendell that they were going to Wagtail at exactly the same time that Cooper would be living there again," said Mr. Huckle.

"Even better, the lunar eclipse event gave Wendell a reason to be up on the mountain. Dinah had too much to drink, so he escorted her to the cliff and pushed her off, ending that problem," said Mom.

Oma sighed again. "Poor, poor Dinah."

"But what Wendell didn't know was that Dinah had already told Percy about the irregularities she'd found, and she brought evidence with her, which Twinkletoes discovered in her room. Percy and Bizzy were now onto Wendell."

"It's a good thing he did not know that. He might have murdered them, too!" said Oma.

"What he did know was that his wife, Ella, was sneaking out at night while he slept. He followed Ella to Cooper's house, carrying a massive knife that he stole from our kitchen. Thankfully, he never had an opportunity to confront them, because Harold Harvey, thinking Wendell was Cooper, beat him to death. Then Harold returned to his restaurant the back way, through Mom's garden, and in his haste, dropped his key chain, which had belonged to his son, Jeff."

"Does Dave know all this? He must arrest Harold." Oma pulled out her phone.

"Good luck, Oma. Dave didn't answer my calls. But I did leave voice mails."

My phone rang then and I excused myself to take the call. I expected it to be Dave, but it was Shirley from the shelter.

"Holly, the man who would like to adopt Squishy is here. Can you bring Squishy up to the shelter, please?"

# Thirty-Three

I had forgotten all about poor Squishy! Ella would be devastated. "It will take me a few minutes."

"Please hurry. He's here waiting."

I disconnected the call and asked Oma, Mom, and Mr. Huckle, "Would you mind if I skipped out on washing dishes tonight? I have to find Ella and Squishy."

"You go right ahead," said Oma. "I think the three of us can handle dishes."

"Is it safe for her to go out?" asked Mom. "What if Harold Harvey realizes she's onto him?"

"I'm taking a golf cart. And I'll be picking up Ella and Squishy. I won't be alone for long." I didn't wait for a response. Trixie and Twinkletoes followed me out of the kitchen. I pulled out my phone to call Ella and realized that I didn't have her cell phone number or Cooper's home phone number. Yikes!

I picked up a golf cart key, and the three of us ran out to the parking lot. It was dusk and a little bit creepy knowing that Harold could be anywhere. Trixie and Twinkletoes jumped into the golf cart, and it only took a second to start the engine and get going.

Ella would be devastated. I didn't know what to say to her.

I parked in front of Cooper's house, ran to the door, and rang the bell.

Cooper opened the door. "Hi, Holly!"

Ella showed up behind Cooper. "Holly! Won't you come in?"

Squishy wedged by the two of them and leaned against my legs while I stroked him. "Ella, I'm so very sorry, but the man who was interested in adopting Squishy has arrived in Wagtail, and the shelter is waiting for Squishy."

"But he's mine!"

"I know. It's not my decision. Did you inform the shelter of that yet?"

"No. It went out of my mind what with Wendell's murder and being arrested and all."

There was nothing I could do. Shirley would make the decision. It was so obvious to me that Squishy loved Ella and that both of them would be heartbroken if they weren't together.

Cooper looked at Ella. "You'll have to tell them that he can't have Squishy."

Squishy gazed up at Ella with those innocent, loving eyes. Shirley couldn't take him from her. Part of me wanted Ella to take Squishy and run away with him. But she wouldn't make it far. One phone call from Shirley, and she would be stopped at the parking lot outside of town.

Tears ran down Ella's face.

I couldn't blame her. If someone tried to take Trixie or Twinkletoes from me, I would be hysterical. To tell the truth, I would pack them up and take them far, far away, even if it meant hiking down the mountain through brambles and snakes to the highway.

Reluctantly, Ella, Cooper, and Squishy stepped into the golf cart and sat together on the back seat.

When we arrived at the shelter, Squishy, Trixie, and Twinkletoes jumped out. A man in a golf shirt and jeans stepped outside with Shirley and walked toward us.

Squishy took one look at him and ran behind Ella. Did the man remind him of Wendell?

Ella approached Shirley and held out her hand. "Hi. I'm Ella Walters. Squishy is my dog. I got him when he was ten weeks old. Maybe I could make a donation to the shelter for all the trouble you've gone to on behalf of Squishy?"

Shirley frowned at her but shook her hand and glanced at me. She turned her attention back to Ella. "Do you have proof of ownership? Who is your veterinarian? And what took you so long to claim Squishy? You'd better come inside."

Squishy and the rest of us trailed behind them.

Cooper let out a big sigh and whispered to me, "Ella loves Squishy. I hope this works out for her."

We sat down. Squishy didn't want to play. It was as if Twinkletoes and both dogs knew this was a place where they did not want to be.

The man called Squishy and held out his hands to him.

Squishy wedged himself behind Ella's legs. He didn't fit there, but feeling her legs touching him must have given him some comfort.

Ella explained about her accident. "I was unconscious when they brought me to the hospital. I'm just now really back on my feet. Holly saw me when I arrived. I was a mess."

Shirley clearly wasn't buying it. "You put this poor dog in a cage by the side of the road! That's abandonment and cruelty. You gave up your right to him when you did that. And allow me to point out that there is a seven-day limit on holding a dog so its human can find the dog. That deadline passed days ago. The law is quite clear. You no longer have any right to him."

"You don't understand. My husband . . ." Ella broke down and sobbed.

"Mrs. Walters," said Shirley firmly, "you don't need to make a scene. It is my job to look out for animals, and you, through your own actions and your own admission, put this dog in danger. He could have been hit by a car or a truck. Someone with malicious intentions could have taken him. What if Holly hadn't noticed him? He would have died in that cage. A long, horrible death without water or food, exposed to the elements."

Ella only cried harder.

Cooper patted Ella's shoulder. "Shirley, on the day in question, Ella was trying to escape from an abusive husband. He was on Ella's trail. She removed Squishy from her vehicle because she was afraid her husband would find her and might be cruel to Squishy. He was only there for a short time. Ella meant to return to get Squishy but was broadsided by a truck that knocked her car down an embankment. As she mentioned, she was unconscious. So you see, she was doing what she thought was best for Squishy because she loved him so much. And one more thing. I'd like you to notice where Squishy is right now. He could be playing with Trixie. He could be going from person to person to be petted or for treats, but he's not doing any of that.

He's giving his mom, Ella, emotional support by pressing his body against her."

I thought it might be the other way around. Ella was giving Squishy emotional support. Or maybe they just needed each other.

Shirley's mouth pulled into a bitter line. "Ella, I understand that are you a suspect in a murder case. What will happen to Squishy when you go to prison?"

The man in the golf shirt gasped. "Uh, I believe I might be able to resolve this matter. As I have no interest in losing sleep out of fear someone will murder me because I adopted a dog, I would much prefer to choose another dog. There's a German shepherd in the kennels whom you are calling Zeus. If I may, I would like to have an opportunity to meet Zeus."

Shirley said, "Of course. That can be arranged. If you would just give me a minute here. Ella, if you are a murder suspect, it doesn't make sense for you to keep Squishy. Will he be abandoned again when you go to prison?"

"Excuse me," I said. "I don't think they will be suspects much longer. I'm sure you know Harold Harvey, who owns Tequila Mockingbird with his wife?"

Shirley looked confused. "Yes."

"It now appears that Harold murdered Wendell. I expect all charges to be dropped against Ella and Cooper." At least I hoped so. What if I was wrong?

Ella gasped. "I told you we didn't kill anyone. Cooper! You're not going back to prison!"

The man in the golf shirt looked increasingly uncomfortable. "I'll, uh, just step out. Maybe someone else can help me with Zeus." He ran for the door.

"Harold? Are you sure?" asked Shirley.

"What if I buy a home in Wagtail?" Ella blurted. "You would be welcome to check up on Squishy all you want."

"You're moving to Wagtail?" Shirley asked.

"Yes! If that's what it takes to keep my Squishy boy, then I will move to Wagtail. I hope to move my mom to Wagtail as well. She will be thrilled to take care of him if I have to go out of town. And you can come by and check on his welfare every day if you want to. I'll have coffee waiting for you in the morning."

"That won't be necessary." Shirley studied Squishy, who was well-fed and nicely groomed. He still leaned against Ella's legs.

In the end, I was completely convinced that it was the way Squishy looked at Ella with those adoring puppy eyes that sold Shirley.

"All right. I'll get the paperwork ready for you." Shirley left the room.

Ella slid down to the floor and hugged Squishy. "It's going to be all right, baby boy. Everything is going to be all right."

Cooper sat on the floor with her. He looked up at me. "Are you sure about this?"

I told them about Wendell and why I thought he had murdered Jeff and Dinah.

"And all this time, I thought Wendell was on my side. Fighting for me!" Cooper ran out.

"Twelve years of his life wasted in prison for nothing," said Ella. "I wonder if he'll ever be able to get over this."

"He might have trouble trusting people," I said.

"You know, when I heard that Wendell had been beaten to death, I actually felt sorry for him. That must have been horrible. But now I think he deserved it for inflicting so much pain on everyone else. He killed two people! He sent poor, innocent Cooper to prison! I think Squishy and I are lucky that we made it out alive."

I thought so, too.

Shirley returned with two sets of papers. "Sign here and here, please."

Ella dutifully signed them.

Shirley spoke firmly. "Now, I want you to take Squishy to a Wagtail vet within one week. And if I ever hear that you left him somewhere, you will lose all rights to him. Is that understood?"

"Now that my husband is dead, I don't think that will be a problem. What are those other papers for?"

"Zeus. Thanks to you and Squishy, Zeus will be going to his forever home tonight, too."

Shirley bent and let Squishy smell her hand before petting him. "Good luck to both of you."

When we walked out of the shelter office, I realized that Ella would have a big problem helping Cooper recover from Wendell's betrayal. But maybe the fact that Wendell had mistreated both of them would bring them closer together. Not all wounds showed.

Luckily, Cooper waited for us. I drove them home with Squishy wagging his tail the whole way, as if he understood that he was finally officially back with his mom.

I parked in front of Cooper's house, which was completely dark.

Trixie barked. For a moment, I thought she was barking at Squishy, but then Squishy flew off the golf cart, followed by Trixie and Twinkletoes. They ran behind Cooper's house.

# Thirty-Four

Ella gripped Cooper's arm. "Someone is out there!"

"We'll be safer inside the house," whispered Cooper. "I'll make a run for the front door. When I turn on the outdoor lights, I want the two of you to come as fast as you can."

"No! Not without Squishy."

I felt the same way about Trixie and Twinkletoes. Trying to hide the light on my phone, I called Dave. He didn't answer. I left a voice mail.

"Dave, I'm outside of Cooper's house with him and Ella. We think someone is lurking around the house. We could use some help here!"

"They're not barking now," I said. "Maybe it was only a skunk or something. I say we find Twinkletoes and the dogs and get out of here."

"That's too dangerous." In the moonlight, I could see the fear in Cooper's face. His breath came hard and fast.

Some people didn't want him here. He had every reason to be terrified. Especially if he hadn't murdered Wendell. My greatest concern was that Harold could be lurking for an opportunity to murder Cooper.

"Squishy!" called Ella. "Squishy baby, come to Mommy!"

"Whoever it is can see us. The moon is like a spotlight. And now they hear us, too." Cooper's hand trembled.

I tried my best to soothe him. "Look, Cooper. I totally understand how you must feel, but they really could be chasing a squirrel or a raccoon." No one meant to kill me. I could sneak up to the house and peer in the backyard. "Here's what we'll do. You stay here. If someone shoots or threatens you, take off as fast as you can in the golf cart. I'm going to find Twinkletoes and the dogs."

Before they could object, I bounded from the golf cart and ran toward the house, calling the dogs and Twinkle-toes in the loudest voice I could muster. I reached the wall of the house and edged along it to the back corner. Then I quickly peered around the corner and ran into someone's chest.

He grabbed hold of me, and I screamed. Squishy, Trixie, and Twinkletoes came to my aid immediately. But in-stead of barking or jumping on my assailant, they acted happy.

"Thank you very much," said an annoyed familiar voice as he released me.

"Dave? What are you doing here? Why did you grab me? You scared me to death."

"I *was* on a stakeout. Thank you for alerting the entire neighborhood to my presence."

"Ohhh. So that's why you weren't responding to my

calls. I should let Cooper know that it's only you. He's terrified."

We walked out to the golf cart. The dogs and Twinkletoes ran ahead of us.

"Sorry I frightened you," Dave said to Cooper and Ella. "I called the house phone so you would know I was the one hanging out in your yard, but no one answered. The house is dark, so I figured no one was home."

"We were at the shelter. It's a long story, but Squishy is officially Ella's dog now," I said.

"What are you doing here?" asked Cooper. "Were you waiting for us? What did I do now?"

"I was keeping an eye on your house."

"You thought someone was coming to kill me," said Cooper. He turned to Ella. "I told you so."

"You don't have to worry," Dave assured him. "With all the barking and screaming, if anyone was here, he's long gone by now."

"You came to protect us?" asked Cooper in a tone that conveyed his disbelief. "You usually drag us to the police station."

Dave nodded. "Both things are my job."

"Holly," said Ella, "could we stay in my room at the inn tonight? I had promised to get my things out, but now I can't imagine staying here. We would sleep better at the Sugar Maple Inn."

"That's not a problem at all. Do you need to get anything from the house?"

They shared a look. Cooper shook his head. "What if someone is inside, waiting for me? I'd rather go straight to the inn."

Dave wished us a good night and stayed behind.

Exhausted, I drove home, glad that I could soon crawl into my bed and relax. I parked the golf cart, and we walked to the inn's main entrance.

"Thank you for helping me get Squishy back," Ella said. "I owe you!"

"You don't owe me at all. I'm glad Squishy is back with the person he loves."

It was late enough for the lobby to be very quiet. Most of our guests were probably settled for the night.

I said good night and proceeded to the registration lobby to make sure Ella's room was marked as occupied on our computers.

Casey was there, getting bills ready for those checking out in the morning. "Hi! Oma said to tell you that she went up to bed. It's been a very calm night."

"I'm happy to hear that. I'm pooped. Ella Waters is staying in her room tonight, but I think she'll probably check out tomorrow morning."

Casey nodded.

Someone rapped on the sliding glass doors and motioned for us to let them in.

"Can't they read the sign?" Casey muttered as he pointed his finger to the right.

The guest was insistent.

Casey groaned.

"I need to take Trixie out before bed anyway. Lock the doors behind me." I unlocked the sliding glass doors and a cute couple hurried inside.

"Thanks! You really should leave that door open all night," complained the woman.

I simply smiled and walked out with Trixie. If she were the person who had to stay up all night watching that door, she would sing a different tune.

I waited for Trixie at the dog potty area.

Twinkletoes hissed at something in the dark.

# Thirty-Five

I turned around just in time to see Harold coming at me, brandishing his baseball bat. I screamed and ran for the front door of the inn. But I tripped on the stairs and fell forward, and in a second, Harold had a grip on my ankle.

"Where is he? Which room is he in?"

I played dumb. "Who?" I screamed again and kicked my free leg like a madwoman. I looked back at him.

His baseball bat was in his right hand, and he grinned at me, sinister and malicious. "Cooper, the man who killed my son."

"It wasn't Cooper," I yelled, twisting to face him.

He clutched my ankle tighter. "Do you think I'm stupid? I was there in the courtroom when they found him guilty." Harold pulled me closer to him. I balanced as well as I could on the steps, and just as I kicked him in the head with my free heel, sorry that I wasn't wearing stilettos, Twinkletoes jumped on his head. I could have sworn I saw her claws extended.

Harold screamed this time.

He momentarily loosened his grip and seized my foot by the shoe. I was able to slip out of it. I crawled forward up the stairs, anxious to get away, at least far enough for him not to be able to reach me. Trixie barked and snarled at him.

Just as Harold lunged toward me, I rolled to the side out of his reach, struggled to my feet, and dashed up the staircase to the front door. Thank heaven it wasn't locked.

I opened the door. Trixie and Twinkletoes shot inside. I pulled it closed behind me and locked it. I could hear his heavy footsteps on the stairs.

"Casey!" I screamed.

"Do you need help?" a guest shouted from the second floor. I looked up and saw guests gathering on the grand staircase.

"Call the police."

The glass sidelight shattered as the baseball bat hit it. Harvey stretched his arm in through the jagged shards.

Why didn't I have a weapon? I looked around. The knives were in the kitchen. I didn't have time to go in search of one. He could unlock the door before I returned.

He waved that awful baseball bat around. I dared to get as close as I could to the broken sidelight, grabbed hold of the baseball bat, and chomped down on Harold's hand. I could taste blood. Ick, ick, ick. But he had released the baseball bat, and I was now in control of it.

His bleeding hand came through the shards again, searching for the lock. I slammed the baseball bat on the side of his forearm with all my strength. I thought I heard something crack, and I didn't think it was the baseball bat.

I heard someone shout outside. "Put your hands in the air." Then louder and fiercer, "Hands in the air!"

Casey came running. "What's going on?"

I could hear Harold's footsteps as he walked down the steps, and then there was a scream and the sound of something falling.

I peered out the sidelight. He wasn't on the porch.

One of the guests watching from the hallway window shouted, "He's on the ground being cuffed!"

I dared to open the door and very cautiously walked out on the porch.

Harold lay on his side, moaning. "She broke my arm. I'm telling you, she broke my arm, I can't move it." One of the officers tried to help him up. Harold screamed in pain like I'd never heard anyone scream before.

While Dave waited for the rescue squad to arrive, he took my statement about what had happened. "He's a murderer. Whatever you do, don't leave him unattended."

When I went inside and locked the door, people applauded. Oma and Mom had finally been awakened. They rushed toward me.

"You're bleeding!" said Mom.

"Actually, I think that's Harold's blood." I excused myself to wash the blood off. I returned, expecting everyone to be gone, but Oma and Mom were in the Dogwood Room serving drinks and desserts to all the guests. We had to do something to make up for this very scary event.

I phoned Shadow and told him what had happened. "Do you think you could bring over a piece of plywood or something to nail over the sidelight?"

Always a good sport, he promised to come immediately.

I fell into bed with Trixie and Twinkletoes in the wee hours of the morning.

# Thirty-Six

The dining area and terrace were abuzz with guests talking about what happened the night before. Only those sleeping in the cat wing missed Harold's madness. And that was what I thought it was. The loss of a child had to be emotionally overwhelming. I reasoned that Harold had dreamed of taking revenge on Cooper for years until it became an obsession and he lost his mind. Dave was furious with himself. Harold had seen us leaving Cooper's house in the golf cart and followed us.

Shelley and Mr. Huckle had wisely closed off the terrace to everyone except those involved.

"You can't possibly eat a decent breakfast if everyone is watching you," she said, setting a mug of tea on the table for me. "That must have been so scary!"

Cooper sat across from me. "I'm very sorry to have brought my troubles back to Wagtail. I came here because I remember Wagtail being peaceful, and all I wanted was to live a quiet life. I never imagined anything like this would happen."

"No need to apologize, Cooper," said Dave as he took a seat at the table next to Oma. "In every way, you are the victim here, not the perpetrator."

Ella stroked Squishy, who leaned against her chair. "It was all Wendell, then?"

Dave sipped the coffee Shelley brought him.

"From the very beginning, he lived a deceitful life. We were able to confirm that Wendell supplied Jeff Harvey with pot. We will never know the exact reason why Wendell pushed Jeff off the cliff, but given that Wendell was a young lawyer who would lose his license to practice law if his drug dealing became known, I think that's a good bet. He probably had no idea how many kids buying pot at the time knew that he was the source."

Cooper said, "What a scum bucket! First he killed Jeff, and then he offered to defend me free of charge so he could make sure that I went to prison instead of him!"

"And when he found out that Dinah was checking into the billing at the law firm, he remembered how easy it was to murder Jeff by pushing him off the cliff," said Mom.

Dave smiled at Shelley when she brought him a country ham and eggs breakfast. "Thanks, honeybunch." Dave and Shelley had been debating wedding dates, and Oma had offered the inn for their wedding.

"That was also when he received the notice that Cooper would be released from prison. It was perfect timing," said Ella.

"Apparently so," Dave said. "Bizzy and Percy confirmed that Wendell was the force pushing for a meeting in Wagtail. Naturally, they had no reason to think he had ulterior motives. It's a shame that Dinah didn't have a handle on the billing issues sooner. Percy wants to think this could all have been avoided if she had, but Wendell had hidden his swindle so well that it was difficult to unravel the trail. Given Wendell's history, I'm of the opinion that Wendell was confident that Dinah couldn't pin anything on him. If she had figured it out sooner, he would have found another way to kill Dinah before she could reveal what he had done."

"He was good at figuring things out," said Ella. "This is my fault, too. I never should have gone to see Cooper."

"I'm glad you did," said Cooper softly, gazing at her.

"But I led him to you," she protested. "Right, Dave?"

"That's how it looks. We checked with Cook and determined that the knife Wendell took to Cooper's house definitely came from the inn kitchen. He didn't go to Cooper's house with good intentions. Harold confessed that he went to Cooper's house intending to murder Cooper that night. But in the darkness and his hysteria, he mistook Wendell for Cooper and attacked him. If Wendell and Harvey hadn't intersected that night, the two of you would probably be dead right now."

Ella shuddered.

Chills ran through me, too.

Oma finally spoke up. "How ironic that Harvey wanted to kill the man who murdered his son, and in the end, he did just that."

"What will happen to Harvey?" asked Mr. Huckle.

"It's early days," said Dave. "But I imagine he'll go to prison for a very long time."

# Thirty-Seven

Wagtail was a media zoo for the next couple of weeks as Cooper's story made headlines. He was offered jobs, people sent him cards and gifts, and reporters couldn't get enough of the soft-spoken man who had been wrongly convicted.

Ella came by on a regular basis when she was walking Squishy. He was always thrilled to see Trixie and Twinkle-toes again.

One afternoon, over iced tea on the front porch, Ella said, "I've decided that I'm not going back to the house of horrors. That's what I'm calling it. I hired a Realtor and sent her my key. We already have three offers on it! It's a beautiful place, but I don't want anything that's inside. Not my clothes or anything that could remind me of Wendell. I hired an agency that's going to empty the house and sell the contents. Every single thing."

"Are you sure you don't want anything?"

Ella snorted. "If you check the window at Diamonds in

the Ruff, you'll see my engagement ring and my wedding band. There's nothing from my life with Wendell that I want. Some people will get great bargains, I'm sure, but I don't want anything from that time to even touch my skin. It's all just stuff, anyway. It can be replaced. I've bought a house on Maple Street. My mom will be moving in with us next month. It's the cutest bungalow I've ever seen. All I need is some cross-stitch to hang on the wall. I'm working on one of Squishy. And best of all—you won't believe this, but Shirley is letting me volunteer at the shelter!"

"That's great! I'm so happy for you. Who'd have thought Shirley would change her mind about you? How's Cooper holding up under media scrutiny?"

"We think the hubbub is dying down now. He took a computer job and does something I don't understand at all. He works from home, which gives him time to garden, and his mom is coming for a visit soon. She seems really nice and is overjoyed that her son isn't a murderer after all and that his name will be cleared. So we're doing okay."

The Wagtail Murder Club continued to meet for dinner in the private kitchen. My mom, Oma, Mr. Huckle, and I were a team. The murders had been solved, and we hoped there wouldn't be more. Now we had fun together.

On Saturday, I offered to pick up Dad at the airport. Mom and Oma appeared relieved that I was bringing him home. But the truth was that I looked forward to spending a little time alone with him. I knew that once he was in Wagtail, Mom and Oma would keep him busy.

When he walked into the terminal, Dad looked great,

better than the previous year. He held out his arms and said, "My little girl" when he hugged me.

Only a parent could get away with that when their child was an adult. I hugged him tight. "I missed you, Dad."

He brought a lot of luggage with him. We loaded it into the car and started for Wagtail. I asked about his other two children, my half siblings. They were well and doing fine in college. His second wife, now his second ex-wife, had made some overtures toward a reconciliation, but he had declined. She was the one who'd left him for a younger man. He wasn't going to go through that again. The divorce was final, and he felt great about it, except that his kids missed their mom.

He had seen Cooper interviewed on TV and was shocked to learn that it had all taken place in the tiny town where he'd grown up.

"How would you feel about your old dad moving back to Wagtail?"

We had reached the spot where I had found Squishy. I wondered if I would always slow down and check to be sure no animals were there. "I would love that! And I know Oma would, too."

"It's under serious consideration. There's nothing left for me in Florida except the weather, which I have to admit is wonderful except for the hurricanes."

When I pulled up in the porte cochere, Oma, Gingersnap, and Mom were waiting for him. Shadow unloaded his luggage and took it up to Oma's guest room.

I was about to park the golf cart when Oma said, "Shadow can take care of that. Would you mind going down to the dock? A gentleman needs a hand."

"Sure." I looked around for Trixie and Twinkletoes but didn't see them. "Where are Trixie and Twinkletoes?"

"Liebling, would you hurry? The gentleman is waiting."

I rushed down to the lake. The gentleman in question sat on the dock with his back to me. His legs dangled in the water.

"Holmes?"

He looked over his shoulder and smiled at me. He reached for my hand. "Come join me. The water is already warming up for summer."

I took off my shoes and sat down next to him. The water was cooler than I expected on my bare feet.

"Do you remember where we had our first kiss?" he asked.

I laughed. "Of course. We were right here, just like this. I was so afraid that Oma might see us!"

"I bet she's watching right now."

Suddenly, Trixie and Twinkletoes appeared, delighted that I was home. Trixie kissed my nose and Twinkletoes rubbed against me.

"What are you wearing?" I asked. They had some kind of signs hanging around their necks.

Trixie wore a sign that read, HOLMES NEEDS US.

Twinkletoes's sign read, CAN WE KEEP HIM? PLEASE?

Holmes said, "Trixie, bring."

She ran over to a small box nestled in the middle of a life jacket. Very carefully, she plucked it out and delivered it to Holmes in her mouth.

Holmes opened the box and extracted a ring. "Trixie and Twinkletoes wanted to adopt me. But I thought it might be easier if I was their dad and adopted them. Holly Miller, will you marry me?"

# Thirty-Eight

It was the second time in one month that someone had asked me that question. Only this time, it was the
right man, in the right place, at the right time. "I would be
honored to be your wife, Holmes."

The ring wasn't huge like the fake one Ben had given me.
It wasn't big enough to stop traffic. It was perfect. Holmes
slid it onto my finger. "I've heard you have some experience
doing this. Was that a real yes or a fake one and you're
planning to break it off as soon as the opportunity arises?"

I laughed at him. "I love you, Holmes."

He kissed me, and I heard cheers and applause. When I
turned around, I felt like everyone I knew in the world—
certainly my family and friends, as well as Holmes's family
and friends—were watching from the lawn and terrace of
the inn.

People swarmed onto the dock and crowded around us.
We scrambled to our feet. Oma handed each of us a glass
of champagne and kissed me on the cheek. "I am happy

for you, my dear Holly. He is a good man. Now come! Come!"

She ushered us up to the terrace where the sun was beginning to set. Hot Hog had set up a buffet dinner. Trixie could hardly contain herself. I removed the sign from her neck. I hoped there would be pulled chicken for her. Twinkle-toes rode on Holmes's shoulder. He handed me her sign.

"I'm planning to save these and hang them on the wall." I set them aside where I thought they would be safe.

"You must have been pretty sure I would say yes," I said to Oma.

"It was meant to be," she replied.

Dad held out his arms. "I can't believe it."

"You knew about this, didn't you?"

"Holmes called me to ask for your hand in marriage."

"Oh yuck. Like I'm chattel."

Dad laughed. "It was the right thing to do."

"Now I'm having second thoughts."

Holmes smiled. "I wasn't going to start our marriage with a disapproving dad."

Holmes's dad, Doyle, had recovered nicely. He said, "I feel like you have been part of our family for a long time. I'm delighted that I will be able call you my daughter."

Grace whispered, "Thank goodness it's you! I couldn't stand that other girl Holmes was engaged to."

After dinner, when darkness had rolled around, a local band played and everyone danced.

Under the stars and a waning gibbous moon, Zelda hugged me. "I love Holmes. And I'm so glad you're not marrying the Ben." She gestured to the man beside her. "Holly, this is Lars."

He looked like he had stepped off a Viking ship. Tall and strong with hair as blond as Zelda's.

He smiled at me. "I am very pleased to be here at your special celebration. Congratulations!"

He had lovely manners, too. Had Zelda finally met the right guy? "It's a pleasure to meet you."

"Lars, would you get us some champagne?" asked Zelda.

When he walked away, she said, "I told you. The lunar eclipse is a time for new beginnings. A time of walking away from the shadows over your old life and those who oppressed you. It's a time for starting everything anew."

# Recipes

One of my dogs suffered from severe food allergies that did not allow him to eat commercial dog food. Consequently, I learned to cook for my dogs and have done so now for many years. Consult your veterinarian if you want to switch your dog to home-cooked food. It's not as difficult as one might think. Keep in mind that, like children, dogs need a balanced diet, not just a hamburger. Any changes to your dog's diet should be made gradually so your dog's stomach can adjust.

Chocolate, alcohol, caffeine, fatty foods, grapes, raisins, macadamia nuts, onions, garlic, xylitol (also known as birch sugar), and unbaked dough can be toxic and deadly to dogs. For more information about foods your dog can and cannot eat, consult the American Kennel Club website at www.akc.org/expert-advice/nutrition/human-foods -dogs-can-and-cant-eat/.

Do not feed your dog foods that have been seasoned. It's best to use plain food without additives or seasonings.

Please read the labels carefully. If you suspect your dog may have eaten something that will make them ill, immediately call your veterinarian or the Animal Poison Control Center's twenty-four-hour hotline at (888) 426-4435.

I am often asked why I do not include recipes for cat food. Cats must eat taurine to survive and be healthy. Cooking taurine kills it. There are many articles online about taurine for those who are interested. I recommend following your veterinarian's guidance and feeding your cat commercial cat food, which includes taurine. You should see it listed on the label of ingredients. Please note that commercially prepared dog food often does not contain taurine and should not be fed to cats.

## Banana Pancakes

Share with your dog, but you eat the maple syrup.

These are the quickest, easiest pancakes I have ever made. Because of the moisture in the banana, you may not even need milk. I have made them with milk and without. They're a little bit thinner with milk, but my preference is without milk. However, if you make them with bananas that are too green, you may find the mixture too dense. All you have to do is add one or two tablespoons of milk for additional moisture. While these are for people, your dog can also have a bite, just not too much. If you want more than two pancakes, simply double the recipe.

Makes 2 pancakes.

*1 banana, preferably ripe with a few spots on the*
   *peel*
*2 eggs*
*⅓ cup whole wheat flour*
*Canola oil*
*1–2 tablespoons milk (optional)*
*Maple syrup (for serving)*

Mash the banana with the back of a fork in a medium bowl. Add the eggs and use the fork as a whisk, blending the eggs with the banana. It won't be smooth; there should be some lumps. Add the whole wheat flour and whisk it in with the fork. Preheat a stove burner on medium and set a small or medium frying pan on it.

Pour a tablespoon or so of the canola oil onto the warm pan (eyeball it). Swirl to spread it, then pour in half of the banana mixture. You may need to adjust the heat if it gets too hot. When the bottom is set, flip the pancake to cook the other side until it's a light brown color.

Move the pancake to a plate, add more oil to the pan as needed, and repeat the process with the remaining batter.

Serve with maple syrup for humans. Your pups will be thrilled to eat them without the maple syrup. Or for extra banana flavor, slice another banana and sprinkle the slices over the top.

# White Cheddar and Spinach Crustless Quiche

NOT for dogs.

Makes 1 nine-inch quiche. If you don't have a quiche dish,
you can use a pie dish.

*1 tablespoon butter*
*6 large eggs*
*½ cup whole milk*
*¾ cup heavy cream*
*¾ teaspoon salt*
*¼ teaspoon black pepper*
*Pinch of nutmeg*
*Baby spinach leaves*
*⅔ cup shredded white cheddar cheese*

Preheat the oven to 350°F. Grease a quiche dish with the butter and set aside.

Crack the eggs in a bowl and whisk them with the milk and the cream. Whisk in the salt, pepper, and nutmeg. Place the uncooked baby spinach leaves in the bottom of the quiche dish. Sprinkle the cheese over the leaves. Pour in the egg mixture.

Bake 35 minutes or until the edges and center are set.

# Blueberry Oat Treats

For dogs.

My dogs hate blueberries—unless they're in cookies! These are meant as treats for dogs. They are not intended as a meal. Don't give them too many! These are perfectly edible for humans, but unless you're on a very low-sugar diet, you may not find them as tasty as your pooch does. I recommend making these cookies in a stand mixer. The batter gets very thick when the oatmeal is added.

Makes about 54 treats.

*4 ounces plain cream cheese*
*1 cup whole wheat flour*
*2 cups old-fashioned oats*
*⅓ cup sugar*
*2 large egg whites*
*2 large egg yolks*
*1 (8-ounce) package of fresh blueberries, washed*

Preheat oven to 350°F. Line a cookie sheet with parchment paper.

Take out the cream cheese and allow it to soften at room temperature.

Place the flour, oats, and sugar in a bowl and combine.

Beat the egg whites until they hold a stiff peak and set aside.

Beat the egg yolks until blended. Add the cream cheese and beat until smooth. Add the flour mixture gradually and beat it to blend.

Slowly add the egg whites to the bowl and mix in gently. Add the blueberries and mix into the batter.

Take a teaspoon of the dough, roll it into a ball, and place it on the prepared cookie sheet. Repeat with the rest of the dough. Smash the balls flat with the bottom of a glass.

Bake for 15 minutes.

Store in a tightly closed container in the refrigerator, or freeze and take out a few at a time to thaw and serve.

# Peanut Butter Yogurt Cookies

For dogs.

These are meant as treats for dogs. They are not intended as a meal. Don't give them too many! Please read the label on the peanut butter to be certain it does *not* contain xylitol, which is deadly to dogs.

Makes about 15 cookies.

¼ cup natural peanut butter (make sure it does
    not contain xylitol)
2 tablespoons honey

*1 large egg*
*2 tablespoons plain unsweetened yogurt*
*½ cup whole wheat flour*

Preheat oven to 350°F. Line a cookie sheet with parchment paper.

Combine peanut butter, honey, egg, and yogurt in a mixing bowl. Stir until smooth.

Add the flour and blend it into the peanut butter mixture. Peanut butter brands vary. If too sticky, add more flour.

Make 1-inch balls with your hands, flatten them, and place on the prepared cookie sheet.

Bake for 15 minutes and place on a rack to cool.

Store in a tightly closed container in the refrigerator, or freeze and take out a few at a time to thaw and serve.

# Acknowledgments

Some time ago, Sisters in Crime held an auction to benefit the Innocence Project, whose goal is to free innocent people who were wrongly incarcerated. Carol Zebrowski very generously bid on my offer to include a pet in a Wagtail book. You have met her darling black Labrador, Squishy, in these pages. He's quite a character and was a lot of fun to write about. While some of Squishy's behavior in this book reflects the real Squishy, the story is fiction. Fear not, because in real life, Squishy has a very good and loving home. Thank you, Carol, for introducing me to Squishy and allowing me to write about your wonderful dog.

Thanks to my circle of author friends, Ginger Bolton, Allison Brook, Laurie Cass, Peg Cochran, Kaye George, and Daryl Wood Gerber, for their constant support. Every author should be so lucky! Also to my dear friends Susan Reid Smith, Betsy Strickland, and Amy Wheeler, who pull me out of the worlds I create and remind me about real life happening around us.

I had the pleasure of attending a reunion this year (no, I'm not telling you the year!) and must thank my wonderful classmates. I still can't get over the fact that we were all immediately comfortable with one another as though no time had passed at all. A special shout-out to my very tolerant and brave former roommates, Lori Braun Jackson and Sarah Martin Finn, who may need to go on my payroll for their kind promotion of my books!

I cannot omit thanking my agent, Jessica Faust, who is simply the best. I don't know what I would do without her.